MW00713874

FUG 10

FUG 10

*Lost Treasure
in the Hessian Triangle*

JAY OSMAN

YELLOWBACK MYSTERIES
JAMES A. ROCK & COMPANY, PUBLISHERS
ROCKVILLE • MARYLAND

FUG 10: Lost Treasure in the Hessian Triangle by Jay Osman

is an imprint of JAMES A. ROCK & CO., PUBLISHERS

FUG 10: Lost Treasure in the Hessian Triangle
copyright ©2007 by Jay Osman

Address comments and inquiries to:

YELLOWBACK MYSTERIES
James A. Rock & Company, Publishers
9710 Traville Gateway Drive, #305
Rockville, MD 20850

E-mail:
jrock@rockpublishing.com   lrock@rockpublishing.com
Internet URL: www.rockpublishing.com

Front Cover photograph by Dan Smith.
The belltower atop Independence Hall in Philadelphia, PA on a cloudy day.

Paperback ISBN: 978-1-59663-782-5

Library of Congress Control Number: 2006937840

Printed in the United States of America

First Edition: 2007

*Dedicated to all the men and women
who fought and died to secure our freedom.*

Acknowledgements

I would like to thank the following for their assistance and support; James and Lynne Rock; Lilda Rock Wiley; Karen S. Davis, freelance editor; Lea Dailey, Registered Nurse; Pennsylvania State Police; The Gratz Historical Society; David Sklow and the American Numismatic Association; Stewart Huckaby and HeritageAuctions.com; John MacKenzie and BritishBattles.com; The Citizen-Standard; Mark W. Allshouse, Esq.; the Millersburg Ferryboat Association; Troutman Brothers Meats, Inc.; Shirley L. Osman, illustrator and first reader; Jennifer Feaser; Sallie Allshouse; Daniel Osman.

Credits

The author wishes to thank HeritageAuctions.com for their permission to use the images of the coins which appear on page 175.

The author wishes to thank britishbattles.com for permission to use the map of Trenton, New Jersey which appears on page 2. Copyright 2007 by britishbattle.com.

Page x (opposite) The political cartoon 'Join or Die' was published 9 May, 1754 in the Philadelphia-based *Pennsylvania Gazette*, a newspaper owned and operated by Benjamin Franklin. The American Colonies are shown as a snake cut into eight segments, each segment representing one of the colonies.

Part One

Wherever Liberty shines, there people will naturally flock to bask themselves in its beam.

—Benjamin Franklin

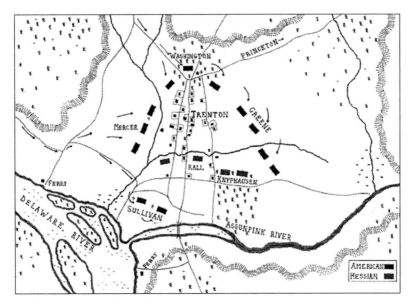

Hessian and American troop deployment at the Battle of Trenton on
the morning of December 26, 1776. Washington attacked from all
directions. The Hessians retreated southeast where they surrendered.

CHAPTER

ONE

Christmas Night, 1776
Hessian Encampment, Trenton, New Jersey

Plumes of their frozen breath grew in length and girth as the exhausted beasts strained against the heavy weight and deepening snow. Their ignored requests for food and rest intensified the memory of a dry stable, fresh hay, and feedbag full of oats. Still, obedient animals they obeyed the stranger urging them through the darkness.

The driver's ability to remove himself from the unpleasantness was not unlike the animals he burdened. He too was preoccupied with a different time and far away place. The horse's agitated whinnies jarred him to the present.

"It won't be long now, my friends," he said, more to himself then his beleaguered team.

The words spoken in a language foreign to them gave little comfort.

The man was Major Johan Conrad Mueller. He thought about home more tonight than at any time since he had arrived in America. Maybe the snow reminded him of his Black Forest youth; maybe it was the prospect of returning to the Fatherland wealthy. He gave the reins another unnecessary slap.

Mueller was a man of meager means. Smart enough to desire what money and power could do but lacking the fortitude to obtain either, the right way that is. Being a professional soldier all of his adult life kept him fed but did nothing to increase his wherewithal. That was about to change. *Those dogs owe me*, he thought.

"Those dogs" were the German government agents who sold his services to the British; the British, who bought his services, and the Americans, who had caused all this trouble in the first place. The thought of one-upping the offending parties helped him tolerate the brutal nor'easter gripping the Mid-Atlantic region.

Mueller was a hulk of a man by eighteenth century standards, six feet tall, two hundred and twenty pounds. His powerful shoulders and arms betrayed the appearance of a man over forty. Other than his bushy eyebrows, a thick dark mustache that extended past the corners of his mouth was the only hair to be found anywhere on his oversized head. His appearance alone was intimidating.

He was relegated to a strange country to fight in a war he could not care less about and kill people he had no grudge against. This had the adverse effect of exaggerating his already irascible nature. As a youth he cajoled his way through adolescence. As an adult he had bluffed his way to his present rank in the German military. All his life he had been an expert at rationalizing his bad behavior and this time was no exception. It was more than justified in his eyes.

The snowstorm slowed his already overweight wagon and reduced visibility, adding to his irritability. He had hoped to arrive long before this. The major had had no problem intimidating the sentries guarding the Hessians garrisoned at Trenton.

"I'm on military business. You don't need to know where I got the wagon or what's in it," he had told them. "Now get out of my way or I'll have you all flogged." When the big German barked an order it mattered little whether he was an officer or the lowly company cook. More than his rank, the *man* was obeyed.

Mueller was reluctant to go into Trenton with his booty but he needed a helper. There was always a risk that he could be spotted by another officer or, worse yet, by Colonel Rall himself. It was a chance he had to take. He had been absent for two days already and he wanted to be finished with his business and make the return trip to Trenton before daybreak. He could do it if he had help. Even *he* wouldn't pull one of the sentries off their post, so he proceeded into town.

"You there. Come here," the major bellowed through the darkness at the first man he saw.

The man quick-stepped over the snow toward the commanding voice. "Sir?"

Private Rudolph Hoppe, at just under six feet, was taller than all his unit comrades except Mueller. He had black wavy hair and eyes so dark you had to be standing close to see they were a deep brown, not black. He was good-natured, intelligent, and the man to beat at arm wrestling. More important to his present situation, he was a good soldier, well liked by the officers and men. Hoppe didn't like fighting someone else's war any better than most of his fellow soldiers, but he was here and he was going to do his duty without complaint.

He had gone outside the commandeered house to relieve himself of some of the night's rum and beer when Major Mueller startled him. Hoppe, like many of his comrades, had had too much to drink as they celebrated all of Christmas Day and well into the night. Now, aside from the snow-muffled chatter of the sentries, the camp was crypt-quiet in the early morning hours as the men slept it off. His bare feet in the snow and Mueller's booming voice had a sobering effect on him.

"Oh ... Hoppe, it's you," a surprised Mueller said.

"Yes, sir."

Mueller hesitated for a moment, and then continued, "I need you to help me with an important mission. It will take us the rest of the night, and above all it must remain our secret. Can you do that?" Mueller said as he stroked the snow and ice from his bulky mustache.

"Yes, sir, I can."

"Well then get dressed, man, and tell no one of this … hurry."

While Hoppe dressed, Mueller untied his horse from the back of the wagon and turned it loose. *I'll tend to you later.* He slapped the animal's rump toward the temporary stable set up in one of the town's barns.

Hoppe would have been his last choice for a helper but it was too late now. Not because Hoppe was deficient in any way; on the contrary. Mueller liked the soldier's enthusiasm and obedience. And he knew what the outcome of tonight's business would be, and it bothered him a little. *Maybe I can trust Hoppe to keep his mouth shut. Maybe I won't have to kill him.*

When Hoppe returned he jumped on the wagon, excited to be included in a secret mission. He nestled his musket under his armpit and across his knee and then sat on his hands to keep them warm. Mueller drove the team. The major knew the horses should have been rested or replaced but there was no time. The pair continued west-northwest until they reached the Delaware River. In the snowy darkness and the bone-chilling cold, they followed the river upstream.

The only light came from a lantern hung on a pole attached to the side of the wagon. The lantern light in the pitch-black woods cast eerie tree shadows on the accumulating snow. As if alive the shadows lunged, froze, and lingered motionless for an instant, then lunged again keeping time with the irregular pendulum motion of the swaying lantern. Hoppe tried not letting the major see him looking over his shoulder at the three long, wooden boxes in the back of the wagon, and the eerie tree shadows. He could tell by the way the small farm wagon lugged that the boxes must be heavy.

"Major, what is our mission, if I may ask?"

Mueller ignored the question at first, and then thought better of not answering.

"Do you see those boxes back there?" he asked, motioning with his head.

"Yessir."

"We must hide them. There are rumors General Washington is on the move with his entire army. Those boxes must not fall into the hands of the Americans ... and nobody can know where we hide them. I know I can trust you, Hoppe, you're a good soldier."

The Major could feign charm when he had to and he was pleased with his short-notice lie. In part he had unwittingly stumbled onto the truth. General George Washington's army of Continentals was indeed out and about tonight.

Mueller had marked the spot where they would have to go on foot. His thinking at the time was that a good hiding place could prove useful militarily at some point. He had no way of knowing then that his fortunes would take a dramatic turn for the better and he would have use of the hiding place himself. He had piled stones in a rough pyramid shape about two feet high along the narrow road. It wasn't far from there to the river and the nearby cave he hoped he could find again.

The cave was small, but large enough for its intended purpose. It was a sinkhole beside a large rock outcropping about seven feet high and fifteen feet in diameter. The narrow entrance fell in at an angle to a small cavern and would not take much to conceal. He had made the discovery while he reconnoitered the area after the Hessians set up camp in Trenton a couple miles to the southeast.

"Watch for the stone pile, Hoppe. We should be getting close. It should look like a pointed mound of snow by now."

There had not been much conversation on the trip partly due

to the miserable weather, but mostly because Mueller was not a trivial man. He had no use for mindless drivel. Hoppe was far too intimidated by the major to engage him in idle chitchat, but he also felt uncomfortable not saying anything at all.

"The Colonel was around camp asking about you, Major."

"What did he want?"

"I don't know."

"Well what kind of questions was he asking, man?" Mueller growled.

"He was wondering where you were, that's all."

"Why would he ask *you?*"

"He didn't. He asked the officers. It's just that the men talk. That's how I knew." After a pause Hoppe asked, "Major, is our mission so secret that even the colonel doesn't know about it?"

Mueller ignored the poignant question. So much for Hoppe's shot at casual pleasantries.

Mueller had already made up a lie to cover his two-day absence. He would tell the colonel that a Tory spy had told him that he could put him in touch with an American deserter who had information on General Washington's plans. He would say the Tory was in a hurry, so there was no time to get the colonel's permission. He'd claim the Tory's informant was gone when he got into Pennsylvania and the return trip had taken longer than expected. *Perfect.*

The truth was he traveled east, not west, and encountered two men and the small wagon almost a day's ride from Trenton while he was foraging for food and looking for mischief. *How clever those Americans think they are—trying to move something this valuable through enemy-held territory in a farm wagon.* Eliminating the two civilians had presented no problem. It was a contradiction, of course. Mueller didn't like killing the Americans who had done him or Germany no harm, but didn't mind killing for personal gain. But that was Mueller.

A little looting by the occupying Hessian army was tolerated, even expected. Most officers turned their heads, especially if it was a fellow officer doing the looting. This was far more than a little looting. He knew he should have turned over a find of this magnitude to the colonel, but Mueller had no trouble convincing himself his actions were justified; *they owe me … the dogs owe me.* It was on his return trip to camp that he formulated his plan. *Now—only to find the cave.*

"There, Major! Is that it?"

Mueller pulled up the team and jumped from the wagon. He brushed the snow off the mound of rocks to make certain. *This is it.*

Pointing to the rock pile Mueller said, "Turn the wagon around and back it to here."

With that done he ordered, "We must move fast now, Hoppe, it'll be light soon. Grab that end of the box as I pull it off."

The wooden boxes were about three feet long, a foot wide, and just short of a foot deep. They had a heavy rope handle at either end. The lid opened by two hinges and was held shut with two latches on the front. Two of the boxes had a padlock in between the two latches. The third did not, the result of Mueller's pistol ball. When Hoppe's end of the first box neared the end of the wagon, he grabbed the rope handle. As the box slid free of the wagon the full weight nearly jarred his arm from its socket,

"Too heavy for you, madam?" the major asked.

"No sir!"

Not at all happy about being called "madam" by a man he respected, and even less happy about the implication, Hoppe doubled his effort. Mueller held his rope handle with one hand; Hoppe needed two. *The major may be able to beat me at arm wrestling.*

Mueller was walking so fast it was all Hoppe could do to keep up. He tripped and stumbled through the snow and underbrush but managed to hold on. He had to. He couldn't risk another verbal assault on his manhood.

"Put it down gently," the major said, much to Hoppe's relief.

Hoppe looked around and saw he was close to the Delaware River. He could make out large chunks of ice as they flowed downstream. Not far from shore he could see what appeared to be the northern point of a small island.

"Pay attention, Hoppe. Get down the hole, feet-first, and I'll slide the box down to you. You pull and I'll push. When you get it down all the way put your back to the wall and push it back as far as you can with your feet," the major instructed.

Hoppe stared at the officer an instant too long.

"Well go on, man," Mueller prodded.

The passageway was just large enough for Hoppe to get through. It was about seven feet long and angled down forty-five degrees. The height and breadth of the cavern was a strong four feet, the depth about seven feet. He could feel the space enlarge when his feet neared the cavern floor.

"I can't see a thing, Major."

"Just do as you're told," Mueller yelled down the hole.

The second trip was as grueling as the first, but went without incident. Hoppe was tired now and his hands were wet and cold. When he grabbed the rope handle on the third box—the one without the padlock—the sudden jarring weight pulled the slippery rope from his grip. With the full weight now on him, the box pulled from Mueller's hand as well and it fell sideways, striking hard on a rock. The lid tore loose from one of the hinges, partially revealing the boxes' contents. Hoppe couldn't believe his eyes. The major's reaction was rage that subsided to a resigned passiveness. There was no question now what must be done and he didn't bother rebuking Hoppe.

"Sorry, Major."

"Just get that hammer under the seat and fix this as best you can. Hurry!"

When the third box was in the cavern Hoppe scrambled to the surface. His mind was racing. *What is going on here? This should have been given to the colonel.* He had always trusted the major, but now something felt wrong.

"Help me move these rocks over the entrance. Mind to hide it well," Mueller said.

The two had covered the entrance with rocks until it blended in with the rest of the outcropping. When Mueller saw the entrance was hidden he jockeyed for position.

Hoppe piled what he hoped would be the last rock in place. Satisfied with his work, he turned toward Mueller just in time to see the major's huge fist on its way to his face. The blow caught him square on the cheekbone. He stumbled backward and fell on the rocks over the cavern entrance. Blood flowed from his torn cheek, his ears were ringing, his vision was blurred, his thinking confused. The snow on the back of his neck prevented him from losing consciousness and he could make out Mueller's blurry image standing over him with a knife in his hand. He thought he heard the major say, "I always liked you, Hoppe, but I have to," or something like it. Just then something else struck Hoppe's face like sand in a windstorm. A split second later he heard the report of a musket. The musket ball missed its mark and struck the large rock beside the cavern entrance, gouging out a long groove and throwing the debris into his face. An instant later, a second shot. This one did not miss its mark and sent more debris into Hoppe's face. This time it was wet and warm and he knew immediately what it was. The ball tore through Major Mueller's head and he was dead before his bulk hit the snow. *The Americans!* Hoppe's mind screamed.

Hoppe was operating on adrenaline now. He scrambled the fifty feet back to the wagon, half stooping and half on his hands

and knees. He no longer felt any pain. He didn't know how he got
on the wagon, but the horses, already jumpy from the musket
fire, sensed it was time to get out of there, now. As he pulled away
he could hear balls of lead fly past him like vengeful bees. Driving
the team as hard as they would go he headed back to Trenton. *I
must warn my comrades!*

CHAPTER

TWO

It was dawn now, and when Hoppe neared the camp he noticed some of the sentries lay dead and the rest were gone, causing his heart to race. He looked for his musket but it was no longer in the wagon. Over the noise of the rig he thought he heard the commotion of battle up ahead. With the deepening snow muffling the sound and his excited state of mind, he couldn't be sure.

Several minutes later when he arrived in Trenton it was in utter chaos. He was too late. He was horrified at the scene before him. All around him there was confusion. His countrymen where running around trying to dress and fire their weapons at the same time. He saw friend Jacob Hermann clubbed on the head while attempting to pull on his boot. He was witnessing the surreal scenes in slow motion.

The Americans were doing most of the shooting, swinging of clubs, and slashing with fixed bayonets. The wet conditions were causing many firearms in both armies to fail and they were using anything they could as a weapon. His comrades were stumbling, spinning, yelling at each other, screaming in pain, and dying. Half-dressed men he had known as friends now ran past him in a wide-eyed trance like he wasn't even there. Hoppe flinched at every cannon blast, something he had taught himself not to do.

The Hessians were running in all directions, some without their weapons. Some were running toward the Americans he just left in the woods. His warning went unheeded, or was never heard, and they continued their flight. In their panic to escape some ran directly into the relentless American charge only to be shot or captured.

A few of the Hessian officers were trying in vain to organize their troops. But defense of this position was as futile as was any attempt to rally the fleeing soldiers. The only thing Hoppe could do now was to escape with his life. But there was no place to run. The Americans were everywhere. There were as many of them in the camp as there were Germans.

His mind reeled. The events of this day were too much for Hoppe to endure. In despair he slumped down in the snow. He looked up to see an American pointing his bayonet at him and yelling in bad German, "Stay, you are my prisoner!" He hung his head and offered no resistance. *Tonight the Americans saved my life and now they'll take it.* He noticed his captor had rags tied around his feet for shoes. *What is this? This is the kind of soldier that defeats our proud army?*

Hoppe heard it start at the far end of town. Cheering. The sound rolled toward him like a giant ocean wave. Now everywhere the Americans where cheering. It was over. *How sad we didn't show the Americans how well we can fight.*

***

The march to interior Pennsylvania was cold and tiring. The Americans were neither kind nor cruel, and so far treatment of their prisoners had been fair. The Hessians were told they would be deposited in prison camps around the state and if they behaved no harm would come to them. Hoppe didn't believe them but was in no mood for causing trouble.

As he walked, he admired the handsome countryside. The blanket of snow dumped by the nor'easter gave definition to the sporadic family farms dotting the rolling hills. It reminded him of home. As a youth he loved exploring the farm country around his birthplace of Hesse-Cassel. *If I survive, someday I would like to live in a place like this.*

"Did you see him, Rudi?" This was friend Jacob Hermann interrupting his daydream.

"See who?" Hoppe asked.

"General Washington."

"You mean the general himself came along? Are we *that* important? No, I didn't see him."

"If he's still with us, you will. He is impressive, Rudi. So tall and straight. And you should see how graceful he sits in the saddle. He has the look of greatness."

"And just how does greatness look, Jacob?"

"Like General Washington."

They both smiled.

"How's your head?" Hoppe asked.

"It hurts, but I'll recover."

"Next time put your boots on *before* you engage the enemy," Hoppe teased.

"How's your face?"

"Sore."

"If it helps, you look good in black and blue," Hermann said, getting in a jab of his own.

"How bad was it … the battle … how bad did we get beat?" Hoppe asked after a few more steps.

"I heard twenty dead and over one hundred wounded. And *us*, the prisoners almost one thousand of us, Rudi."

"What happened to the rest?"

"I guess they got away. God only knows what will become of them."

"Who was killed?"

"Frey, Schlager, Lutz, Brandt, Jost Hoffmann, and Colonel Rall are all I know of."

"And Major Mueller," Hoppe added.

"Major Mueller is dead? I heard he was away from camp and probably escaped."

Hoppe didn't respond. The two walked in silence for the next few minutes.

Hermann broke the silence, "How did this happen, Rudi? What went wrong? How could we be routed in such a short time?"

"Surprise. Cleverness. The Americans must have figured we would celebrate Christmas with drink. Who would have thought they would attack in a snowstorm at Christmas time? They *are* worthy adversaries, Jacob. But for the most part it was surprise."

"Some of the American soldiers said they didn't suffer any casualties. Not a one. Do you think that's true?" Hermann asked.

"Well, they couldn't have suffered many, that's for sure. To have casualties, someone needs to inflict them."

The truth in Hoppe's answer saddened Jacob Hermann and he hung his head.

✱✱✱

An American translator halted the prisoners and told them to stand in place. He worked his horse through the Hessians, dividing them and giving instructions as he went. Standing in his stirrups the translator said in perfect German, "Some of you will stay here, and some of you will go on." He motioned with his arms, "I want all of you on this side to step back—you will stay. All of you on this side will go on." Jacob Hermann was on one side of the imaginary line, and Rudolph Hoppe on the other. Hermann tried to join his friend. The translator pointed at him, "You there! I said stay on that side. Get back. Now."

Another American counted those staying and added a few prisoners from the going side. Hermann wasn't among them. When the division was complete Hoppe watched his friend march away with the others. Hermann looked over his shoulder at Hoppe. They would never see each other again.

"What is this place?" Someone yelled from the group that stayed.

"Reading, Pennsylvania," the translator answered. "Do you know what country you're in?" he sneered, then continued his instructions. "You will be marched to a temporary camp near the Schuylkill River. When it's time you will be moved to another location nearby. When you are moved to the second location, you will be expected to build yourself shelters. You will be under guard at all times. You will be fed and treated fairly if you behave. If you have wounds they will be treated. If you try to escape or cause trouble, you will be shot. Do you understand?"

A few of the prisoners nodded.

Pointing he ordered, "Follow that man on the horse ... Go."

***

The Americans were as good as their word. The prisoners were treated humanely and were fed most of the time. And just as they were told, in the fall of 1777 the prisoners were moved to a new location the Americans called Mount Penn. There they were allowed to build huts so they could sleep out of the weather.

Their spiritual needs were tended to as well as their medical needs. An itinerant Lutheran minister visited the camp every Sunday and conducted an impromptu service in German. All but a few of the prisoners attended.

Other than the brutal boredom, life in the prison was tolerable. Even so, the prisoners, including Hoppe, talked of escape. Although they were under twenty-four-hour guard, escape was not only possible but would have been easy with a little planning. But then what? They were in a strange country. They had no idea where they were in relationship to anything else, they didn't know where their comrades were, they didn't speak the language, and they could have been shot while attempting escape or later if they were caught. Most agreed it was wise to stay put for now and not one attempt was made.

The prisoners were given the freedom to roam around the encampment at will. It was this freedom of movement that allowed Rudolph Hoppe to met Robert Rhone.

***

Rhone was in the Pennsylvania Militia and assigned to guard the Hessian prisoners at Mount Penn. He liked this duty, as it counted toward paying off his indentured servitude, *plus* he could serve his new country at the same time and get paid for doing it. Rhone came to America in 1773 and paid for the trip by allowing himself to be sold as a farm laborer for a period of five years. Landowners and others needing labor came to the immigrant ships regularly to look over the new arrivals.

The person buying his services, Philip Knapp, paid the captain of the ship Robert's fare. After he paid his five-year debt to Philip Knapp in labor, Robert was a free man. An American. Free to buy and own land, something he never dreamed possible before he emigrated. Robert was thankful to Knapp for allowing his militia time to count toward his debt so he always gave him some of his pay when they remembered to pay him, that is. It was a good deal.

The powers-that-be tolerated fraternization between guards and prisoners, very agreeable to both. Robert and Rudi took an immediate liking to each other and became fast friends. They were much alike. Both were twenty-five years old and even resembled each other, except that Rudi had dark, wavy hair and Robert was fair-haired. And whereas Robert was excitable, Rudi was cool headed and steady—their major difference. They had no problem communicating, as Robert was fluent in both German and English. Rudi spoke some English and was getting better as a result of his friendship with Robert, but aside from Robert's English lessons they spoke in German.

"You *say* you're German. Your surname could be German, but it could be French or even Dutch. And your given name is English.

Why is that? No German parent I know would name their son *Robert.*"

"It's a long story. I'll tell you sometime."

"Well, in case you didn't notice I have lots of time on my hands."

"Yes, but I don't. My relief is due any minute."

"Will you be here tomorrow?"

"I will. And maybe I'll bring you a loaf of bread and some apple butter if you like."

"If I like? I think I might."

"Private Rhone." It was the captain of the guard.

"Yes, sir?" Robert stood erect.

"Your relief has not reported in yet, he's late again. You will have to stay until he gets here."

Understanding enough of the English, Rudi hid a smile by turning his head and rubbing a nonexistent itch under his nose.

The captain grumbled as he walked away, "As soon as he decides to show up you can leave. Something is going to be done about that man."

"Yessir."

"It looks like you *will* have time after all. Tell me the story, Robert."

"I will, but don't interrupt me," he said anticipating Rudi's tendency.

"I'll try."

"Before I was born my parents emigrated from Germany to England to escape the religious harassment going on at the time. My grandparents urged them to go."

"From where in Germany?"

"You see? You just got done saying you wouldn't interrupt."

"All right. Go on."

"Stuttgart! They were from near Stuttgart. Just like their parents before them and their parent's parents. When they arrived in

England they were put in a camp for immigrants. Because they were a young couple with no children, this did not present much of a problem. After a while they were relocated to County Armagh in the North of Ireland. They had no say in the matter, but they were happy to be away from the situation in Germany and for the opportunity they now had, so they didn't complain.

"In Armagh they were placed on a tenant farm and got to keep a share of the food they raised; the landlord got the rest. They wanted to fit in and be accepted, so they gave all their children English names. The tenant system …"

"Stuttgart. That's not too far from Hesse-Cassel where I'm from."

"It's not all that close either." Robert was annoyed at being interrupted again.

"So how did you get *here*?"

"By ship," he said, trying to get Rudi's goat.

"No. That's not what I mean."

"Just try listening." Robert said and then continued, "The tenant system was bad. The landlords took a larger portion every year; they call it 'rent.' They left just enough to get by on. My parents worked hard their whole life and died just as poor as the day they arrived on the farm. That is not going to happen to me. So when I heard about the free, well, almost free land in America— I jumped at the chance. The indentured servant system is a gift from God."

Robert explained the indentured servitude system to Rudi and added, "Even a poor boy like me can come here if they aren't afraid of a little hard work. So after my parents died, I came."

"Didn't the English government try to stop you?"

"They discouraged it, but they didn't detain me. They told me if I went I would starve to death or be killed by Indians."

"Did your brothers and sisters come?"

"Just my twin brother, James. He's working on a farm north of here."

"You mean there're *two* of you?"

"Yes. But we don't look alike."

"It's not appearance that concerns me," Rudi joked.

"We don't act much alike either."

Rudi put his hands together in the prayer position and looked skyward. He then asked, "Where are the rest of your siblings?"

"They're still in Armagh working on the farms. I would like to make enough money to bring them all here someday."

"Are they older or younger than you?"

"They're all older, except my sister Margaret. She's living with my oldest brother, Andrew."

"So you *are* German."

"Yes."

"And you learned to speak English from being born and raised in Ireland and German from your parents." Rudi liked to summarize the high points of Robert's stories.

"That's right."

"And your parents gave all their children English names so they would fit in."

"You *did* pay attention."

"Did you know your name is the same as a French river?" Rudi teased.

"The Robert River?" he teased back.

Rudi gave a sideward glance. "No. The Rhone."

"French *and* Swiss river. No matter. It's my blood name and I'm proud of it. And how do you know my ancestors didn't name the thing in the first place?"

Rudi shrugged and said, "You tell a good story, Robert. Someday I'll tell you a *better* one."

"Well, in case you didn't notice I have lots of time on my hands."

Rudi laughed.

"Hey, Shamrock," said the tardy guard. "You can go now."

Robert scolded, "The captain isn't happy about you being late all the time, William, and neither am I. You're going to lose your situation if you're not careful. Or worse."

"Circumstances beyond my control, Robbie me boy. You sound a wee bit annoyed lad," Tardy mocked.

Anybody hearing Robert's brogue assumed he was Irish. He took some ribbing from people like Tardy, but he seldom corrected them.

As Robert walked away he turned to Rudi. "I'll hear that story tomorrow then."

"I don't think so, but don't forget the bread and apple butter."

CHAPTER

THREE

Guards living close to the prison camp had been given permission to go home when they weren't on duty; one less mouth to feed was the reasoning. Philip Knapp gave Robert the use of one of his horses to make the hour ride from their farm to the Mount Penn prison camp. Mrs. Knapp claimed it was not out of kindness that her husband did this but to make sure he got his supper on time. She was only half joking.

Robert was more like a member of the family than an indentured servant. The Knapp's had no children of their own and Robert filled the void. Most of the time they waited until he came home to eat, but this night Philip Knapp's empty stomach won out over his patience. They were almost finished when Robert arrived, thanks to William the Tardy.

"Sit down, Robert, and I'll get you something to eat," Mrs. Knapp said.

Robert wasted no time sitting. Mrs. Knapp was a great cook and he was hungry.

"Can I talk to you about something while you eat?" Philip Knapp asked.

Robert nodded.

"You know Mrs. Knapp and I have grown fond of you," he said.

"I feel the same way about both of you."

"Your servitude will end this spring and your commitment to the militia will end about the same time."

"Yes."

"What will you do then?"

"Apply for a land grant from the Penns."

"All well and good. But that sometimes takes years."

"I'll squat on the land until I get the patent. Others do it."

"Yes they do, but ..."

"I can build a house and clear the land while I'm there."

"By yourself?"

"If I have to. My brother James is northwest of here. He sends word there is good land available near where he is now ... around the Mahantango Creek. His servitude will end about the same time as mine. We can help each other if he can get land nearby. And I've been working on another plan to get help. I'd like to get married and raise children someday too."

"And how will you pay for all this? The Penns do charge a token fee for their land grants, you know."

"I know. I managed to save some money."

"I see," Philip said, rubbing his chin and leaning back in his chair. "It's a good plan, Robert. There's nothing wrong with what you want, but I ... *we*, would like to offer you something else."

"What's that?"

"You stay on here and work for us. The only difference from the way it is now is we will pay you a salary. Under the rules of servitude, you are under no obligation to do that, and goodness knows I understand a young man wanting to strike out on his own. We'll understand if you say no, but we want you to stay."

Mrs. Knapp peeked over her shoulder, waiting for Robert's response.

Robert thought a minute, more looking for the right words than considering the offer, and then said, "Ever since I was old enough to remember anything, I wanted to own my own land. I never dreamed it possible but now it is. I will never forget the both of you and my time here and I will be sad to leave, but I must."

"And there is nothing I can say to change your mind?"

Robert shook his head, "I will always be grateful for what you and Mrs. Knapp have done for me."

"Then Mrs. Knapp and I wish you the best. If there's anything we can do to help you … ask."

"I will," Robert paused, "There *is* something. Can I have a loaf of that bread and some apple butter to take to Rudi?"

Philip Knapp looked at his wife and they both smiled.

✳✳✳

The next day Robert couldn't wait to get to the prison. He had been waiting for just the right time to talk to Rudi about his plan and the time was now. He knew it wasn't going to be easy and he would have to say the right things to convince him. The food under his arm wouldn't hurt.

"Is that my bread?" Rudi yelled from a hundred feet away.

Robert didn't respond. After walking the hundred feet Robert said, "Here. Baked it myself," as he handed the loaf and a jar of apple butter to Rudi.

Rudi tore off a hunk of the bread and dipped it in the jar. When he took a bite a look of ecstasy came over his face like he had just sampled ambrosia.

"Are you *that* hungry?"

"Thank you, Robert, thank you very much."

"I'd like to talk to you about something," Robert said

"What?"

"Don't interrupt and don't clown around. This is serious."

Rudi could tell by the look on Robert's face he meant it.

"Tell me about your family in Germany."

"Not much to tell. My mother died when I was born and my

father never recovered from her death. All I remember of him growing up is that he was always drunk. He was kind to me but he didn't provide well. Many times I had to beg for food. He never accomplished a thing with his life. When he died I worked at odd jobs until I was old enough for the military. Then they came and got me and I've been in the military ever since, and here I am."

"So you have no property or family in Germany?"

"No. I was told I had an aunt, but I never saw her or knew much about her."

"Did you know there will probably be a prisoner exchange sometime this summer and you will leave here?"

"No. I didn't know that," Rudi said through his bread and apple butter.

"Did you know my time in the militia is up this spring and I won't reenlist? My servitude is over about the same time?"

"Didn't know that either."

"I'd like to tell you about an opportunity to get out of prison *and* the military. The American government is offering freedom to Hessian prisoners who will desert. All you have to do is sign a Certificate of Redemption and maybe a few other papers and it's done. You would be my responsibility. I pay a fee and you would be indebted to me but only for three years. Then you're a free man. My government looks kindly at Hessians willing to do this and I hear many of your comrades are taking advantage of it in other parts of the country.

"Eventually you will be able to own land, Rudi; you can start a new life here in America. I am going to apply for a land grant and need help turning it into a working farm. I want you to come with me. If you can get land nearby we'll help each other. I won't be able pay you until I have crops to sell, but it'll be a start for you, and it will be a great help to me. And you know you would be my friend, not my servant."

"Do you want this for you or your country?"

"Both. And for you."

"And *all* I have to do is desert, sign a few papers, and become a traitor to Germany?"

"You can't be a traitor; it's not Germany's war and you were forced to come here."

"I wasn't forced. It … it was just suggested I accept the offer."

"Same thing."

Shaking his head Rudi said, "I can't do it."

"You *can* do it. You have nothing waiting for you back in Germany, you as much as said that. You have to see for yourself the opportunities available here. Is there any chance you will ever own land in Germany? No. Even if you do survive here and return you will be in the military for the rest of your life."

Rudi didn't respond. Seeing he was scoring points, Robert upped the stakes.

"Would you be able to kill me? Because if you get exchanged you will be fighting again, that's for sure. And there is always that chance you will have to point your musket at me and pull the trigger. Could you do it? It will be me or some other American that will die at your hands. I couldn't shoot *you*. Your country sent you here to kill and die for money. You do the killing and risk your life and they get the money. Where's the noble cause in that?"

Rudi looked wide-eyed at Robert, but again didn't answer.

"What would my comrades think of me?" he said after a moment in thought.

"Some will hate you, some will want to do the same, and some will not have an opinion, but they *all* would envy you." Robert had rehearsed his speech well.

"There's truth in what you say. And having you as my master for a time doesn't concern me. But do you know what you're asking of me? I just don't know, Robert. Let me think about it," Rudi said pushing back his wavy hair with his fingers.

Good enough for one day, Robert thought. "Remember this, Rudi. I want you to do this. I think it's the right thing. But it's *you* who will have to live with what you do, not me. I'll respect your decision no matter what it is, and we'll remain friends. We'll talk about it again sometime soon."

"Yes, we will. Thank you for the bread. But I don't believe you baked it."

✳✳✳

For the next few days Robert stayed in contact with Rudi, but most of the time kept his distance. This gave Rudi more time to talk to the other prisoners who confirmed the rumors about a prisoner exchange and the Americans' offer of amnesty. He was surprised at the large number of them who were considering taking the offer. It was like Robert said, some were dead set against it, and others didn't care one way or the other. But those, he noticed, who were against it had families and assets back in Germany.

There had been no official threat, but it had been rumored that the German government would seize the assets and make life rough on the families of soldiers that deserted. Yet the one thing that made up his mind was in this soldier-for-rent situation he was losing his stomach for killing anyone. To him he would be a murderer, no better than the likes of Major Mueller. A sense of relief came over him for the first time since he'd been in America. He felt like a burdensome weight had been lifted off his shoulders. He knew it was the right decision.

"I want to do it, Robert. How is it done?"

"I'll get the captain," Robert said, running before he got all the words out.

CHAPTER

FOUR

Things were going as planned for both Robert and Rudi. Although Robert's servitude was up, Philip Knapp had let him stay on the farm while getting his affairs in order. When Rudi was released into Robert's custody the Knapps let him join Robert on their farm. They paid the Knapps with labor when they could.

The Proprietors of Pennsylvania had allowed Rudi to make application for a tract of land adjoining Robert's just off the Tulpehocken Trail, near Deep Creek, a tributary of the Mahantango Creek, in what was later to become Dauphin County. He would not receive the patent until his responsibility to Robert was fulfilled, but that did not stop him from working his land. Robert's brother James applied for a tract fifteen miles to the east in what would later become Schuylkill County.

In three years the three of them working together, along with any other laborers they could find and the borrowed tools of Philip Knapp, had built three sturdy houses for themselves. Thanks to the practice of barn raising, in another year's time they each had a new barn. And according to the rules of barn raising they had helped build several others for their neighbors.

Rudi was delighted to learn some of his neighbors were also ex-Hessian soldiers. Johannes Schwalm, Nicholas Bohner, Conrad

Dietz, Andreas Schmeltz, Adam Dockey, Gunther Hoffmann, and other Hessians living in the area gave him a feeling of assurance. Hoffmann he had known well on active duty and as a fellow prisoner at Mount Penn.

After the livestock, the next priority for the three was wives, and they all married in 1783 within six months of each other.

Life was centered around the church for most in Colonial America, and the three men traveled every Sunday to the Reformed and Lutheran Church. It was located in Northumberland County, about a twelve-mile ride by horseback for Rudi and Robert, longer for James. It was there they met their wives.

"I see two pretty little heads turned your way," James whispered to Rudi and Robert as they waited for the service to begin.

"You're right again, Brother. On both counts," replied Robert.

"Who are they?" Rudi asked.

"The Kohl sisters. I know their father. Would you like to meet him?" said James.

"We would very much like to meet Mister Kohl *and* family, please," Robert answered.

So after a short but proper courtship, Robert and Rudi each married one of the Kohl sisters, two years apart in age and a mile apart in disposition. Their father, Frederick Kohl, had relocated in Schuylkill County from Berks County when he received his land patent.

Maria Magdalena "Maggie" Kohl, twenty-three years old, was a lot like Rudi, mild-mannered with a good sense of humor, but *she* married Robert. Rudi married Maria Elizabeth "Libby" Kohl Haldeman, twenty-five years old, who was much like Robert, excitable and spontaneous, but loyal and trustworthy to a fault. Libby was a widow with a two-year-old daughter; Maggie had never been married before. It was official now: Robert and Rudi were related, albeit by marriage.

James married Ann Nash, twenty, whose father, Webster Nash, emigrated from Wales and settled in Schuylkill County when she was an infant. James and Web Nash were neighbors and good friends.

The following year each couple produced a baby, sons to Rudi and Robert, a daughter for James. The sons were named Philip, after good friend Philip Knapp; the daughter was Catherine after the Rhones' mother. For now, life was good.

***

It was the summer of 1785. The war was over and Rudi was a landowner with a wife, child, and stepchild in a free and independent country, the United States of America. Over the years Rudi had thought a lot about Christmas night 1776 and Major Mueller. The war, prison, a strange new culture, getting his farm up and running, and major life events being thrown at him one after the other had prevented him from acting on his thoughts. But now they obsessed him. He didn't know what to do and as always when he found himself in that situation he consulted his best friend.

"Robert, do you recall when I was in prison camp I told you someday I would tell you a good story?"

"Yes. Do you mean after all this time I am finally going to hear it?"

"Just before the Battle of Trenton something bad happened to me."

"Plenty of bad things happened to you during and after the battle as well," Robert ribbed his friend.

"Now it's your turn to sit and listen, Robert."

They both sat on the ground on the shady side of Robert's barn.

"Go ahead."

After pushing his hair back with his fingers as he always did when something serious was going on, Rudi told Robert everything that happened that night in detail. When he finished there was silence. He looked over to see Robert staring at him agape.

"Is that the truth, Rudi?" he finally managed to say.

"Every word of it. Do you see this scar?" he said, pointing to his cheekbone, "That's where the major hit me."

Robert sat thinking for a long time, looking at the ground and twirling a blade of grass around his finger.

"Why didn't you tell me this before now?"

"I wasn't keeping it from you. Everything was happening so fast. I didn't think I could do anything about it with the war still going on. Then Libby, and the children. The years just went by."

"No matter. Are you certain the major was dead?"

"His head exploded, Robert. Blood and pieces of him flew all over me. I picked tiny pieces of bone out of my hair for days after. He was dead for sure."

"So now *you* are the only person alive who knows where those boxes are," Robert said, getting the facts straight.

"As far as I know. I don't think the Americans who shot Mueller saw what we were doing. It was still a little dark and snowing hard and they were not that close."

"And you don't have any idea where the major got the boxes?"

"No. They were already on the wagon when he told me I needed to help him."

Robert's mind was on high alert now and he had more questions than he could get out.

"And the coins you saw, what did they look like?"

"They were round and some were yellow and some silver colored. I didn't get a good look at them." Touching the tip of his middle finger to the tip of his thumb Rudi added, "They were about this big and they had writing on them."

"What did the writing say?"

"I don't know. It was in English … I think."

"And you don't know if all of the boxes had coins in them?"

"No, I don't. They were about the same weight though. And they all were *heavy*."

"Do you think the yellow ones could have been gold?"

"I don't know."

"Do you think you can find the cave again?"

" I don't know, it was dark … snowing … I didn't know the area. I don't know if I can."

"For being the only person alive to know anything about this, you sure don't know much."

"What do you make of it?" Rudi asked, ignoring the comment.

"What do I make of it?! The fact that your major tried to kill you tells it all, as far as I'm concerned. If his intentions were honorable there would be no reason to kill you. He stole those boxes from someplace and he wanted them for himself. A payroll shipment maybe, booty from somewhere, that's for sure. And he wanted to be the only one who knew where it was hidden. Didn't you question him?"

"No. I wouldn't have dared."

"And you didn't suspect he was up to something?"

"Not at first. He was a man I always respected. I knew something was wrong once I saw the coins though. What should I do?"

"*We* must try to find that cave."

"But it's in *Trenton*."

"Four, maybe five days by wagon, that's all. One will drive while the other sleeps. We'll use my wagon and team. The roads are good down that way."

"And the horses?"

"Yes, right. They'll need rest. Add another day."

"If the boxes are stolen, shouldn't we return them?"

"To who? We need to get those boxes to know more."

"Could the major have had an accomplice and told him where he was going to hide the boxes?" Rudi asked.

"He could have but I doubt it. He doesn't sound like a man

who trusted anyone. We'll know the answer to that if the boxes are gone. Now think, Rudi. Try to remember everything you can about that night."

Rudi again pushed back his hair with his fingers.

***

Robert was ready to head toward Trenton the same day he heard the story, but Rudi's cooler head prevailed. It was noon the next day when he pulled the team up to Rudi's house. From the porch his friend waved him in.

"*Now* what?" Robert grumbled to himself.

"You two will not leave this house without a good meal in your stomachs," Libby Hoppe ordered as Robert entered the house.

Robert rolled his eyes but knew better than to argue.

"What are we having?" he asked in a relenting but agitated tone.

"Schnitz und Knepp, cherry pie and fresh cool milk for dessert," was Rudi's smiling answer.

Robert's anxiety eased somewhat at hearing his favorite dish was on the menu. To prepare the Pennsylvania Dutch dish, Libby added ham pieces, dried apples, and dumplings to a ham stock and boiled them until the dried apples were soft and the dumplings firm but tender. Rudi didn't mention two things that were automatic at every German meal: fresh bread, and remaining at the table to talk after everyone finished eating.

An hour and a half later the two men were on their way to Trenton with a muslin cloth feedsack filled with bread, smoked meat, and jam, compliments of Libby. That, together with the dried fruit Maggie sent along, would keep the travelers well fed. A keg of fresh water would provide drinks for both man and beast should there not be a stream nearby.

The pace was slow. It was hot and they couldn't risk pushing the horses. Rudi was in a talkative mood. Because it worked best for them they still communicated in German, even though Rudi's English was fair and coming along.

"You know, Robert, before I came here I knew nothing about America or the cause you were fighting for. We were told the American people were greedy and refused to pay taxes and that's why you rebelled. They told us you were barbarians and if we were captured or deserted, we would be tortured and then cooked and eaten. They tried to get us to hate you so we would fight better."

"I know of only a hundred or so Hessian soldiers who were cooked and eaten," Robert quipped.

Rudi laughed, and then continued, "It wasn't until after I was captured that I learned all the Americans wanted was their liberty. Even as prisoners we could see you were hardworking, civilized, and educated. We soon reasoned we had been deceived. Many of us had died believing the lies, though."

"Is that why you defected?"

"That was part of the reason. After I learned the truth I couldn't see killing someone for just wanting to be free."

"Do you ever think about Germany?"

"Sometimes. But *this* is my country now and I don't ever want to go back." Rudi paused and then added, "I never thanked you, Robert. I want to thank you for what you did for me."

"You scare me when you get this serious. Let's talk about something else."

✳✳✳

The routine of driving, sleeping, talking, and tending to the horses put the pair in Philadelphia on the fifth day. As they drove through the city Robert was awestruck by all the new modern buildings and the hustle and bustle of the people. The city had grown since he was last there, twelve years earlier. He wanted to stop and take it in, but Rudi, intimidated by it all, insisted they keep moving. Rudi recalled how the Philadelphia residents jeered the prisoners from Trenton as they marched through the city on their way to the prison camps. He didn't like the memory. They proceeded straight to Cooper's Ferry.

After they crossed the Delaware River they drove north toward Trenton. That town had changed too. While they rested the team Rudi walked around trying to get his bearings and as he did he relived the morning of the battle. He pointed out to Robert where he saw events take place that had stuck in his memory.

"General Washington had cannon deployed at the head of this street and the next one over. It was impossible for the Hessians to defend against them. The Americans quickly entered the buildings and fired at us. The only option was to retreat. They did everything right and we did everything wrong. It wasn't much of a battle, really."

"Where were you?" Robert asked.

"Over there. Somehow I managed to get in the middle of everything ... completely surrounded and with no weapon. It's a miracle I wasn't killed."

Rudi found what he thought was the old road that he and Major Mueller took to the cave. Things looked different now and he wasn't sure. Where there was underbrush that night there were now young saplings. There were many new houses and outbuildings. This was not going to be as easy as the pair had anticipated.

"Rudi, let's just go due west to the river by the best road we can find and then follow the river north," Robert said, growing impatient. "You said the cave was just a short distance from the river."

"That makes sense. We'll have to come across it eventually that way. But if I could find the same road it would save us a lot of time."

"Let's go, Rudi."

When they reached the river they followed it upstream. Robert drove the team within site of the river on an overgrown road once rutted by wagon wheels. Rudi walked between the wagon and the river, confused by the numerous rock outcroppings dotting the river's edge. Nothing looked familiar to him now.

"Rudi, you mean you haven't seen anything you recognize yet?" Robert said after over two hours.

"No, not yet."

"How long did it take you to drive back to the camp from the cave?"

"I don't remember. I was frightened to death that night. Not long."

"It didn't take you two hours did it?"

"No."

"Well then we went by the cave. Let's turn around and go back the same way. Try to remember what you saw that night."

While the two retraced their steps a light came on in Rudi's head. "The island!" he shouted.

"The what?"

"There was a small island a little way out in the river. The cave was in line with the north point of that island."

Their pace quickened now with this revelation. From the wagon Robert saw it first. "Is that the island? I can see some large rocks just ahead."

Rudi ran in the direction Robert was pointing. Robert jumped off the wagon and followed. "This is it, Robert! Look at that groove in the rock. That's where the first shot hit."

They wasted no time throwing aside the rocks Rudi had placed there almost nine years earlier. Using the shovels they brought they cleared away dirt to widen the entrance. Rudi's hand was shaking as he lit the lantern he remembered to bring along.

"It's your treasure," Robert said, motioning Rudi to go down the hole.

Holding the lantern in front of him Rudi worked himself down the hole headfirst. Robert waited for a response. And waited. "Are you all right?" he finally yelled down the hole.

"They're here, Robert! They're still here! Pass me an end of that rope. I'll tie it on and when I tell you, you pull and I'll push."

The oil-treated wooden boxes had weathered well, but years of damp conditions weakened the rope handle and it snapped as soon as Robert pulled. He went sprawling backward and landed on his rump.

"Bloody. They *are* heavy," Robert said to himself.

"I'll have to tie the rope the whole way around the box," Rudi yelled from the cave.

This method worked and the box slowly made its way to the surface. Being the last one Rudi put in, the broken box without the padlock was the first to come out. Rudi didn't wait to retrieve the two others and scratched his way to the surface. Robert already was trying to open the box. The latches were brass and after a little prying with the shovel they broke free and popped open. The two men stared down at the contents. After a few seconds, Robert reached down and picked up one of the coins.

"What are they?" Rudi asked.

"They're coins all right, but I never saw any like this before. It doesn't show a value."

"I don't think the yellow ones are gold—they tarnished," Rudi said, inspecting a coin.

"No, they look like … brass. These look like pewter. I know of no brass or pewter coins."

"Let's get the others and get out of here. We'll have plenty of time to look at them later." Rudi said.

When the three boxes were on the wagon Rudi covered them the best he could with the hay and a bag of oats they brought for the horses. They turned the team toward Trenton.

CHAPTER

FIVE

The routine for the return trip didn't change. Drive, rest the horses, eat, and talk. But now, instead of being full of anticipation, both men felt the sense of satisfaction that comes with success realized. The cool, fresh, early morning air and a breakfast of smoked venison and jam on bread heightened their mood even more.

"The road that goes to Philip's farm is just ahead. Do you want to stop and visit?" Robert asked.

"How long would it take?"

"About an hour each way, plus the visit."

"I'd like to see Philip again but I'm anxious to get home. Let's keep going."

Before Robert could respond, four men on horseback rode past them at full gallop. The pair watched them ride a few hundred feet and stop. As the wagon approached, the mounted men lined up side by side, blocking the path of the wagon.

"Good day, gentlemen," one of them said.

"Good day," said Robert, halting the team.

"Could we have the toll please?" the apparent leader of the group asked.

The leader was dirty and ugly and Robert took an instant

dislike to him. He was bald except for long stringy hair growing from somewhere out of the back of his head. He had a humped back and one arm looked shorter than the other, giving him the sinister appearance of being hunched over forward in the saddle. His beaked nose was crooked, his teeth rotten, and he smelled worse than the horses. One of the other men rode slowly around the wagon looking at the boxes peeking out from under the hay.

"I don't know what you're talking about. Who are you?" Robert demanded.

"Well, what do ya know, a Micky," Ugly said, responding to Robert's brogue, "Are you a Micky too?" he asked Rudi.

"I am German," Rudi said, not knowing he didn't have to be helpful in this situation.

"A Kraut and a Micky," Ugly said, snickering to his friends.

"Two Krauts actually. Now let us pass," Robert said, trying to sound tough.

"What's in the boxes?" asked the man looking over the back of the wagon.

"Not your concern," Robert said, still doing the talking.

"This be a toll road and we're the toll collectors. Ya needs to pay us," Ugly said.

"This is no toll road and we wouldn't pay you even if we had any money."

"Then we must confiscate your wagon," he said, grabbing the bit of one of the horses.

"Mister, hear me clear. We're hard from working all our lives and if you don't let go of that bloody horse we'll show you how hard."

"Tough talk for there bein' two of you and four of us."

"I figure that makes us about even."

"You gotta smart mouth, Micky-Kraut."

"And you're going to have a sore mouth if you don't let go of that bloody horse."

The ugly one let go of the bit and reached inside his shirt to retrieve a pistol. As he did, Robert gave the reins one big slap and yelled "Yaw." The horses lunged forward and Ugly's horse bolted, nearly knocking him off. Robert whipped the reins again and the horses took off at a full gallop. The four thieves gave chase.

Robert managed to stay ahead of them for more than a half mile but the thieves gained ground and pulled even with the team. Rudi had been trying in vain to reach his musket in back of the wildly pitching wagon.

One of the thieves grabbed a harness and brought the horses to a stop. Before they had completely stopped Robert jumped off the wagon at one of the men, knocking him off his horse. Rudi joined his friend and for a while the two held their own, landing more punches than they received, but they couldn't overcome the odds. One of the men pointed his pistol at Rudi's head and ordered both men to lie down on the ground.

"Don't waste the gun powder on these two, take the knives to 'em," Ugly ordered.

As they reached for their knives the report of a rifle caused everyone to flinch. They turned to see three men on horseback and two rifles pointed in their direction.

"Get on your horses and get out of here now," Philip Knapp ordered.

"Just tend to your own business and leave us be," one of Ugly's henchmen yelled.

"This *is* my business … go *now*."

"You got two more shots, mister, then whatya do?" Ugly responded.

"Then two of you will be dead and it will be five against two. Who wants to die first?" Philip said.

"Ugly, rethinking his predicament, motioned to his friends. They mounted their horses and rode back from where they came.

"Glad to see you boys are staying out of trouble," Philip said.

"You come yust in time, yah," Rudi said, trying his English.

"I've never been so glad to see you in all my life, Philip," Robert said, getting to his feet. "Who were they?"

"Bandits," Philip said. "They've been working this road. They stop travelers and threaten them if they don't pay a toll. They pay up, of course. I never travel alone anymore," he said, motioning to his two hired men.

Robert saw Philip looking at the boxes in the back of the wagon. He would never tell Philip they were not his concern, nor could he tell him the story either, not now at least. Philip sensed this and never asked about the boxes or why the pair happened to be in the area. Robert was relieved.

Philip was in a hurry to get home and he couldn't stay and talk. Robert gave him a quick summary of the news. Philip was delighted to hear Robert and Rudi named their sons after him. He was also pleased his two friends were doing so well. He told how Mrs. Knapp was sick and the doctor said she could make a complete recovery if she had a certain medicine of which he had none at the time. It could take weeks to have it shipped from Philadelphia, so Philip volunteered to go get it. He was returning home with the medicine when he interrupted the robbery attempt.

He told Robert and Rudi they could visit and spend the night at his place, but they declined. He apologized for being brief; the pair said they understood. After well wishes and promises of visits the men parted company.

Exhausted, Robert crawled in the back of the wagon, and soon fell asleep. Rudi drove the team with his musket across his lap.

✳✳✳

The two friends made good time, leery to tarry after their encounter with the bandits. By evening they were approaching the outskirts of Harrisburg. Robert was hungry and he had a plan.

"Rudi, have you ever had a bought meal?"

"No."

"Are you hungry?"

"Yes, but we're almost out of money."

"Oh no we're not," Robert said, holding up one of the coins he had pocketed from the wooden box. "It's getting late. We'll rest the horses here and find someplace to eat."

"You want to just walk away and leave the boxes unattended?"

"All figured out—leave it to me."

"I don't think so, Robert. We have no idea what those coins are worth, and they're not ours to spend even if we did."

"We'll replace the value of it later. The proprietor of an eating establishment should know what they're worth."

"But we can be home by daybreak tomorrow."

"Yes, but I'm hungry *now* and we have no more food."

Rudi's empty stomach softened his resolve and he relented. After finding the livery the two men tied the team in front where they could watch it and walked through the large double doors.

"Maybe one of us should stay with the wagon while the other eats."

"No. Just trust me, Rudi."

Rolling his eyes Rudi said, "How many times have I heard that before?"

"Good evening. Are you the proprietor?" Robert asked of a strapping young man.

"Pa is; I work here," said the young man, who was no more than eighteen.

"What's your name, lad?

"Samuel Alt. My Pa's Moses."

"Nice to make your acquaintance, Samuel. I'm Robert and this is my friend Rudi."

"Pleasure," said Sam Alt.

"Our team is out front; would you feed and water them and if you have time rub them down? We'll be gone in a couple of hours."

"Sure will."

"Is your father about?"

"Went home for supper. He'll be back later."

"And you're not afraid someone will start trouble with you while he's gone?"

"Nah, not as long as I have the swoosh-whomper near by."

"The what?"

"The swoosh-whomper," Samuel answered, putting emphasis on and drawing out the "swoosh."

He reached behind a support post and retrieved a fearsome looking club. It was about two feet long and three inches in diameter at one end, tapering to about one inch at the other. Fitted at the thinnest end was a leather loop for the wrist. It had nails driven through the thick end that protruded about half an inch out the opposite side. The nails were arranged so they completely encircled the top of the club. The mere sight of the brutal-looking weapon caused Robert and Rudi to back up a step.

"Did you every hit anybody with that thing?" Robert asked.

"Nah, never had to yet. Just wavin' it about does the job."

He'll do just fine, Robert thought.

"Will you do us a favor, Samuel? We have valuables on the wagon. Can we pull the wagon inside and have you watch it for us?"

"Sure. What are the valuables?"

"Rattlesnakes," Robert fibbed.

The young man's eyes twitched. "Rattlesnakes?"

"Not to worry; they're in boxes. If you stay away from them and let them sleep you'll be fine. Don't let anyone near the boxes though. Do you have a couple padlocks and a chain we can borrow?"

Robert and Rudi walked the team into the stable and added a padlock to the box that had none and chained all the boxes to the wagon, securing them with the second padlock. Robert put the keys in his pocket and paid young Sam Alt his fee. He gave him an extra pence for watching the wagon. This left them with no money but the coin.

"What do you do with the rattlesnakes?"

"A man pays us to catch them for him. He likes to fatten them up and eat them. Then he tans the skin and makes things with it," Robert answered. "Where's the best place to get a meal nearby?"

"Hallsey's Inn. Just down the street. But they don't fix rattlesnake."

Robert didn't respond.

Setting out in the direction Samuel Alt had pointed, Rudi commented, "That sure was a lot of trouble to go through just for a meal."

"Not if you're hungry enough," was Robert's retort.

***

The proprietor of Hallsey's Inn was a brawny man with thick arms, a round face, and no neck, wearing a white apron spotted with food and beer stains. He looked up when a floorboard creaked as Rudi and Robert entered.

"Good evening, gents. Is it a meal or drink you want?" the brawny man said in a gruff but cheerful voice.

"A meal, please," Robert answered.

"Well then, have a seat at the tables. I'll be right with ya."

The pair sat and waited, content watching the other patrons and looking around the inn. The interior was all wood with a bar to one side behind which were double doors that led to the kitchen. High wooden stools lined the front of the bar. At the far end of the bar was a staircase the patrons used to access the sleeping quarters. Eight square tables in two rows with four chairs each lined up six feet back from the barstools. Candle sconces lining the walls, two large lanterns at each end of the bar, and a candle in the center of each of the tables supplied the lighting. The candlelight on the oil-polished wood walls created a warm and comfortable glow. The effect put Robert and Rudi at ease. They thought they were in the lap of luxury.

"Well then, what will you be havin'?"

They looked at each other and said nothing. Seeing they needed help Brawny added, "How about a nice plate each of fried chicken with biscuits and gravy?"

Their faces lit up, and they both nodded, trying not to show their eagerness.

"All right then, comin'right up," their host said as he walked away.

"Can we have a pitcher of stout?" Robert yelled at the proprietor's back.

"Sure can."

When their meals came Robert and Rudi stared at the mountain of food, wondering if all of it was really theirs. They looked at Hallsey, and then each other, and when they were confident a mistake hadn't been made, they ate ... and ate some more.

The chicken was so tender it came free from the bone as soon as it touched their eager teeth. The gravy was hot, brown, and unctuous; the biscuits dripped with butter. They finished every piece of chicken and then mopped their plates clean with the last of the biscuits. They drank every drop of stout.

"That was the best meal I ever had," Rudi said, resting his hand on his stomach.

"Well, be sure to tell Libby that," Robert replied.

Rudi chuckled.

Robert was anxious to pay with the coin and tired of waiting. He motioned the brawny man to their table.

"You're the proprietor I presume?" Robert asked.

"Yessir, Thomas Hallsey, at your service."

"We'd like to pay you, Mr. Hallsey," Robert said, handing him the coin.

Hallsey looked at the coin, turning it over and over again.

"What's this?" he asked, biting the coin.

"We'd like to pay you with that."

"Well, it says it's 'Currency' but it doesn't show a value. I never saw one of these. It looks like pewter."

"What's it worth?"

"It's not worth a thing to me. I'll thank you to pay me in real money," Hallsey said with growing agitation.

"That's the only money we have. We want to pay you with that," a deflated Robert said.

Their conversation had the attention of all the patrons now and with his credibility on the line Hallsey said, "If you can't pay me I'll send for the constable and you'll spend the night in irons." He turned to walk away.

"Wait, Mr. Hallsey," Robert said, thinking fast, "Are you a betting man?"

"Well ... ahh, I've been known to make an honest man's wager now and again," Hallsey said, his eyes darting from side to side.

The crowd snickered.

"I'll wager you my friend here can beat you at arm wrestling. If you win we'll pay you in labor at twice what the meals are worth. If he beats you, the meals are free. And no matter who wins your patrons will be entertained."

The crowd approved and someone yelled, "Go ahead, Tom. I'd like to see you work up a sweat for a bloody change."

The room erupted in laughter.

A stunned Rudi looked at Robert and then at Hallsey's tree trunk arms. He pushed back his hair with his fingers.

Hallsey eyed Rudi's lanky appearance and said, "Agreed. I have a lot of work needs done around here," then yelled over his shoulder, "Martha, fetch me two fresh eggs."

When the eggs arrived Hallsey laid down the rules like he had done this before.

"Whoever breaks the egg with the other man's hand wins.

Someone will steady the eggs. Elbows must stay on the table, and no stopping. If you stop or lift your elbow, the other man wins. And if you lose you pay for the egg too. Agreed?"

"Agreed," Robert said before Rudi could respond.

Hallsey sat down opposite Rudi, flexing his arms and cracking his fingers. The two wrestlers locked their hands together, each readjusting until they were comfortable.

"Everybody ready?" Robert asked.

Both men nodded.

"Then on my word begin," he said. "Readyyy … now!"

Both men pushed with all their strength on the other's hand, hoping for a quick victory. Their arms never moved off center, a sign of two well-matched opponents. They held that position for several minutes. Hallsey's expression showed surprise at the younger man's strength. *I won't be able to stick with him long,* Hallsey thought. *I better end this now.* With a grunt he pushed with all his strength and Rudi's arm inched backward. Rudi knew that if his arm passed a certain angle recovery was almost impossible. He pushed against Hallsey's tree trunk stopping his own arm's descent, then moved Hallsey's arm to vertical. Beads of sweat formed on Hallsey's forehead and both men's faces glowed red, veins in their necks swelling.

After several more minutes of their arms being stalled in the vertical, Rudi sensed a slight weakening in his opponent. He grabbed the end of the table with his free hand and pushed with the other as hard as he could. Hallsey's arm now passed vertical and descended toward the egg. Rudi never let up the pressure but Hallsey refused to go down. *This is the toughest man I ever wrestled,* Rudi thought.

The crowd was excited and boisterous as they cheered on their favorite. Rudi thought of home and his wife and children, and then of spending the night working in a strange town or worse yet, in irons. With a great continuous grunt building in intensity he pushed Hallsey's trembling hand down just far enough to crack the egg's shell. The crowd cheered the victor but nobody louder than Robert.

"Good show, Rudi, you had me worried there," Robert said.

"I had *you* worried?"

"You're as strong as an ox, mister, and you beat me fair you did. I hope you fancied your meal," Hallsey said, wiping the sweat from his forehead with his apron and slapping Rudi on the back. "If you're ever in Harris' Ferry again ... no, excuse me. We're to be called Harris*burg* now ... stop by and we'll have another go at it."

The two men shook hands with Thomas Hallsey and walked back to the livery stable. They removed the chain and padlocks and returned them to the young man with the swoosh-whomper.

"Anybody bother the wagon?"

"Nah. Nobody was here except Pa and he left again. He doesn't like snakes."

"Thank you, young Sam Alt," Robert said, then turned to Rudi. "I'm tired now, but I guess there's no use trying to spend the coin on a soft bed for the night."

Rudi looked sideways at Robert and jumped in back of the wagon.

"Your turn to drive, Robert."

When the two arrived home the next morning they unloaded the boxes in Robert's barn. They hammered the padlocks off the other two boxes, finding the contents the same as the first.

Maggie came to the barn and they showed her the treasure, informing her that the coins were not theirs to keep, not yet anyway. Robert instructed her to say nothing about this to anyone. Holding one of the coins Maggie's only comment was, "They're pretty," then testing the weight added, "and heavy."

The men agreed the best course of action was to talk to the Overseer of the Poor for their township (Upper Paxton at that time, later to be Lykens), part of the newly formed Dauphin

County. The Overseer of the Poor, or Township Supervisor, tended to the business affairs of their district, and saw to it that the poor and downtrodden were cared for. That included assuring illegitimate children were supported by their father, or some other agreeable party. Robert and Rudi reasoned the Overseer should know about the coins, or at least know who to ask about them.

The next day they went to see Overseer John Klingman and show him the coin. He had never seen any before and knew nothing about it. He said the best he could do was take the coin to Harrisburg on his next trip to the courthouse and ask around. Robert told him he need not bother asking Thomas Hallsey.

He instructed Klingman that if he found someone who knew anything about the coin to ask if they also knew of any that were missing or stolen, but he didn't tell him why. He also asked him if he would report their encounter with the bandits near Reading to the proper authorities.

A few weeks later, Klingman visited Rudi and told him no one in Harrisburg knew anything about the coin. He said he had passed the sample on to a friend, William Hoy, who was going to Philadelphia in a few days and would seek out the Treasurer of Pennsylvania or some other knowledgeable party. Hoy asked Klingman to write a letter of explanation to accompany the coin, which he said he did. Rudi thanked Klingman and then walked to Robert's house to give him the news.

When Rudi was finished explaining what Klingman said, Robert's hands fell to his sides. They would have to wait some more.

✳✳✳

Almost two months passed with no word on the coin. It was harvest time and as usual Robert and Rudi helped each other with their crops. They were in Robert's field picking winter squash and pumpkins when John Klingman rode toward them.

"I have a letter for you. It's addressed to me but it's about the coin. It's from Philadelphia. They held it for me at the courthouse in Harrisburg and I picked it up yesterday. Might as well keep it, it's no good to me. The coin's inside," Klingman said as he reined his horse to leave.

"Wait, John," Robert said. Handing him a large squash he added, "Thanks for your help. Here, take this to the wife."

"Sure thing, Robert," Klingman said and rode off.

"I'm thirsty, Rudi. Let's go to the house and read this."

The pair sat down at the kitchen table with the letter. Maggie served them each a cup of cool spring water and a pitcher for refills. When Robert unfolded the letter the coin fell on the table. He translated to German for Rudi.

To My Esteemed Friend John Klingman, Overseer of the Poor Upper Paxton Township, Dauphin County, Pennsylvania

Greetings

Received yours on behalf of your constituents Messrs. Robert Rhone and Rudolph Hoppe on Tuesday last along with the coin in question. I will not speculate from where Messrs. Rhone and Hoppe obtained the coin but I have endeavored at your request to establish its value unfortunately with no success. I have no personal knowledge of such a coin being minted at any time for the Government of the United States or for any of the Colonies for that matter, even though information on the coin itself suggests otherwise. However, finding it intriguing I sought further assistance from my colleagues with knowledge of currency, two of which are members of the present Congress. They too were baffled by the coin. Therefore it stands to reason without any knowledge of said mintage there can be no knowledge of any quantity missing or stolen. Please accept my apology and know I did my best for you.

I can tell you this, however, with all the assurances of my Office and Position and that of my colleagues as well. The coin has no

value as legal tender in the United States of America and I would
caution against any attempt to use it as such. It is our collective
ruling that you are free to keep the coin and do with it as you wish.
I would suggest if you have any quantity of coins you could do your
best by reforging them into something useful. I regret having to
report in opposition of your favor but I trust I have been of some
assistance in this matter. I am herein returning the coin and will
consider this matter closed.

I Remain Your Obedient and Humble Servant,
David Rittenhouse, Treasurer
Commonwealth of Pennsylvania
Philadelphia 14th Day of September 1785

Robert and Rudi didn't know if they should laugh or cry.

"They're worthless!"

"All that for nothing? I was almost killed for nothing?" Rudi added to Robert's conclusion.

"We might as well throw them in the bloody Mahantango for all the good they'll do us," Robert said in frustration.

With a glint in her clear green eyes, Maggie Rhone responded with a comment she hoped would lighten the mood. Rudi started to laugh but stopped short when he saw Robert's disapproving glare at his wife.

"Could he be mistaken?" This was Rudi changing the subject.

"He's the treasurer of the whole bleeding state of Pennsylvania; he should know, I'd say."

Robert got up to leave.

"Rudi, will you stay for supper?" Maggie asked.

"Thank you, but Libby's making Hasenpfeffer."

"Aah ... Mother taught us how to make good Hasenpfeffer."

"She did, yes. What are you having?"

"Roasted venison, baked squash with honey, buttered noodles, and gravy."

"That sounds just fine, Maggie."

Robert was leaning on an outstretched arm with one hand on the door and the other on his hip, staring at the floor. *These two can talk about food at a time like this?*

"Rudi! If you two are finished with the supper arrangements, can we go now?"

The two men returned to the fields, Robert more dejected than Rudi. Rudi attempted conversation, but Robert was in no mood. The men worked in silence for a long while.

When he felt it was safe to speak Rudi said, "Robert, you are more disappointed about this than I, and I'm the one who almost got killed over them. What were your plans with the coins had they been worth something?"

"No, you almost got killed twice and I once, and the both of us almost spent a night in irons over them. The truth is, Rudi, I hoped we would *not* be able to find the owner, which means they would have been yours to keep. And I hoped you then would share enough with me so I could bring my brothers and sisters and their families over here from Ireland. Think ill of me if you must, but that's the truth."

"I don't think ill of you, Robert. I would have given you half. As it is, you can have them *all*. I just want one of the brass to keep." He paused, then added, "I see why your feathers are ruffled, but you're doing good with your crops. It won't be long now until you can bring your family here." Holding a large, round squash in front of his face Rudi asked, "Do I look like Thomas Hallsey?"

Robert managed a crooked smile.

CHAPTER

SIX

As years passed Robert and Rudi thought less and less about the treasure that almost was and the rich men they almost were. They were farmers, after all, and farmers are busy people, no time to fret about much of anything except the business at hand.

They got on with the serious task of raising their families and improving their land. Both increased the size of their families. They also increased the size of their farms by buying adjoining acreage as it became available. They were able to buy more and better equipment and with the help of their growing children soon had profitable farms that were the envy of their neighbors.

And in time, with the help of his brother James, Robert brought their eager brothers and sisters to America one by one and helped them get established in the area. A few decided to stay in Ireland.

Aside from the tragedy that struck Robert's family in the spring of 1788, he and Rudi lead calamity-free lives and were contented men.

***

Robert was slow to recover from Maggie's death on June 7, 1788. He tended to the needs of his children and that was about all. He started to drink to drunkenness. Rudi was determined not to sit by and watch what happened to his father happen to his friend.

Every chance he could, Rudi saw to it that Robert was in the company of a prospective wife. Robert showed little interest. This time it was an invitation to Robert and the children for supper at the Hoppe's house. What they didn't tell Robert was that another person had also been invited.

"Robert. You know Catherine Bingaman, don't you?" Libby asked.

"Yes, I do. Nice to see you again, Catherine."

It worked.

In the fall of 1789, Robert married the midwife who had delivered his and Maggie's two children. Catherine Bingaman was a strong woman eleven years his junior, with a temperament as fiery as her red hair and Robert soon learned his limits with her. Being married to a man who drank to excess was not in Catherine's constitution and that was the first thing to change. She was a hard worker, tending to her midwife duties as well as the needs of her ready-made family. Catherine Bingaman was just what Robert needed.

As happened with Maggie, over time Robert fell in love with her. They would add ten more children to the Rhone family. Robert told Rudi and Libby years later, had it not been for their help and friendship he never would have made it through his loss.

When the Rhones and Hoppes socialized, as they often did, it was in front of one or the others' fireplace, telling stories over warm apple cider and a delicious new crop Rudi raised called popcorn. The most requested story by their children and grandchildren, although they heard it dozens of times before, was how Robert and Rudi came to own thousands of worthless coins.

Worthless, at least, during their time.

Part Two

O that moral science were in a fair way improvement that men would cease to be wolves to one another and that human beings would at length learn what they now improperly call humanity.

—Benjamin Franklin

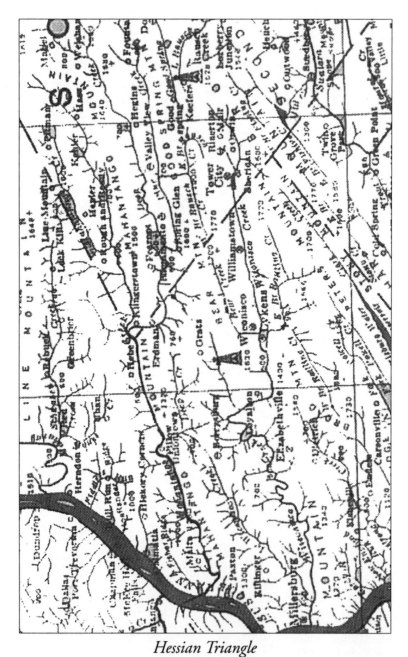

Hessian Triangle
The junction of Northumberland, Schuylkill, and Dauphin Counties,
Pennsylvania, named for the many ex-Hessian soldiers who settled this area.

CHAPTER

SEVEN

March 2004
Lykens Township, Dauphin County, Pennsylvania

They lived in a rural setting a couple miles southwest of the small town of Gratz. It was a beautiful area with small family farms and rolling strip-farmed fields that somehow had managed to resist change. Aside from a few dozen new homes and the inevitable convenience mart gas station here and there, it looked much the same as it had fifty years ago. The area residents liked it that way.

The old man and old lady sat in the small living room of their refurbished two-hundred-year-old farmhouse. Beau, the three-year-old black Labrador retriever was asleep on the floor by the old lady's feet. It was late evening. The cuckoo bird in the antique clock on the wall had just earned its keep by singing out its two-tone name nine times in succession. Beau lifted his head, gave a disinterested glance at the bird, and then resumed his nap.

The cool windy weather had kept the couple inside most of the day, although there was plenty of spring yard work to be done. March is always temperamental in central Pennsylvania. It gave them a chance to do just as they pleased.

The man and woman had long passed the point where words were needed to talk to each other. They were long past the point where they needed to communicate at all, telepathically or otherwise, to be content in one another's company. Just knowing the other was nearby was enough. Tonight she was happy in her Stephen King and he poring over the family group sheets. As usual the TV wasn't on.

They had had a good fifty-six years of marriage and a fruitful life together. They both knew it and didn't have to say it and never did. Their four surviving children and eleven grandchildren all made periodic visits. They would have liked to see them more.

Seventy-six-year-old Melchoir Rhone had been working part-time on their family tree for almost thirty years. Since his retirement as a Conrail engineer fourteen years ago he worked at it full-time. His wife of the same age, the former Mary "Polly" Wolfgang, had helped when she could. Polly enjoyed their trips to the quaint historical societies and old county courthouses. She also enjoyed going to the secluded cemeteries—few knew even existed—to photograph the ancient tombstones of their ancestors. She liked meeting the "cousins" she never knew she had, the result of all the contacts they made seeking family information.

Much progress had been made, but a family genealogy is something that is rarely completed. Everyone has two sets of grandparents, and working back that number doubles every generation. By the time a line of descent is traced back just seven generations there are well over two hundred ancestors involved. Considering there are siblings and *their* families for each individual, and some paper trails are hundreds of years old, it can be a daunting task.

The rumors of a family treasure had persisted through the generations. Mel never paid it much attention until recently. Just a romantic family story passed from father to son that was exaggerated every time it was told, had been his conclusion.

Mel Rhone hoped someone in his family would continue his

work after he was gone. But now, after the unsettling information he uncovered, he had to make sure they did.

Mel and Polly had made more progress on their genealogy in the last ten years than all the previous years combined. Internet access was the biggest boon ever to the genealogically inclined. Email enabled "cousins" from all parts of the world to swap notes in real time.

They were of the generation not born with a mouse in their hand, and it took them a long time to learn how to use the PC even with the tutelage of their grandson, Will Rhone. But once they learned, real progress was made. The number of resources online was staggering and it was growing on a daily basis. With the addition of a genealogy software package Will had bought them, keeping information organized was a breeze. Mel still had some of the old school in him though and he liked using the family group sheets as well.

It was online that Mel made contact with Morris Anthony from Oregon, a distant cousin. The ancestor they shared was Robert Rhone, Mel's third great-grandfather, Anthony's forth. They shared a lot of family history and it was through Anthony that Mel learned two invaluable tidbits. One, that stories of a treasure filtered down through Anthony's line *independent* of Mel's line, and two, that the 18th-century family Bible of Robert Rhone still existed as late as 1939 and Anthony had the documentation to prove it. The proof was in the form of a letter written by Anthony's granduncle to his grandmother. His granduncle had seen the Bible and named the person who had it in his possession in 1939. Mel knew the custom was to pass on the family Bible to the oldest son and using that scenario he had tracked the Bible to a living cousin, Delbert Rhone, from Austin, Texas. This had taken him nearly a year. During their initial contact Mel was surprised to find a reluctant Delbert Rhone. Delbert was not sure he wanted anything to do with lending out his priceless family heirloom, or giving out the information it contained for that matter. Delbert told Mel he was interested mainly in the later genealogy rather than the very early family. Something Mel could not comprehend.

Through personal phone calls and a lot of coaxing email Mel finally received a promise from Delbert to try and work out a way to share the Bible information. That is where he stood now. Delbert Rhone had said, in essence, don't call me, I'll call you. Mel found that nerve-racking.

To a genealogist the discovery of a family Bible is major. The old Bibles contained pages intended for entering family births, baptisms, weddings, deaths, and other important information. Someone in a position to know the truth—making it an accurate and reliable primary source—usually entered the information in the Bible at the time of the event.

As great a tool as the Internet is, Mel felt the information gleaned there should have corroboration from another source. The Bible could be that other source and maybe provide new information as well. The thought of having just what he needed in the hands of someone not willing to give it up made him nervous indeed.

***

From a dead sleep Beau jumped to his feet with a great bark. As always when Beau did this, the couple jumped in unison.

"Beau! You're going to be the death of me yet," Polly scolded. She said that every time it happened.

"What is it, boy … what's out there?" Mel opened the front door to let the excited dog outside.

Beau was a good watchdog and a great friend. Mel had developed a strong attachment to him. He was fascinated how Beau could be sound asleep but yet on full alert at the same time. Scents and sounds detectable only to the vigilant dog crept into the ancient house through dozens of minuscule cracks and crevices. It got so Mel could tell from the tone of Beau's bark the degree of seriousness of the offending noise or whiff. This one was real and serious in Beau's eyes. *Deer, dog, or some other critter*, Mel guessed. He didn't hear a car come up the driveway, so he ruled out people.

Before Mel had returned to his Easy-Lounger, Beau let out a loud, sickening yelp. He turned and ran out of the house as Polly watched from the window. When he rounded the corner of the house he saw Beau lying on his side, motionless. Before he could reach the dog a strong arm grabbed him around the neck from behind and a gloved hand put a pistol to his head.

"Into the house now," the man said through his ski mask.

When they entered the house Polly was fumbling with the phone.

"Put the phone down now, lady, or he's a dead man."

Polly's shaking hand returned the handset to its base. The intruder released Mel and told him to go stand with his wife.

"Who are you? What do you want? We don't keep any money here," Mel said.

"I don't want your money."

"Well then get out of here," Mel ordered, "And what did you do to my dog?"

"Your doggy is dead, and the both of you will be too unless you give me what I want."

"What do you want?"

"I want all your research on Robert Rhone … *all* of it."

"What?!" Mel couldn't believe what he was hearing.

"You heard me. Get me everything you have on Robert Rhone. Now where is it?"

"Are you out of you mind? All you would've had to do is knock on the door and ask. I would have copied it for you … you stupid jerk."

At hearing that the masked man buried his fist into Mel's stomach and the old man doubled over in pain.

"Where is it?" the annoyed intruder said.

Mel was unable to speak so Polly answered, "It's … it's in the filing cabinet in the office."

"Show me. The both of you. Lets go."

When the three entered the office the intruder ordered Mel and Polly to stand where he could see them as he stood in front of the filing cabinet.

"Where is it, under 'R'?"

"No, I filed it under Arthur Godfrey ... Einstein," Mel chided.

"Shut up!" he yelled as he delivered another blow to Mel's midsection.

"Please don't say anything more, Mel," Polly sobbed.

The man retrieved the file of Robert Rhone and Philip Rhone and shoved them into his jacket.

"Is this everything you have?"

"Yes, that's all there is," Polly said.

"It better be or I'll be back."

He then turned to Polly and eyed her up and down. Using his pistol to push the hair away from her eyes the intruder said, "You know you're not too bad for an old gal."

"Leave her alone, you freak!" Mel yelled and lunged toward the man. The intruder pushed Polly backward, and as she fell her head struck the seat of the wooden desk chair. Before Polly hit the floor he swung the pistol into Mel's temple. He dropped to the floor in a heap.

***

Will Rhone watched the ambulance weave between the police cars and disappear after it pulled onto the Gratztown Road. He had found his grandparents unconscious when he stopped by for an early morning visit; alive only in the sense that they were still breathing. The police wanted to talk to him now.

"Mr. Rhone, I'm Trooper Wilber Krull of the Pennsylvania State Police. I'd like to ask you a few questions."

"Yes. Okay."

"You're the couple's grandson, is that right?"

"Yes."

"Do you come here often?"

"Yes, as much as I can."

Will spent more time with his grandparents than the other grandchildren. Partly because he only lived two miles away, but mostly because he liked their company. His grandfather's stories about their ancestors had sparked an interest in genealogy and he helped his grandparent's research whenever he could. Will was the son of Mel and Polly's firstborn, William Rhone, Sr., deceased. When Will was born the family called William Senior "Bill" and William Junior "Will." It stuck.

"Please look around the house to see if anything is missing or disturbed," Trooper Krull said.

"Of course."

Will carefully looked all over the house but didn't see anything out of place or notice anything missing. When he looked in the office the file cabinet was closed and it never occurred to him to check inside, it was just family information of no universal value. He got out of there fast; the room gave him the creeps now.

"Officer, everything looks in order and I don't see anything missing. What do you make of this?"

"It's hard to say right now. I see no signs of forced entry. It looks like whoever did this ran into the dog first, took care of him, and then entered the house. Did your grandparents keep valuables here, in a safe or hiding place?"

"No, they don't like keeping a lot of cash here."

"Do they have enemies, or does someone have a grudge against them?"

"No, they get along well with everybody."

"And there was no family trouble?"

"No, none."

"Sorry, Mr. Rhone, but I need to ask ... do they get along with each other?"

"Very much so!" Will didn't like the implication.

"Can you think of anyone who may have done this?"

"No."

"And you're sure there was no family discord?"

"Yes, I am."

Trooper Krull thought a minute, then said, "It's peculiar, Mr. Rhone. The perpetrator or perpetrators didn't even take the money from your grandfather's wallet, or anything else, so you say. We have to rule out robbery as a motive at this point. I can assure you we will do everything we can to find who did this."

"Thank you, Officer. Can I go to the hospital now?"

"Yes. That's all for now. Thank you. We'll be in touch, Mr. Rhone. Oh, one more thing," the policeman said as Will walked away. "Was the dog kept outside?"

"No. He was a house dog."

**

The Dauphin County Hospital in Harrisburg was almost an hour's drive from Mel Rhone's house. The drive gave Will time to think about his grandparents. This kind of thing just didn't happen in rural upper Dauphin County. He tried to think of anything that would have prompted the attack but came up blank. He was worried about them both, but his grandmother most of all. Though she was breathing she looked awful: her color wasn't right.

The tragedy making him reflective, Will had time to regard his own life too. Thirty-five years old and single, he was a cabinetmaker by trade and had started *Rhone's Woodworld* shortly after college. He had earned a degree in history, but he discovered he liked working with his hands more than he liked his major. He had God-given talent and he felt he should use it. Even at an early age he liked working with wood. At age six he made a cutting board to give to his mother for Christmas. Using a coping saw he had cut it out of an old used pine board he found in the basement and sanded it smooth. It had taken him weeks. The soft pine was a bad choice of wood for a cutting board and it was dotted with rusty nail holes. He had the cutting board now and he could see from the wear in the center his mother had actually used it in spite of its shortcomings.

He built the reputation for excellence his business enjoyed with a strategy of selective hiring. He looked for the right attitude more than skill. Skill he could teach, attitude he couldn't. The result was he now had employed thirteen devoted craftsmen producing work that drew customers from all over the state and beyond.

When he arrived at the hospital he gave his name at the information desk and the pleasant receptionists directed him where to wait. She told him a doctor would be with him as soon as possible.

In the waiting room were a dozen comfortable chairs, a couch, a few magazine racks, and seven people. A young couple sat in silence on the couch facing each other, their four hands intertwined. There was soft easy-listening music playing in the background. Will pretended to read a magazine at first but then just sat and watched the others once they became used to his presence and he their's. *Nobody here looks happy. Surely hospital stays turn out happy sometimes.* He had a sickening feeling in the pit of his stomach.

"Mr. Rhone?"

Will stood.

"I'm the Emergency Room Doctor, John Packard. Will you come with me please?"

They entered a small office with an acoustic ceiling, smooth white walls, a light bar used to view x-rays, a small desk, and a few chairs.

"Have a seat, please."

The doctor sat on the corner of the desk facing Will.

"I'm afraid I have some bad news for you, Mr. Rhone. We were unable to save your grandmother."

Will's heart sank.

"It appears right now she died of a heart attack. It's my understanding that she lay unconscious for hours before you discovered her. Is that correct?"

Will didn't respond.

"Mr. Rhone. Is that correct?"

"Ah … I don't know. I talked to them last night about eight."

"If she had received attention sooner we may have been able to save her. We don't know now when she may have suffered the heart attack. The contusion on her head was serious but in my opinion, not fatal. We'll know more after the autopsy. I'm very sorry." After watching Will's reaction he added, "Are you okay, Mr. Rhone?"

Will gave a not-so-sure nod.

The doctor continued, "I'm afraid I can't give you much information on your grandfather right now other than to say he is holding his own. He is still unconscious, but his vitals are good. The trauma to his left temple and bruises to his stomach area are the only injuries we can find. Thankfully, his skull is not fractured. I'll be able to tell you more tomorrow."

"Thank you doctor."

"If you would like to sit here awhile, please feel free," the doctor said as he left the room.

Will nodded. When the doctor was gone he buried his face in his hands. After sitting in the office for a few minutes Will left. *I have work to do.* When he arrived home he started the awful task of notifying his family.

***

The funeral of Polly Rhone was like all funerals, unpleasant but necessary. Friends and loved ones need closure. In this case, closure to a life only a handful of those attending knew anything about, or so Will thought. He felt like he was the only one who knew what a saint his grandmother was and the lonely feeling made him numb.

The whole scene was surreal to him and he wanted it to be over as soon as possible. He missed his grandmother already. He didn't like feeling cynical. Other than grief, that was the only thing that surfaced through the numbness. *Why is it families wait until someone dies to get together?*

Someday, Will would see things for what they were. He wasn't the only one who knew the kind of person his grandmother was. Hundreds of relatives, friends, and neighbors came to pay tribute to a woman who had led an exemplary Christian life. They came to celebrate that life and see Mary "Polly" Wolfgang Rhone off to her just Reward.

Will had a lot on his mind. His grandfather was still unconscious, although the hospital had called and left him a message just before the service began. "Come as soon as you can," was the only part he remembered. He didn't like the sound of that. *Why do hospitals never tell you what to expect over the phone?*

Will stayed at the post-funeral gathering until just past the point it would have been considered in bad to taste leave. He didn't tell anyone about the phone call from the hospital. He was not sure why. During the drive to the hospital he thought about his grandmother and all the loving things she had done for him as far back as he could remember. He had to redirect his thoughts; it was too painful. *There's time for memories later.*

When he arrived on his grandfather's floor he ran into Dr. Packard.

"Oh, Mr. Rhone, thank you for coming. Good news. Your grandfather has partially regained consciousness. We're optimistic about his recovery. It would be good for you to see him now and talk to him even though he may not be very responsive."

"Yes, of course."

"I wouldn't tell him about your grandmother just yet. We moved him to Room 202 just down the hall. Go ahead. I'll be there as soon as I can."

When Will entered Room 202 his grandfather didn't look any different than he had the day before. Tubes going in and out of him, his face shades of yellow, black, and blue. Will couldn't be sure if his grandfather was sleeping or unconscious. He spoke to him anyway.

"Grandpa, it's Will. How are you feeling?"

Mel's eyes fluttered, then opened halfway.

"Will?"

"Yes. How are you feeling?"

"A guy came to the house and ..."

"I know, Grandpa; we won't worry about that now."

"How's Polly?"

Will didn't answer, and didn't like doing it.

"Your grandmother, how is she? They won't tell me anything here."

"Are they taking good care of you?" Will made a feeble attempt to change the subject.

Mel wasn't fooled. He knew the answer to his question at that point and he closed his eyes again.

"Will you come back later?"

"Of course, Grandpa; you rest now."

When he left, Will met Dr. Packard on his way to Room 202.

"How did it go?"

"He was speaking well, Doctor."

"Good. I'm going to see him now."

"Doctor, he asked about my grandmother and I didn't answer him. But I think he knows."

"Okay. I'll talk to him."

"Thank you, Doctor."

CHAPTER

EIGHT

The police had visited Mel Rhone as soon as they learned he was conscious and speaking. The hospital had been instructed to call them right away. Mel told them everything he could remember about the attack and the intruder. They were baffled by what the intruder stole. They also visited Will, hoping he could tell them why anyone would go to such extremes for two files of family research. Will didn't have a clue.

Will visited his grandfather every day for the next five days and saw he was becoming more alert each day, aside from the periods of silence now and then when his mind seemed to wander. Will surmised it was at those times thoughts of his wife crept into his consciousness.

On the sixth day Mel was coherent and talkative. He was excited because the doctor said he could be released in two days. The doctor had alerted Will to that possibility the day before, and he wanted to know what provisions were being made. Will said he had hired a visiting nurse to check on Mel daily, and that he was going to move in with him for a while. The doctor was satisfied with that arrangement. Today Mel wanted to talk about the night of the attack.

"The police were here to talk to me a few days ago, Will."

"Yes, I know. They visited me too."

"Did they tell you about the files?"

"Yes. I have no idea what that means."

"I think I do, and I am going to need help. Can you get some time off work?"

"I'm the boss, Grandpa, so of course I can."

"Good. Here's what I want you to do. Contact Karen Holtzman and tell her I need her help."

"Isn't that Keith Holtzman's sister?"

"Yes, she's been staying with Keith."

"I thought she moved out west someplace?"

"Washington, but she moved back a couple of years ago. Karen looked me up when she found out I was interested in genealogy. We worked together on both our families for over a year."

"That's right, I sorta remember that now that you mention it."

"She's a great researcher, Will. Excellent reasoning ability and good instincts. Ask her if she has time to spend helping us solve this. I want the three of us to work together. I can't get around like I used to. Now go. We'll talk more when I get out of here."

✳✳✳

Will went from the hospital straight to Keith Holtzman's house in Wiconisco Township. Like Mel Rhone's house it was a refurbished old farmhouse in a country setting. Keith's nineteen-year-old son Jason answered the door.

"Hi. I'm Will Rhone."

"Yeah. I know who you are. I'm Jason."

"Nice to meet you, Jason. Is your Aunt Karen in?"

"Yeah. I'll get her. You can come in."

Will stepped into the beautiful modern kitchen. The floor and countertops were ceramic tile. In the center was a rugged rustic oak table designed much like a picnic table, complete with benches. The cabinets were well-crafted oak, but the work was not his. He ran his hands over the fine workmanship.

"Beautiful, aren't they?" This was Karen Holtzman.

"Yes, they are."

"I don't think your business was up and running when Keith had them made."

Karen was a year younger than Will and Keith was a few years older. She was right; Keith Holtzman married soon after graduating high school and remodeled the old farmhouse soon after that.

"Whoever did them did a beautiful job."

"I haven't seen you for years, Will Rhone. I'm so sorry to hear about your grandmother. What an awful thing."

"Thank you."

"How about a cup of coffee?"

Will nodded, and then regarded Karen Holtzman. The only recollection he had of her was as an awkward but fun-loving teenager. Her adult years had been good to her; she was now a beautiful woman. She was about five feet seven, he figured. Her thick, sandy-colored hair with soft waves fell a little past her shoulders. It was the kind of hair that develops blond streaks when exposed to the summer sun. There was a natural healthy tone to her skin, which overstated her blue eyes and snow-white teeth. Her voluptuous figure would claim she was slightly overweight on the weight-to-height charts, but she was not. She still had the pleasant disposition he remembered. Will was partial to pleasant, voluptuous women with beautiful teeth. He thought she was perfect.

As Karen served the coffee she asked, "I'm going down to see Mel on Friday. How's he doing?"

"He'd like that, but he's coming home that day. You're welcome to come over to the house and see him. As a matter of fact I need help with a surprise I have planned for him. Will you help?"

"Sure. I'd be glad to."

"The reason I'm here, Karen, is Grandpa wants me to ask you if you can help us with some research. He didn't go into detail. I'm sure he'll get into that, but he wants to know if you have some time to spend on whatever it is he has in mind. I think it has something to do with the attack."

"Okay. I have until this fall. I applied for a teaching position on Long Island, New York. It's looking good for me right now."

"Great. Here's what I need you to do on Friday."

Karen was delighted with the surprise Will had planned. She came to Mel's house about eight on Friday morning.

Will explained the day's agenda. "I can pick Grandpa up any time after ten, and you'll be here a couple of hours by yourself. Is that okay?

"I don't mind."

"Why did you move back East?" Will asked.

"It's complicated. I needed a change and a rest."

"You taught in Washington state too?"

"Yes, I taught high school history in Tacoma."

"Oh, my major too," Will said.

"Did you ever teach?"

"No, I started my business right out of college. I like history, but I like what I'm doing better."

"You never married, Will?"

"No. Did you?"

"Close, but ... no."

With that Will noticed a change in Karen's demeanor and figured that subject had something to do with her moving east. He changed the subject. "Did you hear what the assailant wanted the night of the attack?"

"No."

"The file of Robert Rhone. That's it. He also took Philip Rhone's file, Robert's son."

"What? That's bizarre. Robert Rhone that's your immigrant ancestor, isn't it?

"Why, yes," Will said, surprised Karen knew.

"Mel and I worked on our genealogies for about a year after I came back."

"Yes, he mentioned that. I take it from your reaction you don't have any idea what that guy might have wanted with those files."

"No, none."

"I get the impression Grandpa knows much more about this than he's saying."

"I think you're right. His mind's as sharp as the mind of a man half his age."

"Yes, it is." Checking his watch he added, "Time for me to go, Karen."

"Okay, I'll get everything ready and watch for you."

"I'll give you the signal from the kitchen door. Oh, did you ever find a connection between our families?"

"None that we've uncovered so far."

✳✳✳

The hospital attendant delivered Mel Rhone to Will after the usual ride in a wheelchair and gave instructions for him to take it easy and rest for a while. The attendant requested that they have the visiting nurse contact Dr. Packard. Both men agreed to all.

"Did you talk to Karen?" was Mel's first question.

"Yes. She said she could help out until this fall. She'll be by the house a little later."

"Good. How about your work?"

"Already taken care of, Grandpa. I put my foreman, Ed Klinger, in charge; he said he would take care of everything for as long as I wanted. I'll make spot checks when I can."

"Ed Klinger. He's a good man, isn't he?"

"Yes, he is. He's been with me from the beginning. I trust him completely."

As Will pulled up to Mel's house he gave a quick toot on the horn. Mel gave him a questioning glance. He entered the house

with the help of a cane supplied by the hospital and Will support-
ing the other arm. Once inside he settled into the Easy-Lounger.

"Do you need anything, Grandpa?"

"Yes. A cup of that instant cappuccino stuff." Mel had become addicted to the hot beverage.

"I'll make you a cup. But first I have a surprise for you. There's
someone who wants to see you."

Will went into the kitchen and motioned through the door
window to Karen, who had been waiting on the closed-in porch.
When she opened the door he stepped back so the surprise wouldn't
knock him over.

"*BEAU!* But how …"

The black Lab didn't wait for Mel to finish. He jumped on his
lap and licked every inch of his face.

"Oh, Beau. I thought you were a goner."

"When he heard the car he went crazy. I didn't think I would
be able to hold onto his leash," Karen said.

"Karen, you're here too. Nice to see you again." Hugging the
dog and fighting back tears Mel added, "Will, how … ?"

"When I arrived here that morning the first thing I noticed
was Beau didn't greet me at the car or at the front door. Then I
found you and Grandma and called 911. I told the dispatcher to
send an ambulance and the police. The police arrived about the
same time as the ambulance. By then Ed Klinger had arrived. He
heard the ambulance dispatched to the house on his scanner and
came over to see if he could help.

"The police told us that they found an injured black dog lying beside the house. I was in the house with you and Grandma
and I didn't want to leave you, so I asked Ed if he would take Beau
to Doc Philips and tell him to do whatever it took to save his life.

"Later Doc Philips called and said Beau had been struck on
the head with something hard and had a bad concussion, but he
thought he would be alright if he could make it through the next

few days. When I picked him up this morning the Doc said he made a steady recovery, just like you, Grandpa. Karen said she would watch Beau and help me with this little surprise."

"This *big* surprise. I don't know what to say. You have no idea what this means to me. Thank you both. I'll call Ed and Doc Philips tomorrow."

Will said, "While we're all together I want to explain the Bobcat Security System I had installed. There's an interior keypad at each door. When you leave the house you enter our code and press 'arm system.' When you return, you enter your code and press 'disarm system.' You have thirty seconds to disarm the system after you enter the house, and to leave the house after you have armed it. If you don't, the alarm will sound and the police will come and they won't be happy. They don't like responding to false alarms, so remember to do that.

"When you go to bed at night, you arm the system by pressing 'arm occupied.' It works with sensors on the doors and windows. The security company monitors everything twenty-four/seven.

"You can even alert emergency services with it by punching in 911 on the keypad. The company will dispatch the police immediately.

"If someone forces you to disarm the system when you enter, there is a special code you enter that alerts the monitors you are under duress. The alarm won't sound, but the police will come. The intruder will think the system has been disarmed. I'll give you those codes. Memorize them and tear up the paper.

"I also had security lighting attached to motion detectors installed outside, and deadbolt locks installed for each door. The folks with Bobcat Security were great. They put us at the top of their installation list due to the circumstances. They completed the installation in two days."

"Thanks for doing that, Will. I'll reimburse you. But do you really think all this is necessary?"

"Yes, I do. Here, memorize your codes. Here's your keys. I'll get you that cappuccino now."

"Make that two," said Karen.

CHAPTER

NINE

Beau had not moved away from Mel's feet. He, like Mel, was not a hundred percent. Yet Will had never heard his grandfather speak with more resolve.

"I'm going to tell you what I believe is going on here. Will, I'm sure you recall me telling you the family rumors of a buried treasure."

"I do. But you said you didn't think there was anything to it."

"That's right. I never put much stock in it until recently, but now since this happened, I'm *convinced* there's something to it. I think somebody else is convinced also and that's why the files were stolen. It was well known throughout the family I worked on our genealogy. We find who else believes there's a treasure, and we find … Polly's … killer," he hesitated; the words were foreign to him. Mel found it hard speaking in terms of Polly not being around.

He continued, "This is where you two come in. I can't get around much anymore. You will be my legs. You're both smart and I've seen a real knack for research in both of you, so I need your minds too. We'll work together, and we'll find that …" Mel remembered in time he was in mixed company. "We'll find this

guy and maybe find the treasure too. Sometimes you'll work together, sometimes apart. We'll meet here to discuss everything we
find."

"Mel, I'll be glad to help, but I think we'll need to be completely honest with each other, so I'm just going to say it. Don't
you think this is a matter for the police?"

"Yes, I do. But the police can't do what we can. I think the
answers will come from our genealogy. I have no intention of
interfering in any way with their investigation, and we'll cooper-
ate with them and keep them informed if we come up with something. The more people working on this the better is the way I see it."

The answer satisfied, and both Karen and Will nodded.

"The first thing I want you two to do is swap genealogies.
You'll need to know about each other's family. Also we'll exchange
all our contact information, and, Karen, I'll give you a key to the
house. You already have the security code."

"*You* have our genealogy, Grandpa, and now its gone. I have
nothing on paper."

"The *hard* copies were stolen, and believe me, he didn't get
much. Most of my work is on the computer, and they didn't get
that. Karen, I'll print our genealogy for you as soon as I can."

Mel proceeded to tell Karen and Will about Morris Anthony
and Robert Rhone's Bible. He told them about the problem he
ran into with Delbert Rhone and his unwillingness to share the
Bible's information.

"After you get familiar with each other's genealogies, Karen, I
want you to contact Delbert Rhone by phone, a fresh voice might
soften him a bit. Don't tell him what happened here just yet. I
don't feel right using that to influence him. Just tell him you're
helping me out. Feel him out and see if you can come up with
something to dissolve his reluctance.

"Will, I want you to hit the courthouse; deeds, wills, Orphans
Court records, estate papers, criminal records, anything you can

think of on Robert Rhone *and his neighbors* in the Hessian Triangle, particularly land that adjoined his. Then I want you to track ownership of his original grant up to the present day."

"The Hessian Triangle?" Will questioned.

"Yes, that's what it's called. It's the region surrounding the point where the counties of Northumberland, Schuylkill, and Dauphin intersect. There was an unusually large concentration of ex-Hessian soldiers who settled that area. They either deserted the Hessian army or didn't go home after the Revolutionary War was over. I would imagine it was the land grants that drew them, or maybe the geography reminded them of home, or maybe that's where the government promised them land for deserting. I can't be sure, but come they did.

"While you're working on your end, I'll be reviewing everything I have. I'm also going to make a disk and keep it updated and hide it. So if that jerk comes back he won't get everything." Mel took a sip of cappuccino and continued, "One more thing. I want to get your thoughts on how to approach this problem. There is evidence of a cemetery on Robert Rhone's original tract. The locals called it Henry's Patch because the Henry family owned the land for a time. They are the ones who tore down the cemetery. I believe Robert Rhone is buried there, and his first wife, and who knows who else, but I have no proof. To make a long story short, I know about the cemetery because some pieces of the headstones were thrown in a hollow beside a large cultivated field on Robert's tract. The pieces were found not too long ago. The person who found the pieces turned them over to the Gratz Historical Society and they showed them to me. One of the larger pieces showed only the last name of Rhone.

"It makes sense that the stones came from somewhere in that field beside the hollow, but it's a big field. The 1875 Dauphin County map marked the spot of the cemetery at that time, but that doesn't help much because the identifying features have changed. Also, I know from my research that a 'family burying site' is mentioned as the place my great-grandfather wanted to be planted.

"From the county cemetery inscription work done by that retired teacher, what was her name ... Martha Workman, we know that the cemetery was destroyed some time in the late 1930s. No inscription of those buried there was ever found. It would be great if we could find those names and the exact location of the cemetery."

Mel was right. If they can be found intact, cemeteries are a major source of information, and the older the better. Birth and death dates, as well as maiden names, married names, parentage, and more could be engraved on the tombstones. If a cemetery is destroyed, information it contained could be lost for all time. In the case of the Rhone cemetery, it could be the *only* record of this information.

"The late '30s ... that means someone could still be alive that saw it before it was destroyed. Maybe someone has the inscriptions. Have you ever placed an ad in *The Citizen-Standard*?" Karen asked.

The Citizen-Standard in Valley View was founded in 1929, and is still one of the area's oldest newspaper. Published once a week, it has been in continuous operation since it was founded. The paper had on microfilm a copy of every issue they ever published, and Mel had viewed some of them on occasion in the course of his research.

"No, I didn't. Good idea, Karen. I knew getting you on board was a good move. You handle that too, please. Put the contact information for the three of us in the ad."

"How about those Internet genealogy mailing lists you subscribe to, Grandpa?

"Another good idea. I'll handle that one."

Mel was planning with all the precision of a military operation. He sounded like a general inspiring his troops. "Someone willing to go to the extremes they did to get Robert Rhone's files tells me that they know something and have a head start on us, so we need to catch up and fast … stay focused. I'll reimburse your expenses, so record them and submit to me every week or so."

"That isn't necessary, Grandpa."

"Yes, it is. Don't argue. We'll get together once a week, sooner if something comes up. Let's get to work," Mel said with a clap of his hands.

✳✳✳

The Dauphin County Courthouse is a magnificent structure in a picturesque setting. Built in 1943 of white Georgia marble near the site of the original courthouse, it overlooks Riverfront Park and the Susquehanna River on the corner of Front and Market Streets in Harrisburg. Engraved in the stone facade around the perimeter of the building are the names of all the county's townships.

Aside from conducting the county's legal business, the courthouse attracts, from all over the country and beyond, those with Dauphin County roots researching their genealogy. It is the repository for legal records dating back to 1785 when Dauphin County was founded.

After Will emptied his pockets into a tray by the entrance, he walked through the upright metal detector. Not setting it off, he went to the opposite side of the table and reclaimed his possessions. He then picked up his leather-covered notepad from the conveyor that had passed through an x-ray machine, all under the watchful eyes of several uniformed security guards. He then walked to the Recorder of Deeds office.

Will loved coming here. He loved the pristine appearance of the wide hallways and the sound his shoes made on the marble floor. He even liked the sternness of the security check and the sober faces of the guards.

He had researched deeds before when helping his grandfather and in college, so he knew how it was done and didn't need to consult an attendant for instructions. He went straight to the records. The time-consuming task of tracking the subsequent owners of Robert Rhone's land and recording the owners of land adjoining his at any given time would take him the better part of two days. He didn't mind. This kind of thing was in his blood. His background in history once again proved beneficial.

The deeds sometimes provided more information than just a land transfer, stating family relationships and sometimes even how family members felt about each other. With the large number he had to research he just copied the deeds from microfilm and would study the hard copies later.

Meanwhile, Karen Holtzman was also busy with her assignment. She called Delbert Rhone in Texas from her brother's house, mindful of the time difference.

"Delbert Rhone, please."

"Speaking."

"Mr. Rhone, this is Karen Holtzman from Pennsylvania. I'm ..."

"I'm not interested, thank you."

"No, no, Mr. Rhone, wait. I'm not selling anything. I'm a friend of Mel Rhone."

"Oh. How is Mel?"

"He's fine. I'm helping him with his genealogy. He asked me to call you and try to work out a way he ... *we* can see the information in Robert Rhone's Bible. It's my understanding you two discussed that at one time. Can we talk about that?"

"Well, Ms. Huntsman ..."

"Holtzman. You can call me Karen, Mr. Rhone."

"Okay. If you call me Del."

"Agreed."

"Karen, the problem is and has been the condition of the Bible. It's very old and fragile and I'm afraid of moving it around. It would be hard on it if I had it photocopied, as I'm sure you can imagine. Most of it's in German, and I resisted taking it somewhere to have it translated for that very reason. I just can't seem to find the time to look for someone who is willing to come here to do the translating."

"So it's not that you want to keep this information to yourself?"

"Heavens, no. Mel is a nice guy and I enjoyed talking to him, but he can be pushy, and that turns me off a little. But I have been meaning to do something with it. He seems to have a much greater interest in that stuff than I do. In all fairness I suppose I've been procrastinating."

"What about if we *photographed* the pages?"

"Photographed ... as with a conventional camera?"

"Yes. I find a photographer with experience in historical documents in your area and have him come to your house at your convenience. It would be much easier on the Bible and it never has to leave your sight. You can oversee the whole operation. Of course, we pay all expenses. And if you want something for your trouble, I'll talk to Mel about that too."

"And the photos would be readable?"

"Yes. If the photographer knows what he's doing. We would insist they be readable."

Delbert Rhone thought a second, then said, "I don't have a problem with that. I do want something, though. Are you from Mel's area?"

"Yes. What would you like?"

"A couple of rings of that homemade ring bologna from that butcher in Klingerstown. Double garlic, please. I had it years ago when I visited your area, and haven't been able to find anything like it since. I forgot the butcher's name, though."

"I know who you mean. You got it, Del. I'll overnight it to you. Let me do some homework and I'll get back to you."

"Okay. Nice talking to you, Karen."

"Same here. Thank you very much. Mel will be delighted. Good-bye."

Karen hung up the phone and exclaimed, "Y-Y-Yes!"

She didn't waste time. Her thinking was to get this done quickly before Del changed his mind. She called the Chamber of Commerce in Austin, Texas, and explained to them what she wanted. They gave her the name of three possibilities.

The first photographer explained he would do it but had work booked for the next three weeks. *Not quick enough.* The second one said she had done work like that for a couple of historical societies in the area and had a degree in historical preservation. She would be glad to do it in the next few days. *Perfect.* Karen gave her Delbert's contact information and instructions on exactly what she wanted: eight-by-ten photos of every page with script, which must be readable; a photo of the front cover; and the finished work sent to her as soon as possible. She asked the photographer to set up a time with Del and contact her if there were any problems. After they made payment arrangements, Karen wished her good luck.

She then drove to the butcher shop—Troutman Brothers Meats—in Klingerstown and explained what she wanted to do. She had envisioned herself packaging ring bologna in dry ice and preparing it for shipment to Texas. She was delighted to learn the butcher sent his products all over the country on a regular basis and would take care of everything. She ordered three rings of double garlic ring bologna and gave him Del's address. *Piece of cake.*

She then called Delbert Rhone and told him everything she had accomplished in the three hours since they had last spoken. He was impressed with her speed and efficiency. He was excited about getting the ring bologna.

Karen was on a roll and wasn't about to stop now. She went to

the office of *The Citizen-Standard* but the person she needed to
see to place an ad was gone for the day. She returned home and
thought more about what she wanted to say in the ad. It had to
get the attention of as many readers as possible. She thought a
humorous approach might work best.

DEAD PEOPLE WANTED

The Rhone family is seeking information on the dearly
departed interred in the old Rhone cemetery, AKA 'Henry's
Patch,' in Lykens Township just north of Gratz. If you have
seen the cemetery before its destruction in the 1930s, or
know where it was located, or have an inscription of those
buried there, please contact one of the below-listed per-
sons. Any information is greatly appreciated.

The next day Karen went to the newspaper office first thing
in the morning and spoke with the ad person.

"Are you sure you want it worded just like that?"

"Yes, just like that. Can you do it?"

"Sure. Do you want it to run two consecutive weeks?"

"Yes, for now. Make it larger than your usual ad, with bold
print please."

"How about a sixteen … a sixteenth of a page?"

"That should do it. Thanks."

Her assignments now completed, she called Will and asked if
he wanted some help.

"Okay. I was just ready to leave for the courthouse. Come on
over."

During the ride to Harrisburg, Will and Karen filled each
other in on their progress and got to know each other better. Will
was excited about the prospect of seeing what the Bible contained.

"Nice truck. Crew-cab, four-wheel drive … nice. Why do you
drive a pickup?" Karen asked.

"Thanks. Comes in handy for my business. I haul materials, make deliveries … things like that."

"You don't own a car?"

"No."

The two sat in silence for a few miles.

"You're kind of a quiet guy, Will."

"Until you get to know me. How did you ever accomplish that with Delbert Rhone?"

"Elementary, my dear, Rhone, elementary." Karen laughed. "Well, maybe it was the ring bologna."

"Grandpa guessed right by giving you that job."

"Did you know I had the biggest crush on you when we were in school?" Karen asked out of the blue.

"No. Really?"

"I used to watch you out of the upstairs window when you and your friends came to play basketball with Keith. I'll bet you never knew I was alive."

"How could I? You were too busy peeking out of the upstairs window."

Karen chuckled in her usual devilish way. "You *do* have a sense of humor."

"When I'm in good company."

"Hard to believe you never married, Will."

"Well, it's not by design. College, then starting my own business. The years get away from you. I dated several women for a time, but really never got close to marriage."

"How many at a time?"

Giving Karen a quick glance to see if she was serious, Will said, "Just one at a time, thank you," then added, "You said you were close to marriage. How close?"

"About a month away."

"That's close."

With this subject, again Will noted a change in Karen's lighthearted demeanor. *Okay, still not ready to talk about it.* He explained to Karen where he was with the deed research and asked her if she would start looking at wills.

"Sure, I love the old wills. Does Will have a will?" said Karen.

Glad to see her serious moment pass he answered, "He certainly does. But you can't see that one. Get a copy of anything that looks important. I'll give you the names of Robert Rhone's adjoining land owners that I'd like you to check."

"Will Will be willing to will me his will, that is the question," Karen said, not ready to let the wordplay end just yet.

"*Will* would like to ask, *will* you drop that now?"

Karen giggled.

CHAPTER

TEN

It was Friday, the unofficial day Mel, Will, and Karen met at Mel's house to discuss the previous week's progress. Will and Karen had finished their research at the courthouse.

"Hello, Beau. How are you feeling?" Karen asked the dog as she entered Mel's house.

"Don't ask Mel how he's feeling, though."

"Sorry, Mel. How *are* you feeling?"

"We're both doing much better, thanks," Mel said, smiling. "By the way, how are your parents doing? Do they like Florida?"

"Yes, they love it down there. They're both doing great. I'll tell them you asked."

"While we're on the subject, Will, how is your mother doing?"

After Will's father died, Elizabeth Rhone found it too painful to remain in the house she had shared with her husband for almost thirty years. She sold the house to Will and moved in with his younger sister and her family in Maryland. They were glad to have her.

"She's doing great. She was sorry she didn't get to see you when she was here for Grandma's funeral. She said she'd give you a call."

"Good … that's good." Mel then opened the meeting with some thoughts. "Karen, Will and I went over some of this, but we'll start from the beginning for your benefit. First I'd like to say that we're probably up against a Rhone descendant and I want you to be mentally prepared for that unpleasant reality. Could be someone in our line, or a different line. Could be a close relative or distant, but I think whoever it is got their hands on some provocative piece of family history. Okay. Having said that, how did you make out?"

Karen told of her conversation with Delbert Rhone and the plan they worked out, the newspaper ad, and of her helping Will at the courthouse.

Mel said, "I saw the ad in yesterday's *Citizen-Standard.* Very clever. That should get somebody's attention. I can't believe you accomplished in one conversation with Delbert what I failed to accomplish in months of trying. Good work. As soon as you get those photos, we'll have another meeting. And thanks for helping Will."

"That's okay, we had fun. Will asked me to check the wills for Robert Rhone's neighbors and I found something curious in Philip Hoppe's. He's the child of landowner Rudolph Hoppe."

"Yes, Rudolph Hoppe. He is believed to be one of the Hessians who settled here. He was also Robert Rhone's brother-in-law. They married sisters. What did you find?" Mel asked.

Karen handed the copy of Philip Hoppe's will to Mel. "I underlined the part I thought interesting."

Mel read, "Item: I bequeath the sunshine coin to my eldest son, Philip Junior."

"What do you think, Grandpa?"

"The sunshine coin? What in the world is that? We'll come back to that one. Will, what did you find?"

"I traced Robert Rhone's original tract through all its subsequent owners. You're right; the land was in the Henry family for many years. They sold it ten years ago to Mid-Atlantic Agricultural Conglomerate, or M-A-A-C, pronounced 'mack,' who still own it. I then went online to check out MAAC. Unusual company. The CEO, H. Dallas Fitzhugh, was also the founder … a real colorful character. The company buys family farms when they come up for sale with the sole purpose of using the land for agriculture, not development. They own land in six states. They also buy seed companies, grain elevators, equipment companies, anything to do with agriculture.

"Apparently when Fitzhugh was a child, his parents lost the farm that had been in their family for generations through the shenanigans of a development company. He never forgot the heartache it caused. He vowed to maintain as much farmland as he could and keep it out of the hands of the developers.

"He makes it all work by strategically locating equipment depots as hubs to service their land within a certain area. He also contracts local labor and equipment as needed. Last year MAAC's gross revenue exceeded a billion dollars that's *billion* with a B. They own tens of thousands of acres in New York, Pennsylvania, New Jersey, Delaware, Maryland, and Virginia.

"They also experiment with something they call 'custom planting' by planting, say, alternating rows of marigolds and soybeans to help reduce the use of pesticides on the soybeans. They then harvest both the marigolds for seed and the soybeans. Plus, they only post their land as needed, otherwise it's open to the public for hunting, fishing, hiking, whatever. Quite a company."

"Wow. We may get a chance to deal with them if the treasure is buried on their land," Karen said.

"They're right in my own backyard and I never even heard of them," Mel added.

"Yes. Because of their commitment to maintain the status quo. Let's get back to the sunshine coin," Will said.

"I haven't got a clue about that. I don't think one coin makes a treasure, though I could be wrong. But how did the Rhones get involved if the Hoppes had the coin?" Mel asked, then asked again before anyone could answer, "Karen, will you go in the office and get online and see what comes up for 'sunshine coin'? Just turn it on. I have DSL."

Will went to the kitchen and made three cups of instant cappuccino.

Ten minutes later Karen returned to the living room and reported, "I couldn't find anything specific. The sun-with-rays icon was used on a lot of U.S. currency, both paper and coinage. There's a wide range of possibilities. It could be one of those or something else entirely."

"It's still a good clue," Mel commented, then issued an assignment. "This week I want the both of you to concentrate on the relationship between Robert Rhone and Rudolph Hoppe. Find out everything you can. I would start at the Pennsylvania State Archives in Harrisburg. The staff there are great, and they may have some suggestions. It may be helpful to start a chronology of time and place for these two. We pretty much covered the primary sources, but we'll have to dig deeper. We had a good first week. We'll get together again next Friday unless something comes up in the meantime."

"Tell Karen what you did, Grandpa."

"Oh, yes. I posted a query for Rhone cemetery information on several of the county genealogical email lists. Also on a few message boards. No responses yet. But that's okay. You don't always get an immediate response. They keep the postings forever. I've already received responses from queries I posted years prior.

"Now ... Will. Can I have another cup of cappuccino? And get Beau one of those doggy treats in the cupboard above the stove. Tomorrow I'll look over all your material before I file it."

✳✳✳

As Will entered Keith Holtzman's kitchen Jason offered a cup of coffee.

"No thanks."

"Karen said to tell you she'll be right down."

"I heard you're going to Penn State, Jason."

"Yeah. I'll be a junior next year."

"You're on spring break now?"

"Yeah."

"What's your major?"

"Pre-med."

"Pre-med? That's great. You looking for a summer job?"

"Not lookin' yet, but I will."

"I could use some help for the summer in the shop. You interested?"

"Sure. I'd like working there."

"Okay. Go see Ed Klinger. Tell him I said to put you on for the summer. He'll give you all the details."

"I will. Thanks a lot. Wow! I thought I'd have drive to Harrisburg to get work."

"You ready?" Karen asked as she entered the kitchen.

"I've *been* ready," Will joked.

As the couple walked to Will's truck Karen said, "I heard that conversation. You sure made him happy."

"Just doing my part to help educate the youth of America."

"You're a nice guy, Rhone."

"I am indeed," he said grinning.

The two drove to the Pennsylvania State Archives at Third and Forster Streets, parked, and after walking the ivy-flanked stone path through the narrow courtyard, entered through the two sets of heavy double doors.

Two sections of the Archives are available to the public: a large microfilm library with two rooms of viewers and a secure, enclosed glass-walled area, complete with surveillance cameras, for viewing rare documents. The secure viewing room has its own archivist and sign-in and -out log.

They signed in at the first log by the main entrance and told the archivist on duty, whose name tag said he was, "John," what they knew about Robert Rhone and Rudolph Hoppe and what they wanted to know. John suggested they begin with the Colonial Records in the main search area and the rare documents in the secure area. John asked if Robert Rhone and Rudolph Hoppe could possibly have met while Hoppe was a prisoner and Rhone a guard. He commented it was not unusual for prisoners and guards to develop friendships. Will told him they were not even sure Rhone was in the military, or that Hoppe was a prisoner. John suggested they assume that this premise was correct and try to prove or disprove it. It was a good suggestion. Will found a record of Robert Rhone's service in the Pennsylvania Militia and of him serving as a guard at the Mount Penn prison camp.

Karen searched the Hessian records in the secure area and found Rudolph Hoppe listed as a prisoner from the Battle of Trenton. Hoppe was also on the Mount Penn prisoner list. He was not, however, on any of the prisoner exchange records. They approached John the Archivist with that information and he said Hoppe could have died while a prisoner, or deserted and been released, or a dozen other things. They knew he hadn't died.

Will and Karen searched the old land records together. There they found both Hoppe and Rhone made application for their land *before* the end of the war, suggesting Hoppe must have deserted. They signed out and thanked John for his help. As the couple was leaving, John recommended they visit the David Library in Washington Crossing, Pennsylvania, explaining that they had excellent records of the Battle of Trenton and the American Revolution in general, plus a knowledgeable staff.

"So Robert and Rudolph may have known each other before they became brothers-in-law," Karen said as they drove home.

"It looks like a good possibility. They applied for their land about the same time; their land adjoined each other; and they were both at the Mount Penn prison at the same time."

"So what does all that tell us about the treasure?"

"Not much right now, but it gives us a good start on their chronology."

"One more piece of the puzzle."

"Yep. One more drop in the bucket."

"One more link in the chain."

"One more chocolate chip in the cookie."

"One more …" they both started laughing before Karen could finish.

***

Will turned into the supermarket parking lot in Millersburg. "Grandpa asked me to pick up more instant cappuccino. Want to come along?"

As they walked toward the entrance, Will noticed a man looking and walking toward them at an angle. The fortysomething man walked with a limp, aided by an imported Irish Shillelagh made from blackthorn wood.

"Karen, I didn't know you were back East," the man lied.

"Hello, Charles. Yes. I've been back awhile. Do you know Will Rhone?"

"I've seen you around, Will, but I don't believe we've ever met. I'm Charles Holtzman, Karen's cousin." The two men shook hands. "I'm sorry to hear about your grandmother."

"Thank you. Do you live around here, Charles?"

"Yes, just outside of Valley View."

"Will, we'd best be getting those things for your grandpa. Sorry we have to run, Charles. Nice seeing you again." Now Karen lied. As they parted company she said under her breath, "Scumbag."

Hearing the out-of-character comment, Will raised his eyebrows. "Scumbag?"

"I'm being nice. Bad actor, Will. Black sheep. Alcohol, drugs, did time for hit-and-run, always in trouble of some kind. The only one in the family who bothered with him was Grandma Holtzman when she was alive. He sure had her fooled."

"Was that the hit and run on Route 209 just outside of Lykens several years ago when an old man was hit? The driver just drove away and left him lying on the road to die."

"One and the same. Thank God the old man lived."

"Where did Charles get the limp?"

"Car crash years before the hit and run. Too bad he wasn't … that one wasn't his fault. The other driver was drunk. The trucking company he worked for paid up big time. Charles hasn't worked a day since. Did you see that club of a cane he uses?"

"I noticed."

"He worked on our genealogy for a time during one of his rare good spells, and then just stopped cold. I believe Mel worked with him for a while. Just before Grandma Holtzman died she gave him an old trunk filled with family mementos. Dad remembers seeing inside when he was a kid, and said it held old letters, documents, books, old photos, things that would have helped me with the genealogy. Dad was furious about it. It should have gone to him. And do you think Charles would ever let us see that stuff?"

"I'll guess no."

"No, he didn't. Said there was nothing there of interest to us. When I insisted, he got belligerent. I don't like him, Will. Never have."

"I guess there's one in every family."

"There's none in your family."

"Aah … no … none that bad, anyway. Just trying to make you feel better."

Karen smiled and touched Will's arm. Even though their regular Friday meeting was three days away, Will asked Karen if she wanted to come with him to show Mel the information they gleaned from the State Archives. She did.

As they approached Mel's house they could see Beau running at full speed toward the car with a rubber ball in his mouth. Mel was sitting on the front porch.

"Hi. I think spring is here at last. This is the first warm day we've had in a while. It feels good. Just playing a little fetch with Beau. Have a seat. Watch this."

Beau gave Mel the ball and sat down at his feet with an expectant expression. Mel cocked his arm as though he was throwing the ball and held it in that position. He told Beau to fetch. Beau raced off the porch, down the steps, and into the yard as Mel threw the ball as far and as high as he could. Beau circled, leaped high off all fours, and caught the ball mid-air.

"Wow! How did you teach him that?" Karen asked.

"I didn't. He just started doing it one day."

Beau returned the ball and laid it on Mel's lap, nudging it with his nose.

"We had a good day at the Archives, Grandpa."

"Good. Did you get my cappuccino?"

"Right here. I got four cans since Karen and I are helping you drink it."

"Good thinking. Let's see what you found."

Handing the copies to Mel, Will said, "You were right about Hoppe, he *was* a Hessian soldier. Not only that, he spent time at the Reading prison camp at the same time Robert Rhone served as a guard there. Robert was in the Pennsylvania Militia."

"Good, you proved that. Sorry I didn't tell you. I knew Robert was in the militia, but I didn't know where he served. Sometimes it's best to go in cold."

"Hoppe applied for his land before the end of the war, so we know he deserted," Karen said.

"Great. Another piece of the puzzle," Mel said.

Will and Karen gave each other a quick glance and suppressed a grin.

"Grandpa, We ran into Charles Holtzman. Karen said you helped him with genealogy for a time."

"Yes. A little. Then he lost interest, just like that." Mel snapped his fingers. "It's too bad about Charles." He continued, "Now, I have some news. Karen, two people called in response to your ad. They both remember seeing the cemetery as children. Here's their names and numbers. I want you to call them and ask if they are willing to show you the location. Will, you did say MAAC keeps its land open to the public, didn't you?"

"Yes, they post only as needed. I never saw any of their posts around here."

"Good, I wish I could go ..." The telephone rang and Mel asked, "Will, can you get that?"

Will entered the house. "Hello? This is Will Rhone."

"Will. Good. I heard you were staying with Mel. This is Darlene Henry, Joel's wife. You and my son Rob were in the same grade in high school."

"Yes, I know who you are. How is R ... ?"

"I need to meet with you. Meet me inside the supermarket in Millersburg tomorrow about noon. Get a cart and just walk around like you're shopping. I'll find you. Sorry for the cloak and dagger stuff, but this has to be done my way. Don't tell anyone about this and come alone."

Before Will could respond the line went dead. He returned to the porch.

"Who was it?"

"Strange. I'll tell you both later."

Mel said, "Well anyway, get in touch with these two. One at a time, though. Let's see if they are remembering the same spot."

CHAPTER

ELEVEN

The next day Will entered the Millersburg supermarket a little before noon. He pulled a shopping cart from the stack and walked the aisles as Darlene Henry instructed. When he had gone through all the aisles he reversed directions. He spotted her pushing a cart toward him. She looked nervous.

"Hello, Mrs. Henry."

"How are you, Will? I feel so bad about Polly, it's such a shame."

"Thank you."

"Here, take this. Don't look at it now, put it in your pocket," she said, handing him a folded sheet of paper. "It's a translated list of the people buried in the Rhone cemetery. I saw your ad in the paper."

As Will slipped the paper in his pocket, Darlene Henry looked up and down the aisle before she continued in a soft voice. "Just listen, Will, I don't have much time. When I saw your ad I showed it to Joel. I asked him if he would give you the list. He went ballistic. His grandfather owned that land at one time; he's the one who destroyed the cemetery. Thank goodness he had the sense to record the stones there before he tore it down. He spoke German so he had no trouble translating the ones in German. Joel's afraid, Will. Afraid and embarrassed. It's illegal to destroy a cemetery now, but it wasn't when his grandfather did it. Still, Joel's afraid someone will make trouble for him now, even though he wasn't even born when his grandfather destroyed it. So he figures the fewer people that know about it the better. He feels bad about it, but he would *never* come forward with this. If he ever finds out I did this behind his back ... well, I don't know what he'd do. He can't find out, promise me that. Joel's a good man, Will, he's just embarrassed, is all. Promise me this will stay our secret."

"It will, but I want to tell Grandpa and Karen. I'll tell them it should go no further."

"I'd rather you didn't." She thought a second. "Do you trust them not to say anything?"

"Yes. I do."

"Okay, if you must. But tell them the importance of protecting me. Please do that. I must go now. Don't leave right away. I hope this helps you. I know I feel better."

"Won't your husband notice the list is missing?"

"No. I copied it for you. You can keep that. I must go, Will."

"Thank you, Mrs. Henry. I want you to know I don't hold anything against Joel's family."

Preoccupied with what just transpired, Will went through the motions of shopping as though he thought he was being watched by the KGB. When he arrived at the checkout there were items in the cart he didn't remember picking up. Anxious now to see what was on the sheet of paper, he paid for everything. *What am I going to do with a large jar of baby food ... spinach, no less?*

Will sat in his truck and opened the folded paper. There were thirteen inscriptions listed with a notation at the bottom of the page that said there were "eight sunken spots with no stones— listed as unmarked." Another notation said "names writ where located in cemetery." Will scanned the list. *Robert Rhone; Maria Magdalena Rhone, nee Kohl; Rudolph Hoppe; Elizabeth Haldeman*

Hoppe, nee Kohl, Wife of Rudolph; and some Rhone and Hoppe children and some of their grandchildren, he presumed. He noticed Catherine Bingaman Rhone—Robert's second wife—was not listed. One name jumped out at him: *Catherine Holtzman, nee Hoppe, Dau. of Philip and Mary, Wife of Ziba.*

As Will drove home his mind was working overtime. Something wasn't right. He entered the house and placed the bag of groceries on the counter and went straight for the Holtzman genealogy Karen had given him. Mel came into the kitchen and started removing the items from the shopping bag.

"Baby food? Baby powder? Is there something you're not telling me, boy?"

"I'll explain later. Look at this, Grandpa."

His interest still on the contents of the bag, Mel asked, "What in the world are you going to do with anchovy paste? Mix it with your mashed spinach?"

"Grandpa. That call yesterday was from Darlene Henry." Will told Mel about the call and what had just taken place in the supermarket, then handed him the list."

"Oh my!"

Pointing at the list, Will said, "Look at this. Catherine Hoppe was married to Ziba Holtzman."

"So?"

"Now look at this." Will showed the Holtzman genealogy to Mel. "Look who Karen has recorded as being married to Ziba Holtzman."

"She has Catherine *Wagner*," Mel said.

"Now look at the death date for Catherine Hoppe Holtzman. A day after Karen's second great-grandfather, John Jacob Holtzman, was born."

"Oh my. You'd better call her right away to see if she can come over."

***

When Karen arrived Will told her the story of Darlene Henry and the implications of the new information gleaned from the cemetery list.

"I'm a *Hoppe* descendant? How could that be? How could I miss that?"

Will explained. "Easy. Judging from your sources listed here on your genealogy, you had no reason to think otherwise. As you know, on the 1840 U.S. census the head of household is the only name named. Household members are shown only as numbers in an age group. In your case Ziba Holtzman was listed with one female aged twenty to thirty—his wife—and one female child under five years old, which would have been John Jacob's sister Margaret.

"We now know from Mrs. Henry's list that Catherine Hoppe Holtzman died November 22, 1842, *after* the 1840 census was taken, and *before* the 1850 census. On the 1850 census—the first census on which everyone in the household was listed—you see Ziba Holtzman married to a Catherine—Catherine Wagner, as you learned with your research—which would be correct. Also listed are the five children, including your great-great grandfather, John Jacob Holtzman.

"Then, according to this, you find the church baptismal record of John Jacob Holtzman, born on November 21, 1842, recorded as son of Ziba Holtzman and Catherine. In the absence of any other records why would you think that *this* Catherine was none other than Catherine Wagner? Unfortunately, the pastor at the time did not record Ziba's wife's surname as they sometimes did. If he had, you never would have followed the Wagner line, you would have followed the Hoppe line.

"You had no evidence at all pointing to Catherine Wagner being Ziba's second wife and Catherine Hoppe being his first, and all the evidence you *did* have pointed to him having only one wife, Catherine Wagner.

"If Mrs. Henry hadn't come forward with these inscriptions, you could have gone on forever thinking you were a Wagner descendant."

"Unbelievable! I'm a *Rudolph Hoppe* descendant. All that work I did following the wrong line. You're a genius, Will."

"Elementary, Holtzman, elementary." Will winked at Mel and nudged Karen. "But you need to thank Mrs. Henry, not me. And I'm sure someday the Wagner descendants will appreciate all the work you did for them."

With this revelation Karen's emotions surfaced. "Catherine Hoppe Holtzman died giving birth to my great-great-grandfather John Jacob Holtzman, didn't she?"

"Most likely, yes. The day after he was born."

"There were so many unnecessary deaths back then, so many mothers and babies ... it's so sad."

"It is."

Karen rested her head on Will's shoulder. Will responded by putting his arm around her and patting her back.

"Karen. *Ziba*?" Will asked.

"Biblical name."

"I hope so."

"Let's go over the rest of the list," Mel said, "but first I need to talk to you about something, Will."

Beau barked and ran to the window, putting his front feet on the sill. Will looked out to see a dark-colored car park beside his truck. A well-dressed, distinguished-looking man in his fifties with graying hair and wearing a navy blue suit and red striped tie got out and walked toward the house. Will met him at the door.

"Hi. I'm with the Pennsylvania State Police. Are you Mr. Rhone?"

"I'm Will Rhone. Mel is inside. Come in."

Once inside, he announced to no one in particular, "I'm Detective Lieutenant David Zimmerman. I've been assigned to investigate the death of Mary Rhone."

"Lieutenant, this is Mel Rhone and Karen Holtzman. Please have a seat."

"Mel, you're Mary's husband; Will, you're her grandson; and Ms. Holtzman?" the policeman said as he leafed through his notepad.

"I'm a friend of the family."

"Is this the dog injured in the attack?" The detective scratched Beau's ear.

"Yes," all three answered.

"He looks fine now."

"Yes, he's back to his old self, thank goodness." Mel answered.

"I stopped by to fill you in on the progress so far and to answer any questions you may have, and ask a few myself, if you don't mind. As you know from the autopsy report Mary died of a heart attack at 8:06 a.m. on March 16, 2004. The blow she received to the head was not fatal. Since she sustained her injuries during the commission of a felony, and never regained consciousness before her death, the DA would like us to pursue this as a homicide. That's why I've been assigned to the case. Trooper Krull briefed me, and I have a copy of his report, but I'd still like to go over a few things.

"Mel, you believe the perpetrator wanted your family files because of a rumored buried treasure, and they hoped your files contained information as to the location of the treasure?"

"Yes, that's correct."

"How many people know about the treasure?"

"Not many. The story was passed down from my grandfather, and I'm sure it came from his father, and so it goes. I recently learned of a Rhone line in Oregon that also heard the same rumors, independent of our line here in the East."

"Anyone specific in Oregon?"

"Yes, Morris Anthony from Portland." Mel turned to Will. "Get his contact information for the lieutenant, please."

"Well, I'll tell you, Mel. For someone to commit a crime like this, they had to be reasonably sure there *is* a treasure."

"Yes, we believe so too."

"But you're saying you have no real proof, and you don't know what the treasure is, or where it might be."

"That's correct."

"Do you have a list I could have of your relatives in the area?"

"Yes, I can give you the genealogy I have on the current generation. It has most of their addresses and contact information. Some are out of the area though. Will, again please."

"That would help. So if there is a treasure it would have been buried a long time ago?"

"Yes. We think so."

"One more thing. We found a number of hairs in the sweepings we made of your house. Mel and Will, you already gave a sample of your DNA, and the dog's hair too, but Ms. Holtzman, we don't have yours. Could I get a sample of your DNA?"

"Sure."

Lieutenant Zimmerman went to his car and retrieved a plastic bag and pair of rubber gloves. With a long cotton-tipped stick he swabbed the inside of Karen's cheek and placed the sample in the plastic bag. "OK. That should do it for now. Thanks. Do you have any questions?"

"Yes. Do you have any leads on this?" Will asked.

"Not right now," Lieutenant Zimmerman said. "I'm leaving you each one of my cards. I'll stay in touch. If you can think of anything, give me a call any time day or night."

Will walked David Zimmerman to the door. "Thank you for coming, Lieutenant." After he closed the door he asked, "Grandpa, don't you think we should have told him about the sunshine coin?"

"We don't know if that's connected in any way," Mel answered.

"But we do know now that the Rhones and Hoppes were close. Some of them are buried in the Rhone cemetery, Rudolph and

Robert were brothers-in-law, and we find out they probably were friends even before they came to this area. I'd say it's a sure bet that Rudolph Hoppe knew everything that was going on with Robert Rhone and vice versa."

"Hey. It just occurred to me. If they were brothers-in-law, does that mean we're related?" Karen asked.

"Through marriage *and* through the Kohls, yes," Mel said.

"What would we be?"

"Very distant cousins to the umpf degree."

"Wow. That's really something!"

"Not really. Truth be known half the people in this area are related if you go back far enough." Mel turned to Will. "What you say about the coin is true, but too vague right now. Back to the cemetery list.

"Now we know most of who's buried there, and even where their graves were located within the cemetery. But we still don't know the exact location of the cemetery. That's a big field. Talk to the two people who called as soon as you can. Try to find the location of Robert's house too. The more we know about the layout of his original tract, the better."

"Who should we call first?" Will asked.

"Call Dorothy Hummel first. She doesn't live around here and it sounded like she'd be leaving soon."

"Mel, what was it you wanted to talk about?" Karen asked.

"What?"

"Before the officer came, you said you wanted to talk to Will about something."

"Oh yes. Will. About the visiting nurse, Mrs. Adams. How long does she need to come here?"

Leah Adams was sixty-five, a registered nurse, retired. Her husband died two years ago, three weeks after she retired from Dauphin County Hospital. Since then she had been a home health care provider and took it seriously. Professional and competent to the point of being a sometime annoyance to her patients, that is until they saw that their well-being was Leah Adams's only concern. Mel hadn't seen that yet.

"As long as your doctor thinks she should. Why?"

"Well, she knows her business but she's bossy. And that Dutchified accent! 'Chust sit don nawh and take your medicine wonst.'"

Will laughed. "Pretty good impersonation, Grandpa. I'm not going to fire her because she makes you listen and she has a Dutchy accent. You see the doctor in a few days. Ask him if she's still necessary."

"Mel, what is that accent? Where did it come from? You used to hear it a lot more in the area," Karen said.

"Yes, that's right. It's dying out." And as usual when one of his many pet topics was mentioned, Mel gave lengthy and detailed information in story form. "Soon it will be gone completely. It came from the large number of Germans who settled this area. They learned to speak English, but of course with a German accent. In the absence of the mass media the only reference point for their offspring was what they heard everyone around them speaking. If the only thing you hear is English spoken with a German accent, that's how you'll speak English. It evolved over the generations into what you hear today.

"Nowadays a person with a heavy Dutchified accent may not even speak German; it's English as they know it. But as I said, it will soon be gone."

"Why?" Karen asked.

"It started dying when radio and TV became commonplace and we became a more mobile society. Then children started hearing how English should sound. You still find it in pockets. But notice it's mostly the older generation. There are exceptions though. You two don't talk that way, but down the road ten or fifteen miles you hear it in people your age.

"It's still prevalent in the Amish and Mennonite communities, but their accent isn't quite the same as you hear around here. I think because Pennsylvania Dutch was their primary language at one time. So instead of English spoken with a German accent it was English spoken with a Pennsylvania Dutch accent."

"Why is it still prevalent in the Amish and Mennonite communities?" Will asked.

"Because for the most part they don't listen to the radio or watch TV, and they're taught by their parents and their own teachers who just happen to speak like that. As their restrictions loosen, it's just a matter of time till even they lose it.

"Anyway, you find the Dutchy accent around here and in spots in Berks and Lancaster Counties. Some places in Lebanon County too ... or should I say, 'Leptnon Counie.' Well, that's my theory."

"Pennyslvania Dutch isn't German?" Karen asked.

"No. It's called Pennsylvania Dutch but it's neither Dutch, German, nor English. It's its own dialect. I think they adopted it way back when, so nobody they didn't want to could understand them."

"That's interesting. I always wondered where that came from," Karen said.

"It is interesting. For instance, Mrs. Adams has a heavy Dutchy accent and I don't, even though we're from the same general area and roughly the same age. Which brings us back to Mrs. Adams."

"Grandpa, Mrs. Adams stays until the doctor says otherwise. I like her, I like the job she's doing, and I like the way she talks."

CHAPTER

TWELVE

Valley View is rural western Schuylkill County, Pennsylvania, at its best. The small town's name had been changed from the original Osmantown in 1875. The name was chosen because it's situated on a wide ridge that runs down the center of the narrow valley, giving a scenic overview of the surrounding area. A descriptive name, if not creative. A few miles to the east is the town of Hegins. Several miles west is the town of Gratz, just over the county line in Dauphin County.

The modern saltbox was erected in the middle of two acres at the western edge of Valley View in an area that wasn't quite town but wasn't really country either. The two acres adjoined the macadam road that ran the length of the ridge. The owner had planted fast-growing poplar and spruce trees all around the house, save for the narrow walkway to the front door. As a result of the tall trees the interior of the house was dreary even on the sunniest of days. A small price to pay. The owner needed his privacy.

When the man walking down the driveway to the house was a couple of dozen feet off the macadam road, he couldn't be seen unless someone happened to be driving by on the main road and turned to look toward the house. When the man reached the porch in the shadow of the trees, no one could see him knock on the door.

"I told you to never come here," Charles Holtzman said as he pulled Socrates Smith through the doorway by a handful of shirt.

"Don't worry about it. I parked down the road and walked."

"You still came to my door."

"Well, you didn't pay me for the week, Chucky."

"Did you check the drop point this morning? No. You couldn't have, or you would've seen I did pay you. Idiot."

Charles met thirty-eight-year-old Socrates "Socks" Smith in prison. Smith was doing time for robbery, Charles for the hit-and-run incident. The day Charles was released he told Smith to look him up after he did his time, and that he might have work for him. Five months later Smith did just that.

They never liked each other much, but they understood each other. Charles needed someone to do his dirty work and Smith needed the money. Charles didn't see any reason they needed to be friends in their symbiotic relationship.

He insisted Socks rent a room in Millersburg, far enough away from him to avoid encounters but close enough to be handy when Charles had a chore that needed doing. Smith found a half-house overlooking the Susquehanna River on River Street, near the Millersburg Ferry. Charles instructed him to call only from a phone in the local dialing area.

Socks was born and raised in Fontana, California. He seldom returned to visit his family. He had brothers, Plato and Aristotle, and a sister, Theano. His parents reasoned that with a surname like Smith their kids needed identity; something to make them stand out from the crowd, so they named them after Greek philosophers. He was the only one in the family of dubious means.

Smith could be polite and personable when he wanted to be, an advantageous trait for the diabolical, so he worked hard at it. He was well groomed and wore a permanent boyish grin. He was a smart dresser, owned a new van—which he drove without a valid license—and came off as your average nice guy. Charles figured Smith could move around the rural area, where everybody knew everybody else's business, without attracting too much attention.

They had each rented a small locker at Lebo's Storage near Gratz and exchanged the keys they had had duplicated. This was their drop-off point. That and the local calls from Smith were the only way they communicated, until Socks showed up at Charles's door, that is.

"Now that you're here ... I thought I told you no one gets hurt at the Rhone's. The old lady's dead, Socks! Dead! What were you thinking? You can't control a couple of old people without killing them? It's murder now, you idiot!"

"You better stop calling me that, Chuck. The old man attacked me. I just pushed her out of the way so I could defend myself. She was alive when I left. She didn't fall all that hard."

"No ... just hard enough to kill her. And you felt the need to pistol-whip the old man? It's a wonder he's not dead too. What were you thinking? 'Defend yourself' ... aaah, you were afraid a little old man was going to hurt big bad Socks?"

"Calm down, Chuck. Just forget about it. You got what you wanted."

"Yeah. Except now I could be implicated in a murder because you couldn't handle a couple of seniors. And there was nothing in those files I didn't already know."

"I got what you told me to get."

"Yeah, right. I still don't know where that horde is buried."

"What makes you think he wouldn't dig them up if he knew where they were?" Smith asked.

"Think, Socks. I have the biggest clue, which I know they don't have. There could've been something in his files he wouldn't associate with the coins. The truth is I don't know how much he knows but I need to find out. Do I have to tell you everything?"

"Look, Chuck. If you don't want my help I'll just walk away."

"Walk away from a million bucks? I don't think so."

"Since you brought it up, a million isn't enough. Those coins are worth ten times that at least. I want ... say, twenty-five percent."

"Forget it. A million is generous. I take the risks and do all the thinking, not to mention all the work unloading that stuff when I get it, which won't be easy. If you don't screw up again, I may give you a bonus. You wouldn't have anything if I hadn't brought you in. Don't forget that."

Socks and Charles found lying to each other easy. Should they find the treasure, neither man had any intention of sharing it with anyone.

"Then just give me some of the coins and I'll worry about selling my share and you worry about yours. I'm taking risks and have expenses too."

"You get a thousand a week until we recover the stuff. Then you get a million when I fence them. Any more than that, we'll see. Now shut up and listen. I want you to plant a bug in their house. I'll show you how to work the receiver."

"Why? I really don't think they know anything."

"Don't question me. Use your head. The old man mentioned it in passing when I worked with him on the genealogy. So I know he knows something. Then someone forced his way into their house and the only thing they take are family files. Then I see an ad they put in the paper for information on the old cemetery, for who knows what reason. They're not stupid. If they weren't looking before, they are now. And it looks like they have my cousin working with them. That's bad. Sooner or later she'll find her mistake with the Wagners and Hoppes. She already knows I have the trunk. I need to know what they're up to. Now plant the bug, and don't get caught. And this time try not to kill anyone."

"Where did you ever get your hands on surveillance equipment?"

"The Internet ... where else?"

"Do you still want me to follow them around?"

"If you can do it without being noticed."

"Before I go, show it to me again."

"You don't need to see it again."

"Show me, Chuck, or plant your own bug."

After Charles Holtzman swore, he got up from the table and reached inside the old trunk his Grandmother Holtzman had given him. He limped back to the table and plunked the two-hundred-twenty-eight-year-old brass coin down in front of Socks Smith.

"Beautiful. But it doesn't look like its worth fifteen grand," Smith said as he fondled the coin.

"That's conservative. This one's in mint condition. If the rest are that good ... well even so I'll only get about half what they're worth," Charles said trying to downplay the bottom line.

"And how many do you think there are?"

"There could be as many as six to nine thousand if my research is right."

"Unbelievable."

Charles gave Socks the surveillance equipment with the ten-cent lesson on how to use it and sent him on his way. After Smith left the house Charles returned the coin to the old trunk, testing its heft and admiring its busy engraving.

To be certain he didn't miss something he reviewed the information that had alerted him to the existence of the treasure in the first place. He had gone over everything in the old trunk a dozen times before but he wanted to make sure one more time. He took out the old letter and read.

To John Jacob Holtzman,
Lykens Township, Pennsylvania

My Dear Nephew:
    I trust my letter finds you well. I have been meaning to write this letter to you but as with all too many things with me now it

was put off. I do apologize for my procrastination. I am getting to be an old man and I thought it wise to get this bit of business done before it is too late. I apologize also for not paying the attention deserving the son of my dearly beloved sister Catherine. She was taken from us at far too young an age, and I do so regret you never knowing her as your mother. There is not a day passes without my thinking of her. Had I not been obligated to remove to Philadelphia I am certain we would have spent time together and got on quite well.

In addition to the above reasons for this letter I am informing you that as I have no children of my own I want to pass on to you the family mementos gathered over the years that have been handed down to me, including the family Bible of our immigrant ancestor Rudolph Hoppe. Included in the Bible's pages is our ancestry dating back to the War of Independence when Rudolph Hoppe deserted the German Army that came to fight against the American cause after being a prisoner of war. You may find of special interest the additional pages he included detailing how he and his good friend and brother-in-law Robert Rhone came to possess three big boxes of worthless coins my grandfather called the sunshine coins. I recall as a youth listening to my grandfather tell this story many times over and I can attest to its accuracy. One of the coins will also be included in the trunk of mementos, which I will send to you posthaste. It is unfortunate that Grandfather never saw fit to disclose the final disposition of the lot of coins other than to say they had been "returned to God's green earth for good cause." In any event I think you will find the story an interesting part of our heritage. Please watch for the trunk addressed to you, which I will send by rail and then by coach to your place. I implore you to pass on the mementos to one of your descendants when the time comes with the instructions for them to do the same. I trust you will glean as much enjoyment from the contents as I have all these years.

I wish you God's Blessings,
Your Loving Uncle,
Philip Hoppe, Junr.
July 23, 1880
Philadelphia, Pennsylvania

From the Hoppe family Bible Charles next read for the thir-
teenth time the translated version of the treasure story written by
Rudolph Hoppe. As with the previous twelve, he found no clue as
to the location of the cache of coins.

CHAPTER

THIRTEEN

Eighty-year-old Dorothy Hummel greeted Will and Karen at the door of her nephew Steven Kulp's home in Berrysburg, a few miles west of Gratz.

"Come in, come in, my goodness, come in."

"Hi, I'm Will and …"

"Oh, I know who you are. Sit down. We'll have tea. I'm Dorothy Hummel. Call me Dottie. My Donald never liked calling me that, now I insist everybody does. Donald was my poor old husband, God rest his soul. Cream and sugar?"

"Yes, please," Karen answered as Dottie Hummel disappeared into the kitchen.

Will regarded their hostess. Dottie Hummel's attire was stylish and had the look of money. She was wearing an opera-length multistrand crystal necklace with matching bracelet. She was a large woman who had long since lost her waistline, but was fit for her age. She walked with a stiff right knee and carried a walnut cane topped with a gold ram's head. It looked expensive. Considering how well Dottie walked despite her stiff leg, Will figured the cane was more a part of her ensemble than for keeping her upright. She spoke with a high-pitched voice that reminded him of Julia Child. When in her presence there was no question as to just who was in charge. Will liked her immediately.

In just under five minutes she yelled from the kitchen, "Will someone please get this tray?"

Karen responded and placed the tray neatly arranged with a pot of tea, three cups and saucers, three spoons, and a creamer and sugar bowl set on the coffee table. Also on the tray was a plate of shortbread cookies arranged in two rows like fallen dominoes.

Looking at Will, Dottie asked, "You're Mel Rhone's boy, right?"

"No, his grandson."

"Yes, yes, that's right. Bill was your Dad."

"Correct."

"How's your grandpa doing? It's so hard losing someone you've been with for so long ... I know. Terrible thing ... terrible."

"He's doing as good as can be expected. Thanks."

"Karen, I'm afraid I don't know your family well ... you're Bob's daughter?"

"Yes, my father is Robert Holtzman and my mother Charlotte Wilkes. They're living in Florida now. My brother Keith lives in the area. I'm staying with him right now."

"Yes, yes, I recall now reading about your parents moving to Florida ... or did someone tell me that ... heavens I don't remember. My nephew Steve sends me the local paper and I try to keep up with everything. Do you know Steve?"

Will and Karen shook their heads.

"Huh?" Dottie asked again.

"No. We don't know Steve," Will verbalized this time.

"Now then, let me tell you a little about ol' Dottie. I was born and raised not too far from here on the Henry farm. Yes, that's right, the one in question ... the one with the Rhone cemetery. When I was nineteen, Donald Hummel swept me off my feet and I married him, much to my parents chagrin. That's why we moved to New York City. Donald didn't like the way he was treated by them … .my parents, that is. Oh, how exciting it was," she said, touching Karen's forearm, "being carried off to the big city by my knight in shining armor … gracious me, can you imagine … a country gal from the rolling hills of Pennsylvania? Well, I lived there happily with Donald until he died three years ago. I still miss the cigar-smokin' ol' goat. Oh my, was he a good provider … successful publisher, you know. Near sixty years of marriage … can you imagine? Well, Donald provided for me in death as well as he did in life. So after he died I started traveling all over the country visiting my relatives before I croak … and his too … don't like most of them though. Anyway, that's why I'm here … visiting Steve and other family. I saw your ad and gave a call. Which gets to why *you're* here … doesn't it?"

"Yes," Karen answered.

"Well, I think I can help you but you're going to have to help me get there."

"We can do that. I have a four-wheel drive. There is a farm road that should take us beside the field where we think the cemetery was located. We are hoping you can show us the layout of the whole farm."

"Goodness, yes. Let's get going. Oh, isn't this exciting?"

Dottie left the tray of tea and goodies where it sat, draped a pink cashmere sweater over her arm, and walked to the truck with Will and Karen without her cane.

"Gracious me, they're building them higher these days, aren't they?" Dottie said, laughing at her feeble attempt to mount Will's truck unassisted.

Will and Karen helped Dottie into the front seat. Karen sat in the extended cab.

They drove on township road T-231 to the access road used by the MAAC employees to service the fields. The access road was kept in good repair and Will drove several hundred yards to a spot just off a large field.

Dottie said pointing, "No. Go farther that way. To the top of that little knoll there." Will did as instructed and asked Dottie if she wanted to get out and walk. "Heavens, young man, I'm eighty years old. I'm not up to hiking hither and yon through the countryside. Go on now. I'll stay here and direct you. Walk in that direction and I'll tell Karen when to stop you."

Again Will followed Dottie's instructions.

"Stop. Right there," Karen yells, "you're standing on the cemetery."

Will was standing just off the access road that had taken a ninety-degree turn to the left from where the truck was parked. He was in a cultivated part of the field. The field had been plowed and harrowed, but as of yet had not received its spring planting. He told Karen to snap a picture of him standing on the spot. After she did Will saw her talking to Dottie, then come bolting toward him kicking up her heels like a young filly released from the barn for the first time.

"Dottie said we should see the foundation of the old barn if we walk about a hundred yards or so north, which is that way. She said stay on the old road and that should lead to where the house was in a little dip at the bottom of this knoll. There should be signs of a spring in the dip."

Will and Karen found the barn foundation and continued on looking for the location of the house Robert Rhone and friends built over two hundred years ago. They found the spring Dottie mentioned and searched the underbrush just where the terrain started to rise again from the spring.

"I think this is it, Will. There isn't much left, but look at the way those stones are lined up. You can make out the rough outline of a house foundation."

"I think you're right. Makes sense. Good location for a house down in this little dip. Just a short walk to the spring; well protected from the winter wind too."

Karen snapped more pictures and they both returned to the truck.

"Did you find anything?" Dottie asked.

"Yes, we did," Karen answered. "We took photos of everything."

"Good, now take me home and I'll tell you more."

No one noticed the man standing beside his parked van almost a half mile away on T-231. He was watching them through his binoculars.

∗∗∗

As Will drove back to Steve Kulp's house, Dottie did most the talking.

"I used to play around that cemetery when I has a kid. There was a wrought iron fence the whole way around it. My father destroyed the cemetery to get more land to plant. I'm remembering he listed the names before he did, but heaven only knows what became of that. Will, I'm sure you don't like the idea of one of your ancestral grandmas pushing up field corn but things were tough then and even just a little more land meant more to eat. I hope you understand. I think it's illegal to do such a thing now."

"Well, let's say it would be ill-advised to do it without pursuing legal channels. But I harbor no resentment," Will said.

"How many stones do you remember being there?" Karen asked.

"Oh, I don't know. Kids don't pay attention to that kind of thing. I'd say maybe fifteen or twenty."

"Were there any other buildings besides the house and barn?" Will asked.

"Oh yes. There was a little workshop beside the barn, a shed where they used to shoe the horses beside that, a hog house, and a springhouse. There was a long chicken coop just to the west of the house too. I guess there's no sign of that now, is there?"

Will shook his head.

"Huh?"

"No. We didn't see any," Will said, remembering too late Dottie didn't respond well to head gestures.

When they arrived at Steve Kulp's house Will helped Dottie out of the truck and the three walked to the porch.

"We can't thank you enough, Dottie," Karen said.

"Oh, no, no, dear. Thank *you*. Sitting in the truck on the old homestead while you two explored brought back memories of things I hadn't thought about in years. It was my pleasure. You did me the favor ... seeing the ol' place one last time. I hope I helped you too."

"You did indeed," Will said.

"Would you like a couple of handfuls of hard candy to take along? You know. The kind you can do this with?" With a cupped hand Dottie made a quick thrusting motion to her opened mouth simultaneously throwing her head back.

"Oh no thanks, not for me," Karen said.

A smiling Will shook his head, and then remembered in time, "No. Me neither. Thanks."

"Okay. I'll be in town for a few more days, so call if you have any questions."

"We'll do that."

Will and Karen said good-bye and thanked Dottie Hummel again, then headed back to Mel's house.

Karen said, "The list Dottie mentioned is the one we have, isn't it?"

"I'm sure of it. She's Joel Henry's aunt."

"I wonder what Joel will think of her showing us the cemetery."

"I don't know. Maybe she already visited him. Maybe he'll never know."

As Will parked by the house Karen said, "I like Dottie. Wouldn't you just love to sit down with her and listen to all the stories she could tell?"

"Yes. But first we'd need to practice our hard candy throw."

***

Mel's first instruction to Will and Karen after hearing of their adventures with Dottie was to draw a rough sketch of the Rhone homestead while it was fresh in their memory. "Include approximate distances from landmarks too. But don't do it right now. Wait until after your second trip."

"I'll get the pictures printed out on Jason's PC when I get home," Karen told Mel.

"Good. I'd like to see them,"

"Grandpa, don't you every remember seeing the cemetery as a kid?"

"No, I don't. I never ventured over that far. I was aware of where the old Rhone farm was, but I never went exploring. I never had any interest in genealogy as a youth."

The words just sinking in, Karen asked, "Mel. What do you mean 'after our second trip?'"

"I'm glad you came when you did; I was just ready to call your cell. Luther Grace called again. He said he is going to the Gratz Historical Society to look around the museum, and if you pick him up there he'll show you the cemetery location. Can you get over there right away?"

"We're on are way," Will said.

***

The Gratz Historical Society had converted an old general store into a research library and museum. Going there was like stepping back in time. The floor had the original wooden boards and creaked as you walked. The research library was heated by a small oil burner in the center and off to one side. Wooden tables with lamps on each side of the long narrow room provided a place to research their collection of material. In the museum, many of the store's original display cases were now the home of artifacts contributed by local residents.

Karen and Will entered and asked the matron if she knew Luther Grace. She pointed to the doorway that led from the library to the museum. They found Luther Grace in the railroad and coal mining section.

"Luther Grace?"

"Yeah. Who wants to know?"

"I'm Will Rhone and this is Karen Holtzman."

"Oh yeah. Your grandpa sent you, did he?"

"He did."

"Ya know I remember using this stuff," he said pointing to an old miner's helmet fixed with a carbide lamp. "Worked at the old Wiconisco Colliery for many years. That's where I lost this," Luther Grace said, holding up his prosthetic left arm.

"Oh, I'm sorry, Mr. Grace," Karen said.

"Ah, don't be. I'm proud of this thing now. Can use it almost as good as a real one, so I can, and I don't have to worry 'bout getting my fingers caught in the car door." Will and Karen tried not to grin. "You can call me Luke by the way ... Mr. Grace is my father. I got this miner's tattoo there too," Luke pointed to a ragged black mark under his skin about the size of a quarter just above his left eye. The result of a chuck of coal striking him and the wound healing before it was cleaned properly. "I guess we better get going."

Will walked to the passenger side of his truck to help Luke.

"No, no, you drive, I'll ride," Luke said and hopped in the like he was thirty.

Will turned onto T-231.

"Where ya goin'?" Luke asked.

"Isn't this the right way?"

"Yeah, if you want to take the long away around. Turn around and get on the Klingerstown Road."

Will did as instructed.

After they'd driven a short distance Luke said, "As you start into the next curve, pull off to the left. There. See that little pull-off?"

Will pulled the truck into what used to be an old wagon road along a fencerow. There was just enough space to get the truck off the macadam road.

"We'll walk from here."

"It's a good hike to the fields, Luke. Are you sure you want to go in this way?" Will asked.

"Sure am. I guarantee you, you'll be huffin' and puffin' a lot more than me when we get there. I may be seventy-six years old, but I walk two miles a day every day, and I can run down an alley cat, so I can."

Luke Grace was right. He led the trek all the way and was breathing normally. When they reached the fencerow at the edge of the field, Will leaned on a tree catching his breath, and Karen sat on a pile of rocks. Luke looked back at them and shook his head.

"Now, let's see. It was right around here. Yep, this is it."

Karen and Will gave each other a puzzled look. The spot Luke Grace picked was about a hundred yards due south and down the slight grade from the spot Dottie Hummel picked on top of the knoll.

"There used to be an old road leadin' from here to that knoll there," Luke said pointing to Dottie Hummel's choice. "It met the road we walked in on. If you keep goin' on that road over the knoll it'll take you to where the barn and house were, so it will."

"You're certain of this?" Will said.

"Yep, this is it. My dad and uncles used to take me huntin' on this ground. They didn't let me carry a gun, but I liked goin' along. There was a fence around the cemetery."

"How big was it?" Karen asked.

"The fence?"

"The area of the cemetery."

"Oh ... 'bout twenty, thirty feet square, I'd say."

"Do you remember the number of stones?" Karen was still asking the questions.

"Wasn't many. Maybe a dozen or so. Most were in German. I don't speak German so I can't tell you about those. Is that all you want to know?"

"Yes, that's it. Thanks a lot, Luke."

"Don't mention it. You can take me back to the museum now, or do you need some time to rest first?"

Will and Karen didn't respond to the jab.

***

After they returned Luke Grace to the museum, Will and Karen went back to the house and reported in to Mel again.

"I was afraid of that. You get old ... the memory fades, you know. They were both just kids when they saw the cemetery last. At least they were in the same field. Make a note of it on your sketch."

"To make matters worse, they both were sure of themselves," Will said.

"Mel, if you don't mind my asking, why is the location of the cemetery so important? I mean, I realize knowing who's buried there *is* important, and maybe the only record of their death. After all, look what it did for me. But we know the names now. I don't understand why the *exact* location is important. I get the impression there's more to it with you."

Mel looked down a moment, then said, "You're sharp, Karen." Looking at Will he repeated, "She's sharp."

"She sure is."

Mel continued, "You're right. I'm sure you've both seen the large memorial stone sitting in the field a few hundred feet off the road to Loyalton. But did you every walk back to look at the inscription?"

"I haven't," Will said.

"Me neither."

"Well, have a look sometime. Get permission first though, it's private property. It marks the spot of the old pioneer cemetery of the Hoffman family. There may be other families there too … I'm not sure. The old cemetery just slowly disappeared over time like so many others. Before everyone was gone who knew the cemetery location, the Hoffman descendants got together many years ago and erected that memorial on the site. It was a great idea.

"That's what I want to do. Erect a memorial on the site of the Rhone cemetery. Now I can have their names and dates engraved on the stone, thanks to Mrs. Henry. I know it's an uphill battle, seeing as the land is owned by MAAC, but I want to try. I won't start that project until we finish this other business, but that's why it's important to me."

"That's a great idea, Mel. I can help you with it. My ancestors are there too."

"I hope everybody thinks it's a great idea. There's no law saying the landowner has to agree to it that I'm aware of. MAAC appears to be a company with a heart. I hope they are.

"Alright. Back to what you learned today. Which of the two spots looks more logical to you? I mean, if you were starting a cemetery, which spot would you choose?"

"I think I would have picked Dottie's spot. Right on top of the little knoll there … it was nice," said Karen.

"I agree," Will said.

Mel said, "No rush on this but keep it in the back of your mind. How does one find an old grave in a cultivated field with no visible surface evidence on land someone else owns?"

CHAPTER

FOURTEEN

Socrates Smith was familiar with the dense woods overlooking Mel Rhone's house. It's where he waited until dark to make his attack on Mel, Polly, and Beau. He saw it as the perfect spot. The old logging road winding through the twenty acres of woods was in good enough condition to pull his van out of sight from passersby on the macadam road a few hundred feet to the rear. His vehicle couldn't be seen from the Rhone house either. All he had to do was park and walk the two hundred feet to his vantage point at the edge of the woods. Another two hundred feet of hayfield gave a clear view of his intended target.

He hoped this parking spot would be close enough to pick up the signal from the tiny transmitter he was about to plant. Charles told him the receiver needed to be within four hundred feet of the transmitter. He figured two hundred feet from the van to the edge of the woods, and another two feet across the open field to Rhone's house. It was marginal, but it was the best he could do and still remain hidden. He would have to try and plant the bug in a spot in the house closest to the van. Every foot counted.

He had been watching for days without any opportunity, but now with the aid of his binoculars he watched as Will Rhone helped his grandfather into the front seat and opened the door for Beau to hop in the extended cab. *This won't take long. Pick the lock, plant the bug, and I'm outta there. Glad they took the dog.*

He hated crossing the open hayfield from the edge of the woods to the house. He was exposed. He couldn't run, he might attract attention should someone happen see him. He picked up a walking stick and causally strolled to the house. *Just a nice nature-loving guy out for a nice walk on a nice day.*

Smith pulled on his gloves as he walked up the steps. The door was open and he entered the enclosed porch and breathed a sign of relief at being in the shadows again. To make certain no one was in the house he knocked on the door and waited. When no one responded he opened the screen door and saw the first thing he didn't like. A deadbolt. He couldn't pick that quickly or easily break through. The second thing he saw was the Bobcat Security sticker in the window announcing they were protecting the property. *Now what?* He stood thinking over his options.

He could leave without doing anything, but what good would that do? He would find the same situation if he came back later. The Rhones just left, so he had time to break in, plant the bug, and steal a few things to make it look like a burglary. Bobcat Security would first try to call the house to make sure the owners didn't trip the alarm by accident, and then call the police if they didn't get a response. *Can't answer the phone they could ask for a code.* He could stay until he heard the phone and be long gone before the police arrived. He liked it.

Smith pondered the best window to break and decided the back window beside the porch would allow the quickest access. *No nosy neighbors close by to hear anything.* He swung his walking stick baseball-style into the window. The blow broke both the storm window and the interior pane. With the stick he cleared the frames of the remaining broken glass. Using his hands to lift himself up, he rolled into the house headfirst. He worked fast. He stuck the adhesive side of the small transmitter under the phone stand beside Mel's Easy-Lounger.

He went through the first floor knocking over everything that wasn't fastened down. He removed drawers and dumped the contents on the floor. He found two 1973 U.S. Proof Sets with the Ike Dollar in a desk drawer, and forty dollars with a short shopping list on the dinning room table. *Nice hat. Might as well have a souvenir.* Just as he thought would happen, the phone rang. He adjusted the hat and put it on, stuck the cash and the proofs in his pocket, and left the house through the window he had broken no more than three minutes before. He never felt the tiny shard of glass at the top of the window sash nick a small piece of skin from the back of his neck.

As Smith reached the cover of the woods, he heard the police sirens. He ran to his van and escaped clean.

***

Mel and Will had received the call from Bobcat Security informing them of a breach while on their way to Doc Philips for Beau's routine appointment. Bobcat told them they had called the police. Will turned around and headed for home.

Trooper Wilber Krull met Will and Mel as they exited the pickup.

"Looks like they broke a window in the back to gain access. I did a search of the house and the perpetrator is gone. It's safe to go in, but I'm going to have to ask you to wait outside until Forensic arrives. They should be here any minute. In light of what happened to you recently, I asked them to sweep your house again. I called the security company and gave them the status here. They took your system out of service for now."

As the Forensic team did their work Mel and Will waited outside. Trooper Krull was using the hood of his cruiser as a desk to write his report.

"Officer, do you think this is connected to the attack?" Mel asked.

"Yes I do. It doesn't have the feel of a routine burglary. Most thieves would have been long gone once they tripped the alarm. And you can't miss those security stickers … I don't think they would have even bothered in the first place. Why take the chance? There's something else going on here. This was made to *look* like a burglary. I think you were being watched, and as soon as you left, the perp came."

"I think you're right. We've only been gone about fifteen minutes," Will said.

"When I'm finished here I'll have a look around all the vantage points with a view of your house," the policeman said.

"Okay, Wilber, all done." This was Trooper Sharon Quill, head of the Forensic team.

"Submit a copy of your results to Dave Zimmerman, will you, Sharon?" Trooper Krull asked. "Get anything good?"

"Yeah. Looks like the perp left us a sample of his skin on top of the window sash. We'll run the DNA. Might match that hair we found the first time around."

"Nice of him to help us out. Thanks, Sharon."

"Sure thing, Wilber. Take care."

Trooper Krull said, "We can go in now, Mr. Rhone. Be forewarned, the place is a mess."

Seeing their space violated in a violent way was disturbing for Mel and Will. All they could do at first was look as they walked through the house, but then Mel started picking things up and putting them back in place. *No matter what the disaster people always start cleaning up right away*, Trooper Krull thought.

"I don't expect you to tell me now, but make a list of anything missing and submit it to me as soon as possible. I'm going to talk to Lieutenant Zimmerman about this. Have those windows fixed right away and call Bobcat. They'll have to install new contacts.

Tell them I asked if they could please do it today. I'm also going to request increased patrols around your house on a twenty-four-hour basis."

Mel said, "Thank you, Officer. The lady mentioned a hair that was found."

"Yes. It wasn't from anybody it should have been from. Lieutenant Zimmerman will talk to you about that at some point. Take care. I must run."

After Trooper Krull left, Mel and Will got to work. The first place they checked was the filing cabinet but nothing had been disturbed. Mel was glad he had copied his research to disc and hid it in the attic. They noted that the two twenty-dollar bills with the shopping list they'd forgotten when they left was gone. Later Mel noted his U.S. Proof sets were missing.

In a solemn mood they began cleaning up the mess made by Socrates Smith. They were almost finished when the phone rang.

CHAPTER

FIFTEEN

When the photographs of the Bible arrived Karen ripped the packet open like a kid on Christmas morning. She scanned the photos one after the other looking for some mention of the treasure. Nothing. The documents did contain a lot of new family information, however, and Mel and Will would be able to fill in gaps, but it was not what she was hoping for. The last photo appeared to be of the back inside cover of the ancient Bible. There was only one entry. Written in pen and ink in the upper right-hand corner was:

> FUGIO
> Mind your business
> With Mother
> 8 June 1788
> RR

F-U-G ten. What's that? Someone's initial, a nickname, ten what? And what business with whose mother? Who was F-U-G? Her mind raced through the possibilities. It made no sense but a red flag went up, a subconscious trigger that told her this was important. It would be rare for her subconscious to be wrong. *June 8, 1788.*

The date sounded familiar but she couldn't place it. The only thing that made sense to her was the "RR". *That must be Robert Rhone.*

She called Delbert Rhone to tell him the photos arrived and were perfect. She asked him if he had any knowledge of what the short entry was on the inside back cover. He did not. She thanked him again. He said the ring bologna was delicious. He was pleased the butcher shop included a catalog and that he could now place a direct order any time he wanted. She then called Mel to tell him she had the photos and asked if they all could get together right away.

"Come on over. We had an incident, but we're getting it cleaned up. I'll explain when you get here," was Mel's answer.

When Karen arrived Beau greeted her in his usual way of presenting his favorite ball and dropping it at her feet.

"Can't play now, Beau. Important business here."

"We had a break-in," Will said.

Will and Mel told Karen the story. Karen forgot for a moment why she was there.

"And you say your files weren't disturbed?" she said.

"No. Nothing missing there," Mel answered.

"All that for a couple of proof sets and forty bucks? It doesn't make sense, Mel."

"And my hat," Will added.

"Your hat? What hat?

"I just received a free sample from a vendor who personalizes wearing apparel. I get things like that all the time. It was a beige baseball style hat with RHONE'S WOODWORLD in red letters. All the O's were shaped like a saw blade. Nice hat. I may get some for the guys next year."

"You mean it's one of a kind?"

"Yes. Until next year, anyway."

"Did you tell the police that?"

"No. I'm not absolutely certain it was taken just yet. I thought it was on the table near the money but I may have just misplaced it. If it doesn't turn up in the next couple of days I'll let them know."

"Why would anybody chance it for so little?" Karen asked of no one in particular.

"No idea," Mel said, "Let's have a look at those photos."

Karen handed the envelope with the photos to Mel. After studying them he handed them to Will.

"Incredible. Thanks a lot, Karen," Mel said. "Lots of good stuff there. Notice Robert's two infants buried in the Rhone cemetery. That explains a couple of the unmarked graves."

"Can you read the German entries, Mel?"

"Enough of it in this context. For example, *geboren* ... born, *sterben* or *starb* ... die, *Taufe* ... baptism, and I know the months in German, things like that. I have trouble with the old German script in general though. When I come across documents in German I have to get my reference material out and really study them one word at a time."

Will perused the photos and handed them back to Karen.

"What do you guys make of this inscription on the back inside cover?" she asked.

"Let me see that again," Mel said.

Passing the photo to Mel, Karen said, "I could only make sense of the 'RR' and the date. I checked the cemetery list Mrs. Henry gave us and June 8, 1788, is the day after Magdalena Rhone died."

"It looks to me like Robert was giving instructions to someone, or making a note to himself. Didn't Robert's mother die in Ireland? Why would he be telling someone to mind their business with her if she's already dead?" This was Will.

"I don't know. Robert's mother *did* die in Ireland. One thing is for certain," Mel said, "The family Bible was important to those people. They wouldn't use it as a notepad. Anything they entered would be important. That's not a casual notation."

"How do you know about Robert's parents, Mel?"

"Well, research in Northern Ireland isn't easy, but it's possible. There was a fire in 1922 in the Public Record Office in Dublin. Destroyed most of the old records making research tough. I finally hired a private researcher for the Ulster region. She was good. She found a lot—not everything I wanted—but a lot. Thanks to her I know Robert and his brother James arrived in Philadelphia in 1773 on the ship *Betsy*, among other things. Robert's parents are definitely buried in Northern Ireland. I can't imagine what that reference to Robert's mother would be."

"Did you notice that the W in 'With Mother' is upper case?" Karen said.

"I don't know if you can read much into that. They capitalized at strange times in the early script and hardly ever punctuated anything," Mel noted.

"You would think Robert would be grief-stricken and preparing for her funeral and not thinking of making Bible entries the day after his wife died. I noticed he did record her death on the 'Deaths' page at some point. But why would he make *that* entry the day after she died?" Will asked.

"Well, a couple of points here, Will. Those people weren't any different than people are today when it came to the emotions of deaths, births, marriage, or anything else. They were hard, but not that hard. He *was* grief-stricken, you can be sure of it. And the day after Magdalena died is most likely the day she was buried. No embalming then. They didn't waste any time getting them in the ground. This all bodes well for the importance of that entry," Mel answered.

"We don't know when he wrote that in the Bible. He could have written it years after his wife died or the day she was buried. Was he saying the date was when he wrote it or was it the day of whatever event he was making note of? We don't know," Karen commented.

"I say that's the day he wrote it and that's the day of the event," Will replied.

"Any thoughts on the 'F-U-G ten'?" Karen asked Mel.

"None. Did you try online?"

"Yes. I couldn't find anything of consequence."

Will walked to the office and returned with English and German-English dictionaries. He paraphrased the English definition of fug. "Used as a noun, it is an odorous emanation; the stuffy atmosphere of a poorly ventilated space; probable alteration of fog. Used as a verb, to loll indoors in a stuffy atmosphere. And let's see ... in German it means, 'rightly, justifiably.'"

"Rightly or justifiably ten? But why would he write the rest of the inscription in English and fug in German?" Karen noted.

"One thing for certain, that inscription makes no sense at this point. Fug just doesn't sound to me like it would be part of the everyday eighteenth-century lexicon, in German or English," Mel said.

"We'll figure it out. While you were talking, Grandpa, I remembered something. What was it you used to call Grandma that got you a scolding every time you did it?"

Mel thought a minute, "Mother! You're right. I only did it to get her going, you know."

"*I* know you did, but I don't think Grandma knew."

"Are you saying that the reference to 'Mother' could be Robert's wife?" Karen asked.

"Why not?" Will answered, "It's used as a pet name. We've all heard a father call the mother of their children that. If it's done in the twenty-first century, why not the eighteenth?"

"Okay, let's assume you're right. That still doesn't tell us much. Why would he be telling someone, or making a note to himself, to mind business with his wife the day *after* she dies?" Karen asked.

"Good point," Will answered. "I don't know. But hear me out. What if the inscription in the Bible was just done for posterity and no other reason? What if 'fug 10' is a reference to the treasure? What if Robert wanted to put it someplace it would never be disturbed? What if that place would be 'With Mother'—his wife—on June 8th, 1788, the day she was buried? What if that *was* the business with her? That would explain why "With" is capitalized.

"Wait a minute. You're suggesting Robert buried the treasure with his wife?" Karen was incredulous.

"Yes."

"Why would he do that? That doesn't make any sense. You mean every time he needed to access the treasure he went to his wife's grave and started digging? I don't think so. As a matter of fact we don't even know if Robert *had* the treasure when Magdalena died. And another thing bothers me while I'm on the subject. We have not seen any evidence at all that suggests Robert or Rudolph, or their children for that matter, were extraordinarily wealthy. Why?"

"Good points all. I can't answer your questions," Will conceded.

"Will," Mel said, "I have to agree with Karen. Burying the treasure with his wife just doesn't make sense. We must certainly keep an open mind and all theories are welcome here, but I think that's far-fetched."

Will replied, "Maybe so. But what else could it mean? I mean really. Making reference to the day he buried his wife. And it doesn't matter when it was written, he's still making reference to that day. Like you said, Grandpa, it has to be something important."

Mel said, "I agree. But we're missing something. We have to keep digging. We'll keep your theory in mind, though."

"I won't *let* you forget," Will said.

"I'm sure you won't," Karen teased. She scratched her head. "I don't know. I have to be honest with you two. Sometimes I have doubts. What if we're just spinning our wheels? What if this whole treasure thing is like so many other treasure stories you hear? Nothing but rumor."

"Well, don't forget. Somebody else believes the rumor," Will said.

"That doesn't make it true," she answered.

Mel intervened, "We can't let frustration get a foothold here. The answers are out there. If we are persistent in pursuing this we will persevere."

Part Three

Natural affections must have their course.
The best remedy of grief is time.

—Benjamin Franklin

*Map of the 1762 waterfront region of Philadelphia, north and south
of Market Street at Front Street. Today this area is the location
of the Benjamin Franklin Bridge, joining Philadelphia
and Camden, New Jersey, since 1926.*

CHAPTER

SIXTEEN

June 8, 1788
The Robert Rhone Farm
Dauphin County, Pennsylvania

This is what she wanted. This is what I'll do, Robert thought. As he worked he regarded life with his wife and the devastating events of the past several days.

Maggie Rhone had gone to a tributary of Deep Creek on a hot afternoon in the spring of 1788 to wash clothes in the small dam Robert built for that purpose. When she finished the exhausting task she removed her outer clothes and washed them too. The water was cold but it felt good on her overheated skin and she sat down in the shallow dam, cupping the water in her hands and allowing it to drain over her head.

The next day she felt tired and chilled and she had a persistent cough. She told Robert what she'd done the day before and was sure that's why she felt as she did and it was nothing to worry about.

Over the next few days her condition worsened. Her breathing became wheezy and labored. Robert was worried and sent

Rudi to try to find a doctor, any doctor, and bring him as soon as he could. Libby watched Philip and Catherine so he could tend to his wife as best he could.

A high fever had Maggie delirious and she rambled on about nothing. She had to fight for every breath until she could fight no more. The doctor never came. She died with Robert by her side at the age of twenty-eight.

Their marriage had been like many others of the time, one of convenience, or necessity, or just because it was time. So what if a couple had known each other for a matter of days rather than months or years? If they approved of each other and he asked, so be it. Here's the surprising part. This practical approach worked out most of the time.

Many times love came, sometimes it didn't. It came to Robert and Maggie. He had fallen in love with her sense of humor and agreeable disposition sometime *after* their marriage. There was never a cross word between them, a major accomplishment on Maggie's part living with the hypertensive Robert, and he knew it. Now his heart was broken, She was gone. He felt like half of him had been torn away and he wanted the pain to stop.

***

When Robert finished filling the large glazed stoneware jugs he tapped the plugs in to about an inch below the top and filled the resulting cavity with melted wax. He then put the jugs on the back of the wagon and returned to the house to tend to his wife's lifeless body. He wanted to do right by her.

He removed her clothes and placed them on the bed in a neat stack. The porcelain washbasin and pitcher set he had given her last Christmas was nearby on the bed stand. A bar of soap Maggie had made was nested in a washcloth beside the basin, and beside that, a towel. He had heated the water to just the right temperature in the heavy cast-iron kettle and poured half of it into the pitcher and half into the basin. He wet the washcloth in the basin, picked up the soap with the wet cloth, and then turned it around in his hand until it made a creamy lather. He made gentle strokes with the cloth over her face as though he expected her to respond to the heat. He repeated this procedure on all of her and then washed her flowing auburn hair. When he was finished he replaced the soapy water with fresh and repeated his steps, rinsing her. With a gentle touch he patted her dry.

The only sound that came from his quivering lips was the sudden intake of air in great gasps. It was the sound made when crying was no longer possible but grief was still lodged deep in the soul.

He dressed her in her favorite blue gingham dress and fixed her hair with the silver barrette inlaid with a mother-of-pearl rose she had worn only on Sundays. She was beautiful.

He carried her downstairs and carefully placed her on the blanket in the long wooden box delivered that morning. He added some of her favorite things beside her, mementos of their life together; things that only had meaning to them.

Memories of favors he'd promised her that remained unkept came to him and he strained with all he had left to keep them away. He hoped she saw him as a good husband and father. He nailed the coffin shut.

Rudi would bring his wagon soon to help him take Maggie to the top of the knoll.

***

There was going to be a service at the grave site. Reverend Snyder said he would come. Robert's children, James' family, Rudi's family, the Kohls, and a few friends and neighbors would be there.

Robert selected the site because he could see it from the house, and it was in full sun most of the day. She had always liked sitting in the sun. The engraved headstone he ordered would be ready in a few days. Later he would buy a fancy iron fence to enclose the burial site and plant the flowers Libby offered him around the fence. He could have buried her in the cemetery by the new church. Reverend Snyder had made the offer but it was two miles away. He didn't want her to be that far from him, so he and Rudi started digging on top of the knoll a few hundred yards from the house. The physical labor helped postpone his grief.

When all were present the service began. Reverend Snyder was solemn and brief. He concluded by telling Maggie's loved ones to "Cleave to each other for comfort and call on the Lord for strength. Grieve, but only for a time, then carry on with your lives. You will be with her again in Glory someday soon. She will not want to hear you squander your days from now until then mired in grief."

As Pastor Snyder sung the John Fawcett hymn "Blest Be the Tie That Binds," six of the men lowered the pine box cradled by three long ropes into the grave. His powerful voice echoed through the hollow beside the field. When he finished he said a few parting words for Maggie and invited everyone to his house for Christian fellowship and a bite to eat. Everyone accepted.

"I want to do this alone," Robert told the men who lingered to help him close the grave. "You go ahead. I'll be along in a little while."

When everyone had gone, Robert went to the back of the barn where he had the wagon loaded and the team already hitched. He walked the team to the graveside and with the aid of a rope slid through the handle, one by one lowered the seven stoneware jugs he had sealed with wax on top of the pine box. With that done he proceeded to close the grave.

When he was finished, Robert stood leaning on the shovel looking at the fresh earth. He regarded the day he had discovered the coins were worthless. In frustration he had commented, *"We might as well throw them in the bloody Mahantango . . ."* He remembered being annoyed by Maggie's strange response. He recalled her words like they were just spoken the day before: *"No.*

They're pretty. When my time comes use them to line my grave." He wondered now if she had had a premonition. After a few more minutes of staring seeing nothing, he said aloud in a soft voice, "I love you, Mother. I'll see you soon enough." He heard a noise and turned to see Rudi walking toward him.

Rudi walked to the grave and stood beside Robert for a long moment, then asked, "Did you do it?"

"I did."

In solemn silence both men stood looking at the mound of earth a little while longer.

Part Four

*In bad fortune I hope for the good;
in good I fear the bad.*

—Benjamin Franklin

Portrait of Benjamin Franklin by J. A. Duplessis, 1783.
An engraving was made from the painting
by H. B. Hall in 1868.

CHAPTER

SEVENTEEN

April 2004
Dauphin County, Pennsylvania

Socks Smith called Charles Holtzman from a local call phone as instructed.

"Chuck. I planted the bug yesterday."

"I'll say you did, and wrecked the house, and had half the police in the county involved again. Why the dramatics, Socks?"

"Don't start on me, Chuck. I did what I had to do under the circumstances. And how do you know about it already?"

"It's my business to know. Did you test the receiver?"

"No. Not yet."

"Well, what's the delay, Socks? Every minute that goes by we could be missing useful information."

"I couldn't very well hang around the area with cops crawling all over, now could I? Let things cool down a bit and I'll go back later and test it. But I'm not hanging out there twenty-four hours a day, Chuck, I'll tell you that right now. I'll get nailed for sure."

"Here's what you do, Socks. I don't know why I have to tell

you everything. You've been watching them for a while now. Try to remember a pattern when they get together and be on the receiver then."

"Friday afternoons. They're in and out all the time, especially that cousin of yours. But Friday afternoon seems to be when they all get together."

"Be there then. Don't screw this up and call me if you hear anything … from a *local call* phone only."

"I …"

Charles hung up before Socks could respond.

✳✳✳

Mel had been making homemade wine for over fifty years. He could legally make up to 200 gallons a year for home consumption, though he never made near that amount, and never drank near what he did make. He gave most of it away to his friends. He had learned the basics from his father and developed the procedure into an art form with the aid of the latest techniques, additives, and equipment. This was not his father's homemade wine. He won ribbons every time he entered home winemaking competition.

With the new vineyard a few miles away now in production he had access to premium wine grapes for the first time in his life. Chardonnay, Marechal Foch, and Joannes Seyve, harvested at their peak, were now available to him and more varieties were pending. He thought he was in winemaker's heaven. Still, strawberry was his all-time favorite and strawberry season was just around the corner. If it was a good season for the berries and the fermentation went well, strawberries made the most exquisite wine imaginable. He was anxious to get a batch in the primary fermenter.

He was also anxious to imbibe the half-glass of two-year-old Concord he currently held in his right hand. The outcome was in doubt thanks to stiff opposition in the person of Mrs. Leah Adams, visiting nurse.

"Ya chust better kuddit ott or I'm callin' the doctor on ya," Mrs. Adams scolded. "Chust look at yur blutt pressure."

"Mrs. Adams, I don't see how a little glass of homemade wine can hurt anything," Mel defended himself.

"Medicine and alcohol don't mix. That's hawh."

"But it *has* medicinal value. That's why I'm drinking it. You don't really think I enjoy this stuff do you?" Mel said, trying a different strategy.

"Oh nawh yur tryin' to be funny, ain't ya? Ya better quidit wonst. This ain't funny."

Will didn't think mixing medication and alcohol, or Mel's elevated blood pressure was funny, but he sure was enjoying the verbal exchange between the two combatants. He was glad he chose the iced tea.

"All right, Mrs. Adams, I'll pour it away," Mel relented.

"No more for ya nawh either. You can drink yurself silly wonst yur off the medicine for all I care."

"Right. No more for now."

Mel walked his half-glass of Concord to the kitchen sink and turned on the faucet. He gave a quick look over his shoulder scouting Mrs. Adams' location. With the coast clear he downed the wine in two gulps, then returned to the living room.

"There now. Are you happy?"

"Humpf."

"So you and Karen are taking the day off?" Mel asked Will.

"Yes, part of the day anyway. Today's her birthday. Believe it or not, Karen has never had a ride on the Millersburg Ferry. We'll park the truck and go as pedestrians. Want to come along?"

"No. I better stay here and take it easy. Right, Mrs. Adams?"

Mrs. Adams ignored the question and gave Mel a stern look.

"Can we take Beau?"

"Sure. He'd love it. Take his long leash … the chain-link one."

"Okay. Time for me to go, Grandpa. I know I'm leaving you in good hands. Mind Mrs. Adams now."

Mel flashed him a frown.

As Will walked Beau out the door he heard yet another volley being fired in the wine wars. He almost hated to leave.

"Maybe if you tried a glass yourself, Mrs. Adams, you might feel better about *me* drinking it."

"Ach! Get ott. Stop bein' funny."

✳✳✳

Will, Karen, and Beau pulled in view of the Millersburg Ferry just in time to see it chug away from its slip. Will explained that it would only be a short wait. Park benches dotted the well-maintained seventy-five-foot-wide (more or less) strip of grass that ran parallel to and between the Susquehanna River and River Street. Will and Karen chose a bench with a panoramic view of the river within sight of the ferry slip. Will told Karen about the wine incident as they waited.

"They're so funny together. He complains about Mrs. Adams but I bet he misses her when she isn't around anymore," Karen said.

"Probably."

"Keith said he and you and your friends used to ride your bikes here and take the ferry to Perry County."

"That's true. Lots of memories of us exploring the west shore. We'd spend all day there and take the ferry back in time for supper."

"This goes to Liverpool?"

"Yeah. A couple miles south of Liverpool, actually."

"How far away is it over there?"

"About a mile. Takes about fifteen, twenty minutes one way."

"I can't believe I never rode the ferry. I love stuff like this. How long has it been in operation?"

"Nobody knows for certain. It's believed it started sometime in the eighteenth century. You'll hear the stories from the captain as we cross. One story that has some credibility is that Thomas Edison, Henry Ford, and Harvey Firestone rode the ferry together on one of their sightseeing treks."

"Wow. You mean if the ferry had sunk that day we wouldn't have cars, tires, or the phonograph?"

Laughing, Will agreed.

"So it *can* sink then?" Karen followed up.

"Yeah, but you can swim, can't you? If it does sink, just crawl to the top of the cabin and stand up. Your head should be above water there. Just kidding. You could probably stand up in the channel. Not deep at all. It's a paddleboat. Works in shallow water. It's the last wooden stern paddlewheel ferry in the country. Before 1875, when they switched to steam power, they used poles to push the ferry across the river."

"I'm impressed with your knowledge. Did you research this?"

"No. I just read it on that sign over there."

After Karen looked over her shoulder she gave Will a playful push.

"Did you know there are two of them ... two ferry boats?"

"No. Did you read that on the sign too?"

"No. I just remember that," Will said, and then asked, "Do you see that white door hung on the post ... the door to nowhere?"

"Yeah. What's it there for?"

"Because sometimes they only run one of the boats. If the boat is on the Perry County side and a passenger wants to cross from this side, the passenger just opens that door. With the broad side facing the Perry shore the crew can see it and they come a'runnin'. There's another white door on the Perry side attached to a tree for someone wanting to cross from that side. High tech, huh?"

"Are they both running today?"

"Looks like it. The Roaring Bull and the Falcon. When one leaves on this side, the other one leaves on that side. The one we get on will not be the one we saw leaving. Speaking of which. . . ." Will said, pointing out in the river.

"Here it comes!" Karen said with the excitement of a kid about to go on her first pony ride. Will found her excitement appealing.

About fifty feet from shore the captain turned the boat upriver as it approached the slip. The first mate hooked a tether rope attached to a long pole extending into the river from the shore and looped it to the boat about mid-ship, then took in the slack. The current of the river caught the bow of the ferry and, turning on the axis of the tether, the stern swung to shore in perfect alignment to the loading ramp. The vehicles on the ferry were now pointing in the right direction to offload. The experience of the captain was the only thing that enabled this difficult maneuver to go off without a hitch. He made it look easy.

After two cars departed and one drove on, Will, Karen, and Beau walked on the ferry.

"You can have a seat up front in the cabin where the captain is," the first mate said.

The captain signaled the first mate to untether and the ferry was under way, her wooden paddlewheels slapping the water.

"You're free to walk around the ferry but I ask that you don't cross over the yellow lines painted on the deck," the captain said.

"I thought it would be bigger than this," Karen said to Will in a low voice.

"We can ferry up to four cars on each boat ma'am," the captain said, used to conversing over the drone of the engine.

"How deep is the water?" Karen asked the captain, knowing now she could heard from twelve feet away.

"Five feet today, ma'am," the captain answered, making an adjustment to the large horizontal steering wheel.

"How does it work in such shallow water?" she asked.

"Because the boat's draft is only fourteen inches. I actually like the river a little lower than this."

"Did you ever lose a car?"

"No, ma'am," the captain smiled. "But we were almost struck by lighting once. We don't operate in bad weather, but the storm moved in so fast we didn't quite make it to shore."

"Oh no. Was anybody hurt?"

"No. But I couldn't hear right for about a week."

"Wow. It must have been close."

Cupping his ear, the captain said, "I'm sorry, what'd you say? Just kidding, ma'am. Yes. It was very close."

The captain talked about the history of the ferry in answer to a question from a passenger of the only vehicle.

"How do you make any money charging just six dollars for a car and driver and two dollars per passenger?" the passenger asked.

"We don't make a profit. The fees help to defer our expenses, but we operate mainly with the donations we receive. That's why the Millersburg Ferry Boat Association was formed. They're the current owners," the captain explained.

Standing on the bow seat, Beau put his front paws on the railing surrounding the open cabin and stood with his face to the wind as though he had been riding ferryboats his whole life.

"This is so cool, Will. Look at this view."

"Beau's enjoying it too. Look there. We're going to pass the Falcon heading to the east shore."

The ferry docked on the Perry County side and the passengers departed, everyone thanking the crew. Will told the captain they would be returning in about an hour.

"What is this place ... a campground?" Karen asked.

"Yes. Equipped with its own ice cream parlor on stilts," Will said. "Come on. I'm buying."

The couple sat on a swing overlooking the river, content eating their ice cream cones and taking in the view. Beau got the last inch of each cone.

"Right in my own backyard and I never experienced this."

"Well, most of your adult life you spent out of the area. And most of your childhood you spent watching me from your upstairs window." This earned Will a restrained elbow to the ribcage.

The couple plus one walked the campground road paralleling the river. Will suggested they browse the souvenir shop, also built on stilts to avoid disaster when the river got high. When they walked to the top of the stairs Karen read the sign on the shop's door, 'No Pets Allowed.'

"Well, Beau, seems you aren't welcome in there," Will said.

"If they knew what a sweetheart you were, Beau, they'd let you in," Karen added, patting Beau's head.

"The ferry just docked, Karen. Let's take it back."

On the return crossing Beau took his position on the bow railing. Karen and Will sat nearby facing the captain.

The captain gestured toward Beau, "You can leave him here when you go; we could use a mascot."

"No. Can't do that," Will said. "I'd never be able to go home."

The captain docked the ferry with the same know-how that had brought him successful results a thousand times before.

Will said to Karen as they stepped on the east shore, "You know, I could do that if I wanted to."

"Sure you could. Do you mind if I wait on shore while you try?" She paused, then suggested, "Let's get a drink from the little store there and sit on the bench again. I'm not ready to let go of this experience just yet."

"Sounds good. Here, hold Beau. I'll go get it."

As he walked away Karen regarded her birthday date. Will's mild manner hid a quiet strength. He had a sense of humor that crept up on you, something she never noticed when they were youths. She never noticed his restrained intellect either. *Where in the world did that come from?* His good looks hadn't changed much, other than to become more rugged with age. She suspected he would be the one everybody would still recognize at his forty-year class reunion. At six feet two inches, 200 pounds, with dark hair and eyes, he fit into the tall, dark, and handsome category, she figured.

On the downside—if it can be considered a bad trait—she got the impression people had to earn his trust. Or maybe it was just a generally cautious nature she was seeing. *Oh well, don't analyze too much, nobody's perfect.*

Childhood crushes were supposed to go away in adulthood; she wondered why hers hadn't.

When Will returned with two cold drinks and a piece of beef jerky for Beau, they settled onto the same bench they used to wait for the ferry.

"This was a great birthday present, Will. Thanks. I really enjoyed it."

"As many times as I ride the ferry I never grow tired of it. Maybe we can do it again this fall. You should see the view from the middle of the river when the leaves have changed."

"Yes. If I'm here."

"What do you mean?"

"The teaching job on Long Island."

"Oh yes. Forgot about that."

Will tried to take the news in stride and not show his sadness at the prospect of Karen going away.

"Speaking of which … I have to go for a second interview June fifteenth."

"That's not far away. What part of Long Island?"

"Terryville. About mid-island on the sound side."

"If you get the position, when will you have to report?"

"Not till the end of August. But I would want to be there a couple of weeks early to find a place to live and get all set up."

"Sure. Well, let me know if you need any help."

"I certainly will, Will."

"Don't start."

***

When Will first heard the sound he wasn't sure what it was or where it was coming from. He listened closer. It was coming from Beau lying at his feet like the Great Sphinx of Giza. Other than the dog riveting his gaze on the man walking toward them and making that sound, Beau appeared normal and calm. Will and Karen gave each other a puzzled look.

The baritone rumble coming from somewhere deep within Beau's jowls grew in intensity as the man walked closer. Beau jumped to his feet, tested the air with his nose held high, and motionless held his gaze.

At fifteen feet away the man was unaware of any danger and stayed on a course that would take him right by the agitated dog.

At ten feet, Beau lowered his head and drew back his ears. His teeth flashed as his face contorted to a snarl. The hair between his shoulder blades stood straight up. His seventy-eight pounds strained at the leash as Will wrapped more of it around his right hand.

When the man was six feet away, Beau lunged.

Surprised by Beau's power, Will grabbed the leash with his left hand too. Beau got to within two feet of a horrified Socks Smith before Will's weight on the leash slowed him. Smith froze in place for a second, and then backpedaled. Will dropped to the ground on his rump and dug his heels in the soft turf in an effort to stop Beau's forward progress.

Beau was making the most ferocious sound Will had ever heard him make. The dog he thought he knew was in full attack mode, snapping, growling, and barking all at the same time. Will was scared, but not as scared as Socks Smith. When Smith regained his composure he shouted an obscenity, turned, and ran in the direction he came from.

Smith crossed River Street and disappeared up an alley. When he was out of sight, Beau's rage relaxed to an excited whine.

"What was that all about?" a shaken Karen asked.

Still on the ground and out of breath Will answered, "I don't know. I don't understand it. I never saw him act that way toward anybody."

"Do you know that man, Will?"

"No. Never saw him before."

The frightening event had damped the lighthearted mood and Will and Karen hurried Beau back to the truck.

Rubbing his shoulder Will said, "You should have felt his power. Beau wanted to kill that man."

The instant those words were out, the reason for Beau's behavior struck them both. They gave each other a knowing look. Will turned the ignition key the same time Karen said, "Hurry, Will! Drive down that way. Let's try to find him."

From his upstairs window Socks Smith watched as Will and Karen drove up and down the street several times. He knew he had been made, but he was sure they had not seen him enter the back door of his rented half-house. He also knew he had to get out of town and fast. *Made by a dog ... a stupid dumb animal. I should have made sure he was dead!*

Will and Karen drove around Millersburg for the next half hour looking for Socks Smith. Not finding him they headed for home.

When they returned to Mel's house they told him the story of Beau's near attack, but didn't tell him the conclusion they drew from it. They didn't have to.

"That was him," were the first words out of Mel's mouth.

"That's what we thought too. We drove around hoping to find him, but he just disappeared," Will said.

"Mel, you said the man who attacked you wore a mask. Can we be absolutely positive that was him?"

"Absolutely. There is only one thing that could have made Beau behave that way. You know he loves everybody. He would *never* do that without reason. He didn't identify this man by sight so it doesn't matter if Beau saw his face or not that night. He identified him by smell. And from the sound of it, he was darn sure of himself. You must have been downwind from the man."

"And there is no chance that a similar cologne, or soap, or something, could have confused him? Sorry, I just want to be sure we have this right," Karen said.

"No chance. A person's natural body scent is unique. As long as there's even a trace of it you can't fool a dog. I have always been fascinated by the canine's olfactory abilities and I've done a lot of reading about it. Virtually every aspect of a dog's life revolves around their sense of smell. It's so complex and sophisticated even modern science doesn't fully understand it. Did you know dogs have the equipment to taste odors? No, Beau wasn't wrong. We need to report this to the police right now."

Mel had done his homework. The canine's scenting abilities are legendary. Dogs can sense odors at concentrations millions of times lower than humans can, and humans have a good sense of smell for the most part. Research into the canine's ability to smell disease, including cancer, in humans before it becomes apparent is being conducted with promising results.

Canines don't use this ability with every breath they take; they control it. When they test the air with a sniff they are forcing the air over their super-sensitive olfactory receptors deep in the snout, sorting out and identifying the scent molecules. This remarkable ability rarely fails them.

Will called the state police and asked for Lieutenant Zimmerman.

"I'm sorry, Mr. Rhone, Lieutenant Zimmerman is on the road. I'll get in touch with him by radio right away and have him call or stop by."

Twelve minutes later Will greeted Lieutenant Zimmerman at the door.

"Hi. I was in the area when I got the call. What's up?"

Will and Karen took turns relating the incident at the Millersburg Ferry to the detective, giving as much detail about Socks Smith as they could.

When they finished, the policeman said, "This *is* important. The state police are well aware of a dog's olfactory prowess and we take it seriously. You did the right thing by calling.

"Here's what I'm going to do. I'll increase patrols in that area and have anybody that resembles the man you described questioned. I'll also have the patrols on the major arteries out of town keep an eye out. I'm going to send the police sketch artist here as soon as she can make it. Her name is Trooper Shirley Mowrey and she's very good. I'd appreciate the both of you working with her and we'll try and get a likeness of this guy. Once we do we'll distribute the sketch all over Millersburg and do a door-to-door if we have to. We'll classify him for right now as 'wanted for questioning.' Speed counts now. This guy is going to run ... if he has half a brain."

✳✳✳

Socks Smith threw everything he had into two suitcases, and then spent the next half hour wiping down every inch of his two-story half-house. He emptied the waste cans into a plastic garbage bag along with anything else that could help identify him. He threw everything into his van and headed to a pay phone to call Charles Holtzman.

"This better be important, Socks."

Smith told Charles what had just occurred at Riverfront Park in Millersburg.

"Why would you take the chance of walking that close to them?"

"I didn't notice them until the dog attacked. I walk up and down the park every day. There's always people around. I don't look at everybody."

"Well you should," Charles paused. "Too late now. You have to get out of here and I mean far out. Get out of state."

"I'm leaving right away. What about the receiver? Oh, and I should tell you I can't get it to work."

Shaking his head in disgust Charles said, "Take the back road to I-81 through Gratz. That'll take you right by the drop point. Put the receiver in my bin. Now listen. When you get settled in someplace put the address on a sheet of paper in an envelope and mail it to me. Not your name, just the address. And don't use a return address on the envelope. Then stay there. When I need you I'll send for you. You understand?"

"Yes. I get it."

"Don't call me. I don't want any record of our connection anywhere. And if you get caught don't drag me into this or I'll get you, Socks. If you do, someday I'll get you. Now get going."

✱✱✱

It had been three days since the state police artist, Trooper Mowrey, came to Mel's house to sketch a composite of Socrates Smith based on Will and Karen's description. They were astonished by how accurate the likeness was. In that time they had not heard from Lieutenant Zimmerman, which meant to them that Socks Smith had not been found. They were right. Smith was holed up in a small apartment in New York City. He would stay there for a few days and then look for a nicer place. Then, as Charles instructed, he would send him the address and wait.

CHAPTER

EIGHTEEN

"We've been invited to a cookout at Keith Holtzman's house tonight. You coming?" Will asked his grandfather.

"Oh, I don't know. I don't want to be the fifth wheel."

"You wouldn't be. It's just a friendly little get-together. You could invite Mrs. Adams to come with you."

Mel made several unidentifiable sounds and mumbled something under his breath.

"I take it that's a no," Will said.

"You go. I want to go over our research again. Maybe we missed something. Leave Beau here tonight, please."

"Okay. I think the Phillies game is on tonight."

✳✳✳

When Will arrived at the Holtzman's, Keith greeted him in the front yard.

"Nice to see you again, Will."

The two shook hands.

"Nice to see you again, Keith. How long has it been?"

"It's been a while. And we only live a few miles from each other."

"Yeah, well, you know how it is. You get involved with your own life. I guess we don't travel in the same circles."

"Yes, and this job of mine keeps me away from home way too much. But you want to sell, you go to the customers," Keith said, raising his eyebrows.

"It looks like it's paying off for you."

"It is. In a couple of months I'll get assigned a new district closer to home. I should be home every night then. I guess where I am now I sold everybody a piece of heavy equipment that needs one."

"That'll be nice."

"I'm looking forward to it. So is Maddy. You can go in the house. Karen's researching as usual. Maddy and Jason are getting things together in there. I'm doing the grillin'."

"Okay. Hey. Jason's going to be a doctor. Bet you and Maddy are pleased about that."

"We are. He's a good kid and smart too. Oh, and thanks for putting him on for summer."

"Sure. Ed tells me he's a quick study. Has some real wood-working talent."

When Will entered the house, Karen looked up from the papers she had spread over the entire table. "Hey."

"Hey yourself. What are you up to?"

"Just reviewing everything. No Mel?"

"No. As a matter of fact he said he wanted to review tonight too."

Jason entered the kitchen with his mother and stood behind Karen.

"Hi, Maddy."

"Hi, Will. You hungry?"

"Always," Will said. "Jason, how's it going?"

"Hi. I love my job. Thanks again."

"Glad to hear it. You any good at riddles?" Will asked.

"Sometimes."

Showing Jason the copy of the fug 10 Bible inscription Karen had laid on the table, Will asked, "How about this one? What does fug 10 mean?"

Jason studied the document, "That's not fug 10. It's written kinda funny, disjointed and all, but I think that's 'io', not 1-0. Looks like 'fugio' to me."

"What?" Will and Karen said at the same time.

"Fugio. Latin. I'm taking Latin courses at State. Fugio means 'I fly,' or 'I flee.'" Karen and Will gave each other a dumfounded look. Jason added, "After we eat, we can go online and see what comes up."

"Yes, please," Will said.

Jason departed the kitchen with a plate of raw burgers and hot dogs, Maddy with an armful of condiments.

"Fugio? Will, do you think Robert spoke Latin?"

"I guess anything's possible."

"'I fly.' It still doesn't make any sense."

"No, it doesn't. But let's wait and see what we can find online."

As they ate the burgers and dogs, Will and Keith did what childhood friends do: talked about their past adventures. Vivid, real, and funny to them, not so much so to anyone listening.

Karen was preoccupied with the prospects fugio held. She couldn't wait for the meal to be over.

When it was she said, "I'll help you clean up, Maddy."

"No, go ahead with the guys. Keith and I will get this. Won't we, hon?"

"Yes, dear," Keith said, rolling his eyes.

Jason sat down at his PC flanked by Will and Karen sitting on chairs they collected from other parts of the house. Jason brought up his search engine.

"What do you want to try?" Jason asked

"Try punching in 'fugio' for now," Will said.

The search engine produced thousands of possibilities in a matter of seconds. Jason scrolled through them.

"There," Karen said, "The 'fugio cent.' Try that."

Jason clicked on the link. Everyone read the information on the fugio cent.

Karen said, "That's it, Will!"

"Wait a minute." Will continued reading the whole page. "No. That can't be it."

"It is, Will. Look what's engraved on the coin. 'Mind Your Business,'" Karen insisted.

"No. See this?" Skipping to the high points Will read, "'*The Continental Congress ... agreed on a design copied from the earlier paper Franklin Dollar ... passed a resolution on April 21, 1787, to mint the coin in copper ... coins were minted May of 1788.*' There. They weren't minted till May 1788 and never left the mint until the end of May."

"So?"

"So that's too late. Remember Magdalena died June 7, 1788. But I do think it's obvious now the Bible inscription is a reference to treasure ... 'Fugio, Mind Your Business.' That's pretty darn convincing evidence, wouldn't you agree?"

"Yes. Looks like Mel and I are eating crow tonight. Are you going to rub it in?"

"No. I wouldn't do that. On second thought, I think I might," Will said, grinning.

"If you must. But I still think the Franklin Cent is it."

"No, it isn't. How could they have learned of the coins, then devise a plan, and then acquire the coins—which were many miles away from them—and had them there for Magdalena's funeral? Impossible. Just not enough time. We're only talking about from the end of May 1788 to June 8, 1788. It just doesn't jell."

"Oh ... yeah. I guess they couldn't just hop on a plane, could they? Wait a second. It said they were copied from the *earlier* paper Franklin Dollar?" Karen said.

"Exactly. Jason. Punch in 'Fugio Mind Your Business Colonial Money.'" Jason's search brought up a new set of results. They scrolled the possibilities.

One of the links leaped out at Karen. "There. That one mentions the ANA – American Numismatic Association. Try that one. They should know."

The page started loading from the top down. Goosebumps formed on Karen and Will as the page unfolded before their eyes. Layer by layer the large image of the coin revealed itself—each layer providing an answer for the clues they had uncovered: Fugio, Mind You Business, sun with rays icon, minted in 1776. When the page was loaded, Will, Karen, and Jason stared in silence at the Continental Dollar.

It only got better as they read page after page of what was known and not known about the antique coin. One link led to another with still more information, and it all fit.

Jason printed everything of importance as the three studied the websites for over an hour.

***

In 1776 the monetary system in Colonial America was nothing more than a hodge-podge of paper money and coinage. The system was—there was no system. In the absence of a national mint most colonies had privately printed and minted their own currency. That, as well as foreign currency—particularly Spanish—thrown into the mix, kept America in money. Often the same currency would have different values depending on where you were when you tried to spend it. Benjamin Franklin wanted to change that. His dream called for a standardized American currency system with a central national mint.

After the Declaration of Independence was signed Franklin intensified his efforts, reasoning that a sovereign nation needed a coin to call its own. He was also anxious to make a statement to the world. Working with renowned engraver Elisha Gallaudet, Franklin used elements of designs from other currency in and out of circulation at the time, including the Franklin Dollar, to create the Continental Dollar.

On the coin's obverse Franklin used the medieval symbolism of a sun with rays shining on a sundial accompanied by the Latin word "Fugio" and the admonition "Mind Your Business." The intended message was that you had better tend to your business and make hay while the sun shines because time is fleeting. Typical Franklin.

On the reverse the names of the thirteen states appeared in interconnected circles, surrounding another sun with smaller rays with the words "We Are One" centered in the sun and encircled by "American Congress." The message was clear. This was Franklin's proclamation to the world.

When Franklin was satisfied with the design he turned it over to Gallaudet to engrave the dies. He then went mint-hunting in New York City.

The metal to be used for the coins was another matter. Silver was Franklin's metal of choice but sufficient quantities did not exist in the Colonies. Early in 1776 he had secured the promise of a loan of silver from France to be used for American coinage. At that time he was content to wait until France made good on their promise. The events of mid-1776 changed everything. By July France had still not provided the silver and Franklin grew impatient. The stakes were now higher.

After the Declaration of Independence was signed, in secrecy he commissioned the Continental Dollar to be minted in brass and pewter—as emergency coinage—until France freed up the promised silver. Almost as soon as the coin was minted it ran into trouble, thanks in part to the British occupation of New York City and New Jersey, and Major Johan Conrad Mueller; and in part to the relatively low value of the metal used.

The coins minted and delivered to Franklin before Mueller got his hands on the second lot saw little, if any, general circulation. They were worthless almost as soon as they came off the die.

In just a few short years not many people ever knew the coin existed—including many members of Congress—due in large part to Franklin's having acted unilaterally and in secret. The few people that did have knowledge of the coin often disavowed its existence. No one wanted to be associated with a failure.

Since its ignoble birth over 225 years ago things changed. The Continental Dollar has gained favor among collectors. It has been researched, studied, and written about in books and magazines. Theories about the coin abound everywhere. Collectors swarm to the auction houses whenever one becomes available. With few known specimens, the price per coin has skyrocketed. Franklin would be pleased to see his darling doing so well.

***

Will and Karen gathered up the printouts, thanked Maddy and Keith for the fine meal and good company and Jason for his revelation then headed to Mel's house.

Will was so pleased with the night's discovery he felt playful. "And did you accomplish anything with your review, Grandpa?"

"Not much. How was the cookout?"

"Good," Karen answered.

Looking up at the grinning duo, Mel said, "All right. What's up with you two?"

Saying nothing Will handed him the picture of the Continental Dollar. Mel studied the image in silence, then exclaimed, "Goodness gracious!" He repeated that two more times, then added, "This is it! How in the world did you ever find this?"

"We owe Jason for that," Karen said.

"Jason?"

"He's taking Latin in college, Grandpa. As soon as we showed him the Bible inscription he said it looked like fugio, not fug 10. We went online and it didn't take long to put everything in place."

"This is incredible. It all fits. We solved this. You were right, Will. Robert Rhone buried these coins with his wife. That has to be it. But it still doesn't make sense to me."

"There's still a pile of questions for sure, Mel, but I'm confident now we can figure out the rest of it."

"It'll make a little more sense as you read all that stuff we printed out about the coin, Grandpa. For instance, the question we had on access to the buried coins. Robert buried them with Magdalena because they were worthless almost from the get-go. He learned that somewhere along the line and he knew he'd never be digging them up again, and he didn't want anyone else digging them up. That's why the Bible notation was so vague. Only someone who knew what the coins looked like would know what he was talking about."

"I don't even know where to begin planning our next move," Mel said.

"Well, let's take some time to learn all we can about the coin," said Karen. "Mel, you can start by reading everything you have there and maybe try to find some of those magazine articles. Me, I think I'll take a look ahead at some of the problems we could face. Will, I suspect, will just gloat."

"No. Too happy about this to gloat." With tongue in cheek he added, "Far be it from me to say 'I told you so.'"

Mel said, "This is a great find. You two came through again. Let's get together, say the day after tomorrow, and go over everything. By then I want each of you to develop a research strategy "

***

The next two days gave Mel, Will, and Karen time to digest the information they had on the Continental Dollar and find more. When they met at Mel's house they all had questions and even a few answers.

Mel opened the meeting. "The first thing that struck me was it looks like whatever those guys were up to, they were in it together; reference the sunshine coin. It was important enough to the Hoppe family to will it to a descendant. Even if it had no real value. That speaks volumes."

"Could Robert just have given the coin to Rudolph?" wondered Karen.

"He could have, but no. I think Hoppe was directly involved. Those people only willed things that had importance. I think there is more significance there than just a simple gift. Keep in mind they most likely knew it had no value as currency, so I think it was willed more as a memento of a bigger event."

"Maybe I should make note of all the conclusions we draw, right or wrong," Will said.

"Good idea. But let Karen make note of it. That way I'll be able to read it."

Karen laughed. "Penmanship's not your strong point, Will?"

"Never has been. I would point out, though, many of the great minds through the ages had horrendous handwriting."

"Yes, well, I'd like to ask the great mind among us if he knows how a captured Hessian soldier and an German-via-Ireland immigrant got their hands on the Continental Dollar."

"Good question," Will said. "Here's what I think based on what we now know. Did you read in the coin info that it is estimated there were only between eight and ten thousand of the coins ever minted? Yet today there are only sixty coins known to exist. What happened to the rest? I think our boys somehow got hold of a large portion of them. Maybe even half or more, which we now believe are buried with Magdalena Rhone. I don't believe Robert would bury just a coin or two and then make a big deal of it by making a notation of it in the family Bible. I agree with you, Grandpa. I think the amount is significant. My strategy is to research the New York City private mints in operation in 1776, more Hessian records, and Benjamin Franklin's involvement with the coin. And I mean gumshoe work here, not just the Internet."

"My trip to Long Island!" Karen exclaimed. "I can stop in New York City on the way back. And it wouldn't take much to swing down to Philly from there."

"Your trip to Long Island?" Mel asked.

"Yes. Next week I have to report for an interview for the teaching job on Long Island."

"Oh, yes. Forgot about that. Sure, that would be great. Maybe you should go too Will."

"No. I'm not comfortable leaving you here alone for extended periods just yet, Grandpa."

"Nonsense. You sound like Mrs. Adams," Mel grumbled.

"Sorry. The decision has been made," Will said. "Karen, will you take my laptop and keep in touch with us via email?"

"Okay. I'll be able to keep better records that way too."

"It's settled then," Will said. "Karen, what did you come up with?"

"Before I get into that, I wanted to show you this, Mel. I clipped it for you from one of the genealogy magazines I subscribed to back when we were working together. I put it away and I forgot about it. I came across it yesterday. I thought you'd get a kick out of it." Karen handed Mel the clipping.

In Pursuit of Ancestors

Great-Great-granddad was a horse thief;
They hung him in the square.
Grand-auntie was a rabbit;
Eighteen children did she bear.

Great-uncle had lots of money;
He made some every day.
When ink stained mister banker's hands,
They hauled poor Unk away.

No more of this I want to find;
I thought my family pure.
But I'm bitten by the diggin' bug;
Please God, let there be a cure.

—*Anonymously Masochistic*

Laughing, Mel handed the clipping to Will. "'Anonymously Masochistic.' I guess so!"

When Will finished reading the poem something clicked. He said, "That's meant to be funny, and it is, but there's truth to that, isn't there?"

"What part of it?" Karen asked.

"Once someone starts working on their genealogy, it is hard to quit. It's addictive."

"Yes, there is truth to that," Mel answered. "When you work on your genealogy your ancestors come alive ... become real people ... and they're family ... your blood. You may get away from it for a while, but you never get it out of your system. You always have one eye open for some new bit of family information. Why?"

"Oh, nothing ... nothing," Will answered. "Karen, I think you're up."

"Yes. I took a look ahead. How do we find the *exact* location of Magdalena's grave? When we do, how do we dig it up? What are the legal issues? Just how are we going to pull this off? I couldn't make much sense of the legal information, but I did find some interesting things on finding old graves. Our choices are limited to three: GPR, ground-penetrating radar; a grave dowser; or metal-detection equipment. With the latter there has to be buried metal of course, which we think there is. No matter what method we consider it's going to be expensive. I made copies for both of you on each."

"A grave dowser?" Will asked. "Same principle as dowsing for water?"

"You got it."

"Let's start there. I have to hear this," Mel said.

"Well," Karen said, "when you read your printouts you'll see that methods vary with the dowser. But most use two wax-coated steel welding rods, two to three feet long, bent at ninety degrees four to six inches from one end. They hold the short end in each hand with the long end pointed straight ahead and parallel to the ground. Then they just walk over an area until the rods cross. The one guy from Pennsylvania claims he can tell if the grave is that of a man, women, or child, and which way the body is oriented: north, south, east, or west."

"That seems so ... impossible. How does it work?" Will said.

"No one knows. Not even the dowsers. 'You either can do it

or you can't' is how they explain it. Something to do with 'sensitivity to a disrupted magnetic field' is as close to a scientific explanation as it gets."

Mel asked, "Do these guys give references?"

"The one from Pennsylvania does. His list of successes is incredible. His clients aren't limited to ordinary people like you and me, but police departments, contractors, churches, and even the courts. For example, he was hired by a group of people who claimed their ancestors were buried in the basement of a church. The church said if anyone was buried in their basement their records would show it, but they still agreed to let the dowser give it a once-over. With news cameras rolling the dowser went to work and discovered seven graves in the basement. Three men, three women, and one male adolescent, he claimed. They started digging and he was right. The church apologized. Eerie, huh? When I first started reading about this, I thought 'No way.' But now ... well, let's say my mind is open."

"Were the people buried in the church basement murdered?" Will asked.

"No, no. They all died natural deaths. They were buried in what was the churchyard at the time of their deaths. The church wanted to build an addition in the early 1900s and needed part of the churchyard to do it. Rather than move the bodies, they just built over the graves. Whether by accident or design, it was never recorded.

"The people who hired the dowser had personal family records that showed where their ancestors should have been buried. That's what started it all. The dowser found the spot in the basement where someone buried the stones too, which looks very much like someone didn't want anyone to know there were graves in the church cellar."

"Well, the dowser could have just taken a chance that the family records were correct," Will said, still skeptical.

"Ah ha ... I knew one of you would deduce that. The dowser was never given any information, by the church or the family members. He was just asked if there were graves in the basement or not. And remember, he told them the sex of each before they uncovered the bodies, and he was right."

"You have to admit, Will, that's pretty convincing," Mel said.

"I guess it is, but ... I don't know. Where's this guy located and how much does he charge?"

"He's from northeastern Pennsylvania. His charge is $1,000 and up, plus expenses. His fee is based on what a customer wants to know and how much land he has to search."

"Does he give guarantees?" doubting Will asked.

"No guarantees. And you pay his fee whether he finds anything or not ... .up front."

"Wow. How can we turn down a bargain like that?"

Karen answered, "Well maybe, Will, you have the ability to dowse. Care to give it a try and save us some money?"

"No, thanks. How would I ever explain it to our good neighbors—me walking around the fields with a couple of bent coat hangers? We'll pay the money if we have to."

"That was actually the cheapest method I found. GPR is effective, but not in all situations, and boy, is it expensive! With that the problem we face is the graves are old and most likely the people were buried in wooden caskets. And I'm sure after 200 years there are no body parts remaining. That reduces accuracy.

"The upside in our case is there are coins in the grave. When there are metal objects like belt buckles, boot buckles, hairpins, and the like, it increases accuracy. Soil type also affects the outcome."

Mel asked, "Is GPR conducted on the surface of the ground?"

"Yes. The ground is not disturbed. And there is portable equipment available, meaning it doesn't have to be mounted on a vehicle, which makes it even less invasive. But again, it's expensive because the equipment is expensive. Plus the people doing the testing have to know what they are doing and how to interpret the results. It isn't a simple matter of going down to the local rent-all establishment and renting a GPR unit for the afternoon."

"Okay. You also mentioned metal detection," Will said.

"Yes, but again there's a problem. Depth. In metal detection it all comes down to the depth the item you're looking for is buried. Your standard garden-variety metal detector isn't going to do. The good ones are only effective up to about a foot. You have to believe Magdalena was buried five or six feet deep. We don't know how the coins were placed in the grave. Were they just thrown in the coffin with her body? Were they put in a container of some kind? We don't know.

"Let me give you the one-minute tour of metal detection. There are just a few types of metal detectors and they all have some things in common. BFO, or beat-frequency oscillation, and VLF, or very low frequency, are the two most popular. Almost all standard detectors are one of these types. The VLF outsells the BFO by far. You can get attachments for them called extra depth coils, among other things, but they still won't give us what we need.

"Then there is PI equipment, or pulse induction. This one has some real clout and it may work, but I'm still not convinced it's the one we need.

"Next is the proton induced magnetometer. This one goes deep, but it's hard to use and very expensive. But I think it's our only real choice if we decide to go with metal detection.

"There is another technique called ground scraping, where the top foot of soil over a suspected site is scraped off. You're supposed to be able to tell by the color difference of the soil if the ground was ever disturbed. Expensive, invasive, and not all that reliable."

"So what's the best approach as far as a magnetometer?" Will asked.

"Hiring someone who has one and knows how to operate it."

"And the cost?" Mel asked.

"Forty-five hundred and up, no guarantees, and they get paid regardless of what they find or don't find."

"So, based on your research, what are you recommending?" Will asked.

"All things considered, I say let's go with the dowser."

"I was afraid you were going to say that."

"We can get references. If we're not happy with them we don't have to hire him. My thinking is to try the easiest and cheapest first. Plus we have the added benefit of knowing two possible locations of the grave site and we have the list Mrs. Henry gave you with the layout of the cemetery. We don't have to tell him that. Let's see what he comes up with on his own. If he identifies one of the two sites, then I say we have something."

"Okay … okay. What do you think, Grandpa?"

"I think I never finished my presentation."

"You're right, Mel. Sorry for being longwinded."

"No, my fault, Grandpa. Go ahead."

"Well, based on what I could find about the Continental Dollar, they now sell at auctions from five to twenty thousand dollars each, depending on condition and type. If you select a rough average price of ten thousand dollars each and there are six thousand buried with Magdalena … have you done the math?" Mel didn't wait for an answer. "Sixty million dollars."

"Sixty million dollars!" Karen gasped. "Are you kidding us, Mel? Are we really dealing with that kind of money here?"

"That may be conservative."

"You mentioned 'type,' Grandpa. What do you mean?"

"Apparently all the coins were not struck with the same die. For instance, on some 'EG FECIT' is struck on the obverse. 'FECIT' being Latin for 'made it.' 'EG' is believed to be Elisha Gallaudet, the engraver. Also some were struck in brass and some in pewter. It's believed a few may have been struck in silver although none are known to exist. If one of them ever surfaces, the sky's the limit. So there are variables that affect the price."

"Grandpa, we need legal advice. We're in over our heads here. With that kind of money at stake, we can't afford to make a wrong move."

"I think you're right," Mel said. "I'll call Al Marcus and explain the situation and ask if he's willing to help us. But let's wait till Karen gets back from her Long Island trip."

"One more thing," Karen said. "Will, something bothered you about that poem. Care to tell us what?"

"It wasn't the poem. I thought the poem was funny. But it caused a light to go on."

"What do you mean?" she asked.

"Charles. You said Charles was working on your genealogy and then just up and quit and wanted nothing more to do with it. That's unusual. Now we know he's a Hoppe descendant and he was given a trunk containing family information, which he won't let you or anybody else see, and he has a history with the law. I'm just piecing things together, that's all. If you recall the police wanted a list of Rhone descendants because all descendants are suspects. We now know Hoppe descendants have to be considered suspects too. Karen, do you recall if Charles stopped doing genealogy about the same time your grandma gave him the trunk?"

After thinking a moment Karen answered, "Yes. It was around the same time. About the same time he ran over that poor old man too."

Mel said, "You may be onto something, Will. But I can assure you Charles was not the attacker. I would have known him, face covered or not. It was the man Beau confronted in Millersburg. Of that I'm certain."

"That doesn't mean Charles wasn't involved in some way. I wouldn't put it past him," Karen added.

"Can we agree that it's time to let the police in on this?" Will asked.

Mel and Karen nodded agreement.

Mel adjourned the meeting. "Karen, good luck with your interview. Drive carefully and keep us informed."

CHAPTER

NINETEEN

It was a beautiful, clear, and crisp morning in late spring as Karen drove out of Keith Holtzman's driveway on her way to Long Island, New York. Her interview wasn't until nine o'clock the next morning but she wanted to leave early for the six-hour-plus drive and not be rushed. She would stay the night at a motel near the school so she could be fresh and alert for the interview, her organizational skills and practicality coming through again.

As she drove she reflected on the astonishing events of the last few months and the twists and turns her life had taken. She felt more alive and important than she had in two years. She needed this. The black cloud that was the tragic death of Polly Rhone did indeed have a silver lining.

Her enthusiasm for the new job had dulled, however. Now the thought of leaving the central Pennsylvania area was not as happy a proposition as it once was. She wasn't sure why, or if it was something she even needed to concern herself with. She would go for the interview and do the best she could. *I'll see what happens after that. Maybe the school is no longer interested in me.*

As she drove Karen relived some of the experiences she and Will had shared: the ferry ride, the grave-site-location adventures with Dottie and Luther, their research trips, and their conversations—especially their conversations—and she noticed she was smiling. She looked down at the laptop Will had lent her for the trip on the seat beside her. Will asked if she would email him as soon as she arrived. *He acts like he cares about me. But in what way? He cares about people in general.* She dismissed the thought. What she couldn't dismiss was that she was looking forward to contacting Will tonight. *I hope he's online so we can chat. Remember to ask the motel if they have a dedicated Internet line.*

***

Mel and Will had settled in to watch the Phillies game. Will had turned on the PC speakers loud enough for him to hear the three-note tone that announced an incoming email. Mel had suggested he do that when he grew weary of Will jumping up to check the computer every five minutes.

The Phillies were beating the Cincinnati Reds three to two at the end of the first, so the mood was upbeat. The teams were in a rain delay now, what would turn out to be the first of many that night.

Will had been a loyal Philadelphia Phillies fan all his life, just like his father, just like Mel. With devotion he rode the team's highs and lows year after year. It didn't matter where the team was in the standings, every game was exciting and every game offered new hope.

And every so often a genuine star came to the Phillies in their long history, intensifying interest even more in the team. Stars like Robin Roberts, Dick Allen, Steve Carlton, Mike Schmidt, and Larry Bowa. The fans were happy they came, but it wouldn't have mattered to them if they hadn't. They would still be loyal to a fault. Such is the nature of a true Phillies fan.

The rain delay was over, and just as the Phillies and Reds resumed play the familiar three-note tone sounded from the office.

"Oh my goodness! That could be her. Better check that quick," Mel said, teasing his grandson.

Will opened the email from Karen Holtzman.

Hi,

I'm sitting in my motel room bored silly, wishing this thing was over. I'll never understand how anyone who travels a lot gets used to this lifestyle. Made it safe and sound. Ran into a lot of traffic in NYC of course. I'm going to get a shower and go to bed early, I'm the tiredest woman in the world.

Tomorrow I hope to get out of town as soon as the interview is over, which should put me in NYC at a reasonable hour, giving me enough time to do a little research. I think I'll hit the Internet and check the best place to start looking. I'm leaning toward the NYC Historical Society right now. While I'm checking on that it'll give you a chance to respond to this if you're online.

What are you guys up to? Don't tell me watching the Phillies game. If I don't hear from you tonight, I'll email you sometime tomorrow. Say hi to Mel.

Take care,
Karen

Will responded.

Hi Karen,

You're right again watching the Phillies game. Thanks for letting us know you made it okay.

Grandpa called Lieutenant Zimmerman today and told him all about the Hoppe connection, and specifically our suspicions about Charles. He said he had some things to report to us and he would stop by later in the week. I hope you can be here when he does.

I helped Grandpa enter a lot of the new family information we have compiled recently in his database. We'll work on it some more tomorrow. If we have another good day like today we should be all caught up.

Mrs. Adams was here today. It was entertaining as usual watching the interplay between these two. I'm beginning to think they really like each other. The doctor said she only needed to stop by twice a week now, and then once a week after a few weeks of that.

Be careful in the big city tomorrow. Keep us informed. Back to the Phillies game.

So long for now,
Will

Karen had lain back on the bed and by the time Will's response came through she was sound asleep.

The next day Will and Mel continued making entries in the family database. Will knew the day would be a busy one for Karen but thought there was a chance she could sneak in an email. He didn't hear from her until seven o'clock that evening.

Hey,
Sorry I didn't get in touch sooner. I fell asleep after I emailed you last night and didn't wake up until two this morning. Today was hectic. The interview went fine and they promised to give me an answer—one way or the other—as soon as they reach a decision.

I arrived in NYC about 1:30. I went to the NYC Historical Society and poked around. I also spoke with their currency expert. The only thing he could confirm is that there were a number of small private mints in New York City in the 1770s. He gave the name of Elijah Birchfield as the man associated with the mint that would be his best guess at the one we seek. He said others suspect that it was Birchfield who minted the Continental Dollar as well. They didn't have any day-to-day operational records of Birchfield's mint. I am going to spend the night in the city and head for Philadelphia tomorrow morning. I'll try and stay awake tonight if you have any suggestions or just want to say hi I'll be online. You should see this hotel ... glitzy.

Later,

Karen

Ten minutes later Karen received a response from Will.

Hey yourself,

Glad to hear all went well on Long Island. Grandpa and I finished entering all the data we needed to today. It's nice to be up-to-date. Doing this also provides a chance to review things. We also went over all the Hoppe information we had. Did you know Rudolph's grandson Philip Hoppe Jr., the recipient of the sunshine coin, died in Philadelphia? If you get a chance tomorrow check his will at the courthouse and see if he passed the coin to someone.

The only other thing I would suggest is you may want to stop at the David Library in Washington Crossing, PA. Remember John from the State Archives suggested we have a look there? You may have to detour a little, but not much.

Remember to check the Franklin papers in Philly. Drive carefully. Looking forward to hearing from you tomorrow. Seems funny with you not around.

Will

It was seven o'clock again the next night when Will opened the email from Karen.

Hi,

Me again. Another busy day, but a good one. Wait till you see this! I went to the library in Washington Crossing as suggested. What a place, Will. You should see all the material they have on the Rev. War and the Hessians. The staff is great ... very helpful.

I poured over the records of the Battle of Trenton since that's where Rudolph Hoppe was captured. One thing jumped out at me as unusual. It was the report of a Captain Samuel Rickert; who led a group of Continentals in support of Washington's main assault on Trenton. The captain's orders after the crossing were to proceed south toward Trenton staying close to the river to guard Washington's flank and prevent any Hessians from escaping north once the main assault began. He reported killing a Hessian major a couple of miles from Trenton at dawn. Since Washington began the main assault around eightish, "at dawn" would have been just before the main assault began in Trenton. Now here's the kicker. The captain reported that another Hessian soldier with the major escaped toward Trenton in a wagon. He said when he first saw these two it looked as though they were fighting and the major, who was killed, was about ready to carve up the one who escaped. With that information I then looked at those killed at Trenton and the prisoner list and the only major I could find that was unaccounted for was a Johan Conrad Mueller. He was classified as "missing." Here's the best part. I checked the unit rosters and guess who served with Major Mueller? Give up? None other than our Private Rudolph Hoppe. Now the questions are why was Mueller so far from the main encampment with a wagon and who was he fighting with in a snowstorm? It doesn't sound like these two were pickets. It doesn't make sense unless these two, or one of them anyway, was up to no good. Pretty good stuff, huh?

This is even better. I then went to the Historical Society of Pennsylvania in Philadelphia. I looked under anything dealing with coinage or currency of the Revolutionary period. I saw some mention of the coin but nothing we didn't know. I then looked over some of the Benjamin Franklin papers as you suggested. I started with his letters. I looked down the index of senders and there it was. A letter from Elijah Birchfield of New York City dated September 2, 1776. It was on microfilm so I have a copy for you, but I can't wait to show you so here it is transcribed verbatim:

To the Honorable Benjamin Franklin
Philadelphia, Pennsylvania

Sir,

I am obligated to inform you of a matter of the utmost importance. I beg your indulgence in the evasive nature of my writing but I am fearful it could fall into the hands of the enemy even though I hope to reduce that risk by sending this by my personal envoy with instructions of handing it to no one but you. In regards to the work you commissioned in July last I have endeavored to make shipment to you as quickly as possible again in fear of the enemy confiscating the work completed since the initial shipment was made in relative safety. I will not give details on when I plan to do this or the method I will employ but I will tell you to expect shipment before the beginning of the new year and that concealment of the cargo will be my foremost priority. I realize what I do is risky business but no more so than having the work remain here with the enemy already within our gates. I request you notify me

when said work arrives at your place and if and when you would
like me to continue to fulfill my commitment in light of the recent
turn of events. Please be advised Sir that I feel to continue my work
would be to do so at great peril for those in my employ and for the
commodity itself.

I Remain Your Humble Servant,
Elijah Birchfield
New York City
Monday September 2 1776

Isn't that something? My feeling is the "recent turn
of events" and "enemy already within are gates" Birchfield
mentions are a reference to the British occupation of NYC
... remember your Revolutionary War history? I strongly
believe, Will, the shipment he speaks of is the coins. What
else could it be? Is it possible Mueller and an accomplice
(maybe Hoppe) intercepted this shipment on its way to
Philadelphia and hid it near where Mueller was killed? Is
it possible the man who escaped was Rudolph Hoppe?
Birchfield said to "expect shipment before the beginning
of the new year". The location and timing are right. I just
made a copy of this just as the Society was closing. I plan
to go back tomorrow to see if there is a record of Franklin
responding to Birchfield or any other related documents.
This is exciting. I can't wait until tomorrow. We'll discuss
this at length later. I have lots of theories. I'll keep in touch.
How am I doing so far?
Karen

Will printed Karen's email and showed it to Mel. It was late
when they finished discussing it and Will decided to wait until
morning to respond to Karen.

Before he had a chance to respond the next day, another email from Karen arrived just after eleven a.m.

Hi,

Went back to the HS of PA early today and glad I did. Look at this response to Birchfield's letter I have attached. That has to be the coins Franklin is talking about. Mueller somehow intercepted the shipment from New York City to Philadelphia. It makes sense if Birchfield shipped it over land, the direct route through occupied New Jersey. Even if he shipped it through Pennsylvania it could have been intercepted. Birchfield would have never shipped it by sea with British ships patrolling the whole mid-Atlantic coast. Over land was his only option. I'm sure of it, Will. Hoppe was the man who escaped the morning Mueller was killed. If it was just the two of them involved, and Mueller was dead, that would make Hoppe the only person who knew about the coins. This wasn't Robert Rhone's treasure; it was Rudolph Hoppe's! And like Mel suspects, Robert and Rudolph were in it together and later it somehow became know as Rhone's treasure. I'm not real thrilled about the prospect of my ancestor being a thief, but that's the way it goes ... remember the poem? Of course maybe Hoppe was betrayed, which would explain why Captain Rickert thought Mueller was trying to kill him. Are there holes in this theory? Yes. But right now anyway it appears clear to me. So many of the questions we have are answered with this scenario.

I'm going to check the courthouse for Philip Hoppe Jr.'s will and then head for home. I'll see you tonight sometime and we can talk about this some more.

Bye,
Karen

Attachment:

To the Esteemed Elijah Birchfield
New York City New York

My Dear Sir
    Having received yours of September 2 1776 last month I was
of mind to delay answering hopeful that shipment as mentioned
should arrive at my place. However, events now dictate that I de-
part for France by the end of the month and will be unable to
await the arrival as anticipated. I have instructed my cohorts to
notify you as soon as possible after said shipment arrives. I am in
agreement with you that to hold the shipment at your place is in-
deed as risky or more so than making an attempt to have them in
my security. I accede also that to continue work on your commis-
sion imposes undue risk to yourself and your workers as well as the
commodity itself. I therefore am requesting that you cease and de-
sist work on the remaining quantity until you receive further in-
struction from me. Furthermore, I beseech you to do your best in
concealing all things related to the commission should your work
place be inspected by the enemy. In closing I commend you for your
devotion to our cause and for the risks and hardships you heretofore
have endured in the name of Liberty.

Your Trusted Friend
Benj. Franklin
Philadelphia Pennsylvania
October 9th 1776

                              ***

It was almost dark by the time Karen arrived at her brother's
house. She was tired but that wasn't going to keep her from going
to Mel's house to deliver the material she had gathered and to

discuss her findings and to see Will. But for now a hot shower was the first order of business.

✳✳✳

"Outstanding work, Karen," Mel said as she entered his living room. "Will, make us all a cup of cappuccino, please."

"Nice to have you home, Holtzman," Will said smiling as he headed for the kitchen.

"Nice to be home, Rhone."

Mel said, "Karen, I think you nailed it. Tracking this down took some excellent reasoning on your part. Anything of importance in the will of Philip Hoppe Jr.?"

"No. The usual. He and his wife never had any children. No mention of the sunshine coin. No telling what happened to it."

"Will and I discussed your theories. I think you very well could be right. A couple of points need to be clarified, though. In the Hessian army, division of the ranks was profound. I find it hard to believe a major would choose a private as a partner in crime. Looting did occur with the Hessian officers and it was tolerated for the most part. Not so much so with the lower ranks. So I think if Hoppe was involved it came after the fact and not as a participant in the crime." Mel paused. "Will. What was the other point we wanted to make?"

Will answered from the kitchen, "The mention of some of the shipment making it safely."

"Oh yes. Birchfield eludes to … let me find this … here, that an initial shipment was made before the one that was lost. That would account for some of the coins surviving to the present day. You said your theory has holes, Karen. I'd just like to say, it doesn't have too darn many. This feels right."

Serving the cappuccinos, Will said, "So what's our next move?"

"Lieutenant Zimmerman called and said he would be here day after tomorrow around ten in the morning. Can both of you be here?"

Will and Karen nodded.

"Good. Tomorrow afternoon Al Marcus will be here. I know you'll both be here for that."

***

Fifty-two-year-old Alistair Marcus knew Mel through the *Upper Dauphin Vintners*, a local home winemaking club. Like Mel and all the other members of the club, he loved the hobby. The club met once a month and enjoyed sampling each other's product, swapping recipes and tips, and telling stories, all with a designated driver standing by, of course.

Al Marcus was of average height, balding, a little overweight, and thanks to his treadmill and dumbbells, was in excellent health. He was intelligent, articulate, and had commanding presence. Law was his passion and he often joked he'd practice for free if his wife would let him.

Marcus was an ex-Philadelphia lawyer and a good one. When he told his partners he wanted out they gave him all the good reasons to stay. He gave them all the good reasons to leave. And as it is with most behavior needing justification, there's a good reason and there's the real reason. The real reason the partners didn't want Marcus to leave was that he was a moneymaker extraordinaire. The real reason Marcus wanted to leave was that he lost his resolve for the kind of law he was practicing. He had hurt people for nothing more than the self-serving objective of increasing his net worth. He didn't like himself much when his moment of conscience struck. There had to be a better way to use his knowledge of the law, he reasoned. So ten years before he had sold his partnership in Strawbridge, Marcus, Reinholdt and Associates and moved to rural upper Dauphin County to practice a kinder, gentler version of the law.

Within six months he was receiving clients in a sweatshirt, and within another six months he was appearing in court in jeans, with a sports jacket, of course. He was now helping people and making a decent living doing it. It felt good and he liked himself again. He even made house calls.

"Hello, Mel."

"Al, nice to see you again. Please come in. We're all here. This is my grandson, Will, and our friend, Karen Holtzman."

"Nice to meet you both."

"Thanks for coming, Al. As I explained over the phone, we're in a bit of a bind," said Mel.

"I don't know about a bind, but you're certainly knee-deep in a conundrum. Your situation gives catch-22 new meaning. But … let's see if we can work it all out."

Al reached in his briefcase and pulled out a stack of papers an inch thick. After organizing the stack and making his body erect, as if to signal something profound was coming, he said, "Before I start let me say this, even though I don't think I have to. You sound so sure of yourself about the treasure being where you say it is, I'm going to assume that you're right. And that means there is a security issue here. This can't get out to anyone or it's good-bye treasure, regardless of what the law has to say about it. That field would have more craters than the moon. Everybody say, 'We agree, Al.'"

Grinning, everybody said in unison, "We agree, Al."

"Okay. Just to confirm what Mel told me. All three of you are blood descendants of Robert Rhone and Rudolph Hoppe; Karen you of Hoppe; and Mel and Will of Rhone?"

"Correct. But that's pronounced *Hope-ie*, not *Hoppy*," Karen said.

"That's right. Sorry. Mel did correct me once. In any event, you can prove you're descendants?"

"Yes. All three of us can," Mel assured.

"Okay. First let's talk about grave excavation." He started at the top page of his stack. "Although specific laws regarding excavation of graves are hard to find, based on the many criminal cases—or precedence—where bodies are sought to prove guilt or innocence, it is clear Pennsylvania places a distinct protection on known grave sites. Generally speaking, if someone desires to excavate a grave, they must petition the local Court of Common Pleas. They must present a compelling reason as to the necessity. The court must then weigh the decedent and family's interest in keeping the grave sacred and intact versus the reason for the request. Being descendants helps you here.

"Equity usually determines the decision, not rule of law. Obviously, it follows then that any excavation not court approved of a known grave site would at least be a trespass and possibly a robbery or property damage claim, not to mention a criminal charge for the act."

Mel looked at Will. Will looked at Karen. And all three looked at Al.

"Whoa, Al. Layman's terms, please," Mel said.

"That *was* layman's terms. Do you want to hear it in legalese?"

"How about layman layman's terms then?" Karen suggested.

"Okay. Bottom line. To play it safe, a good rule of thumb is that you can't dig up a known grave in Pennsylvania without court approval and you'd better have a darn good reason to get court approval."

"You said *known* grave. Not many people know this grave site ever existed."

"Ahh ... but *you* know."

Mel nodded, understanding.

"What about with the permission of the landowner?" Will asked.

"That wouldn't necessarily help you. That might absolve you from any trespass issues, but you would still need court approval. Now the twist in your case—one of many, I might add—is that you know, or at least strongly believe, there is a cache of coins actually buried with the decedent, Magdalena Rhone. And the cache is worth a lot of money. So the reason you would be petitioning the court is to recover the coins. In other words, for personal gain. Probably the worst reason in the world to excavate a grave. Recovery of a family heirloom, maybe, but that would be a hard sell and I wouldn't go there.

"I want to make you aware of something else while I'm on this. There is something called the 'Clean Hands' doctrine, which means you must come to the court with clean hands, not bad faith. Petitioning for any reason other than the absolute nondiluted truth would be an attempt to deceive the court. That's why it's imperative we don't get involved with any shenanigans.

"And before we go any further, would someone please tell me why on earth did the man bury valuable coins with his wife?"

Karen answered. "They weren't of any value then—long story. But we think Rhone learned the coins were worthless. So why *not* bury them with this wife?"

"I see."

"Let me be clear on this, Al," Mel said. "You're saying the only way to get court approval to dig up Magdalena's grave is to tell them the absolute truth and by doing so it most likely will result in the court not ruling in our favor?"

"Yep. Told you. Catch-22. But the denial of your petition is not automatic. Personal gain just isn't the best of reasons. That's why there's lawyers ... to plead your case. I would claim special circumstances, which indeed apply. The court will see that we came with clean hands—we acted in good faith—and that weighs heavily with them. How much are the coins worth, by the way? Do you have any idea?"

"Based on an average price per coin of ten thousand dollars each, we believe between sixty and ninety million dollars," Karen answered.

"What! You can't be serious!" a bug-eyed Al exclaimed.

"We're dead serious," Mel said. "A lot of variables, though.

The condition of the coins. The true number buried, obviously. And what a large cache released to the numismatic community all at once would do to the price per coin. We factored in everything we could think of and we feel we're close."

"Incredible! I had no idea." A rattled Al Marcus inhaled a big breath and took a moment to regain his composure. " Okay. I thought this was complex before, but now … wow. Let me move on to the other issues you mentioned on the phone and then we'll come back to this.

"Erection of a memorial on the grave site in question. This one's easy. The landowner has absolute rights. He can't be forced to do anything to his property except in the case of eminent domain. You, a private citizen, can't enforce eminent domain, only a government can. And if the government was on your side in wanting to erect a memorial, and wanted to enforce eminent domain, they would have to pay the owner a reasonable price for the land in question. Now. The government has to answer to the taxpayers for the money they spent … right? Which means, realistically, you don't stand a snowball's chance of getting them on your side in this situation. However, if you and the landowner can come to an agreement, you can pay him for the ability to erect under easement, or a ninety-nine-year lease. My advice to you? Ask. Don't bully. He just might work with you since it's an unselfish cause."

Mel, Will, and Karen nodded.

"Couldn't he also sell me the land, which would mean I can do as *I* please with it?" Mel asked.

"He could, yes. As a matter fact that's what I would go for. Legally, it's a better deal for you if you can pull it off. But then you have right-of-way issues."

"And there is no problem—from a legal standpoint—in selling a parcel of land, say, twenty feet by twenty feet?" asked Will.

"Yes and no. Not if both parties agree on the particulars, which needs to happen first and foremost. That's why it's important you don't antagonize the landowner, it all hinges on his approval, obviously. The only legal concern is that the township won't let you subdivide such a small parcel. You would have to get a variance or special exception from the township and that's not automatic. And you would most likely have to buy a minimum of a half acre. But that's not so bad, is it?"

"So Grandpa should be able to get his memorial."

"Right now, I would say it's doable if the landowner is willing to work with you. But that's the least of your worries. On to buried treasure," Al said, shifting his body into his something-profound-is-coming position. "In legalese first. In the Commonwealth of Pennsylvania, common law holds that the finder of lost or abandoned property has superior claim to the same against the world, except the true owner. This is commonly referred to as the Finders-Keepers Law.

"In layman layman's, digging up previously undiscovered treasure falls under the category of abandoned property for legal purposes. That means the law is based upon the premise that the treasure was left behind or abandoned and not just hidden or stored in the location by the true owner. In other words, no claimant with ownership interest is alive or discoverable. Which is true in your case, being that your ancestors who put it there are dead. Except—and it's a really big except—the United States government, since the property was stolen from them in the first place, or so you tell me. Also, other possible claimants would be any other descendants of Robert Rhone and Rudolph Hoppe, assuming they, Rhone and Hoppe, did not obtain the coins illegally. But we'll come back to that."

"Excuse me. If I can interrupt here, Al. Are you saying the landowner has no claim to the treasure?" Karen asked.

"That's right. Not if you were on their land legally and acting legally when you found it, unless of course they stumbled onto it first. Now I happen to know that MAAC owns the land in question here, and they don't post it and actually encourage the public to use their land … responsibly. I know that because I hunt pheasants there sometimes and I sought permission to do so even though the land isn't posted, which is always a good idea.

"So legally it's all right for you to be there for whatever legal reason, just as it's all right for me to hunt there. But you do *not* have the right to start digging there without their permission, especially over a known grave, as we've already discussed. That then begs the question of how you would ask MAAC with a straight face if they mind if you dig some holes on their property. They're going to ask why. Then you're going to have to tell them about the treasure, the grave, or both. What are they going to say then? 'Sure, go right ahead, and oh, by the way if you find the ninety mil just keep it, what the hey. We're good sports.' Do you see what I'm saying?"

"Now what a minute, Al. What if we said we would share it with them if we found it?" Mel asked.

"Now you're talking. A joint venture could work. But remember, we still have the grave excavation issue, but to have the landowner on our side is a definite plus. Let me finish and we'll come back to that."

Will whispered to Karen, "We have a lot to come back to."

"I heard that," Al said, then continued undaunted. "Okay. Where was I … oh yes. Now here's where it gets sticky. As I said, it's my understanding your ancestors may have obtained the treasure illegally. If they did, then they would have no claim to the treasure, nor would their descendants. A person committing a crime cannot profit in any way from their crime. 'But this happened over two hundred years ago and the people involved with the theft are dead,' you say. That won't help you. The reality is that in a find of this magnitude Uncle Sam is going to hear about it and Uncle never forgets. They're not going to say, 'Aw shucks. That was so long ago, just go on and keep it.' They're going to claim it's theirs and then all bets are off. They would have a good legal argument for ownership of the treasure if they could prove it was stolen from them.

"Then, on top of everything else, Pennsylvania would file a Forfeiture Petition for the treasure, of that you can be sure. So. Now you have the United States claiming the treasure is theirs; Pennsylvania saying no, it's theirs; and maybe other descendants claiming it's theirs if they can prove it was not obtained in the commission of a crime by their ancestors; and I can't even begin to imagine who else might make a claim. The only one who doesn't have a claim is the poor landowner, assuming someone else found it legally as I've explained, and even he might find a way to make a claim.

"And this all revolves around you seeking and getting court approval to dig up a grave site. No matter what scenario you pick, this most certainly would be decided in the courts and that could drag on for years. Now, there are going to be exceptions, stipulations, and gray areas for many of the things I told you and we can get into them as they come up. I just know you have questions."

"What if the coins were obtained in the commission of a crime by somebody other than Rhone and Hoppe?" Will asked.

"And they somehow innocently came into possession of the coins?" Al followed.

"Yes."

"Good question. I can't imagine how that could happen, but certainly then they could not be held responsible for the crime, which means they could have legally been the owners of the coins. But, that's potentially one of those gray areas."

"What if we dig up the treasure and don't tell anybody about it; the U.S. government, the state government, the landowner, or anybody?" Mel asked.

"Good. I knew that one was coming. Now we can get it out of the way. The first thing that happens in that case is you lose Al

Marcus as your legal representation. Because under that scenario you are lying by omission of the facts at best, and at worst, outright breaking the law. I spent too many years playing that game and I want no part of it. And neither do you, Mel. I know you better than that.

"Let me say this as adamantly as I can. People in these kinds of situations usually have a knee-jerk reaction and it's almost always *wrong*. It's how decent, honest people get themselves into trouble. I'm not going to let that happen to you. No. We follow the letter of the law no matter where it takes us. Everybody say, 'We agree, Al.'"

Karen and Will said, "We agree, Al."

"Yes, yes. Sorry, Al. I do know better. Well, if we have to do this legal-like, that certainly limits our choices," Mel said, embarrassed he even asked the question.

"Al," Will said, "this is one of our 'come back to' issues. What if we went to the landowner, told him the whole story as truthfully as we can, and ask if he would work with us for a share, with the added stipulation that he allow Grandpa to erect his memorial over the grave site, either by the means you mentioned or by purchasing the grave site outright?"

"Good. We're on the right track. Okay. The issues with that are as follows.

"One, we would still have to get court approval to dig up the grave. Difficult, but not impossible, especially with the landowner on board. But I'll tell you this: when equity determines the decision, how the ruling goes depends on the judge we draw. That makes it a crapshoot. You need to be aware of that. Being descendants does help you in that scenario.

"Two, you would be tipping your hand to the landowner. He could say he wanted nothing to do with a partnership, post 'No Trespassing' signs all over the place, and then go treasure-hunting himself, cutting you out of the deal completely. Let's hope mister landowner has the scruples I think he does. Your bargaining chip there is you know where it's buried and he doesn't. You wouldn't have to tell him the township or even the county for that matter.

"Three, you still have the issue of the U.S. Government laying claim to the treasure even with the landowner as an ally. Even if your ancestors had nothing to do with the theft, Sam would want the coins … trust me here. If your ancestors *were* involved with the theft and Uncle can prove it, forget it. It would be better to try and strike a deal with them than go to court. There is only one hope in besting Samuel. If you can prove your ancestors had nothing to do with the theft *and* made an honest attempt to return the coins to the rightful owner, we would have a good argument and I would be optimistic about the ruling.

"I failed to mention another angle Big Brother could use. National treasure. They could claim the coins are a national treasure and they belong to the American people. But we'll deal with that when the time comes.

"And four, you have the issues with the state and other descendants, but I'm not overly concerned about that now."

"Why not?" Karen asked.

"Because if you find the coins by legal means, the Finders-Keepers Law kicks in, excluding any other descendants, or anybody for that matter, except the state and feds. Remember … in Pennsylvania finders have superior claim against the world. Let me say this again in another way. If you find the coins by legal means, Uncle can't just confiscate them. They have to convince a judge that the coins belong to them. It's their responsibility to prove it. And we'll worry about the state when it's time."

"How are we ever going to prove how they came to possess the coins and if and when they ever tried to return them?" Will asked.

"Old documents, public records, private records, whatever you can get your hands on. You know how, you're genealogists, plus Mel said you two are history majors. There are no better researchers than genealogists and history majors … except lawyers, of course." Al winked at Mel. "You have your work cut out for you, that's for sure."

"The trunk! That bloomin' trunk!" Karen exclaimed.

"The trunk?"

Karen told Al the story of the trunk given to Charles Holtzman by their Grandmother Holtzman, and then asked, "Is there anything I can do legally to force Charles to allow me to see the contents of that trunk?"

"Another uphill battle. Let's say we go to court and, through a court order, force him—which is a longshot at best—to show you the contents. What's to stop him from removing any pertinent information before you see it? You don't know what's in there now, so how would you know if he removed anything? Forget it. Why not just ask him again and say please. Honey draws more flies than vinegar … not to imply your cousin's a fly."

"He's worse than a fly. That trunk should have gone to the oldest son, my father. Doesn't that count for anything?"

"No. That's family tradition, not rule of law. You can sue for anything, but don't go there. Possession is still nine-tenths of the law. I'm afraid he's gotcha. By the way, does anybody know where Charles was on the night of the attack?"

"No, it wasn't Charles, if that's what you're implying, Al. I would have known him, ski mask or not. Let's say we have our suspicions about Charles but that's all. Right now, anyway."

"Okay. Just curious."

"Mel asked, "How about the statute of limitations if Robert or Rudolph *were* involved with the theft?"

"That's not going to help you. First of all, the guilty parties are dead and you can't prosecute a dead man. And you certainly can't prosecute a descendant for a crime committed by an ancestor; therefore there is no statute of limitations to run out. The issue here is who has rightful claim to the coins if they ever are recovered, and the statute of limitations has nothing to do with that." Al closed his briefcase. "You know if the coins aren't where you think they are, this is all for naught. Just *how* sure of yourselves are you?"

"We could be wrong, that's for sure. But we don't think we are," Will answered.

"So in a nutshell, you know millions of dollars worth of antique coins are buried with one of your ancestors, but you don't know exactly where that grave is, and when you do find it you can't legally dig up the grave to get to them, and you can't get legal approval without notifying the whole world they're there, and you can't easily ask the landowner for permission to dig up his property without risking him getting to the coins first, legally or illegally, and if you do defy all odds and get the coins in your possession you have everybody and his brother saying they belong to them. Is that what you're asking me to sort out?"

"Yeah. That pretty much covers it," Mel said.

"I have a question, Al," Karen said. "We have reason to believe MAAC does not know the grave site is there. If we did tip our hand to them by asking permission or going for a partnership, wouldn't the law protecting grave sites apply to them as well?"

"Absolutely. But if they wanted to be disingenuous they would have a much better argument as to why they were digging in that spot … I mean, once the discovery came out. They could give an infinite number of reasons to be digging on their own land and say they stumbled on the coins by accident. Even if you *did* tell them about the grave site and the treasure, they could just deny it, or say they didn't believe you, or thought you meant it was somewhere else, etc., etc. Your word against theirs."

"What if they wanted to be honest? Would they have an easier time of it getting court approval to dig the site?" Will asked.

"Yes and no. They certainly could come up with a better reason than personal gain to move the whole cemetery. Then they could say, 'Oh my, looky here. Ninety million in antique coins, imagine that.' They would then claim Finders-Keepers. That's an interesting perspective though. *But,* they would still be deceiving the court by not giving them the real reason they wanted to be digging at the grave site in the first place. To answer your question, if they were to be totally honest, they would stand no better chance than you being totally honest."

"And we would also be indirectly deceiving the court by striking a clandestine deal with MAAC," Mel said.

"Absolutely. Now you're catching on," Al said. "Before I go, how *are* you going to pinpoint the grave of Magdalena Rhone?"

"We're still working on that one," Will said.

Shaking his head in general disbelief, Al Marcus asked, "All else aside, have you thought about how you are going to feel disturbing the final resting place of one of your ancestors?"

"Yes." Karen fielded that one. "We cannot *not* pursue it. Remember, Al, this isn't just a treasure hunt. Polly Rhone was killed because someone else knows about the treasure and wants it. It may be morally and legally wrong to disturb a grave, but it is *more* wrong if we don't find a way to do it, because we know someone else is going to if we don't. Which means the grave will be disturbed anyway and for the wrong reasons. As the law says, no one should profit from their crime. We feel we know more than the bad guy now, and we can beat him to it and do some good with the money in Polly's name. It's just plain unacceptable to allow the bad guys to win in this situation, and if we do nothing, they'll win."

"'All that is necessary for evil to triumph is for good men to do nothing' is how Edmund Burke put it. That's the answer I was hoping for. Count me in. I love a challenge. As a matter of fact, 'good versus evil' is the argument we would use if and when we go for court approval to dig the grave."

"One more question, Al," Mel said. "Did you ever hear of dowsing for graves and GPR—ground-penetrating radar?"

"I've heard of them both, but don't know much about either. Why?"

"Are we within our legal limits to do either on the grave site without asking the owner's permission?"

"I would say yes to the dowsing, since all that's involved is a guy going for a walk with a couple of sticks. Certainly within legal limits based on MAAC's current policy on usage of their land, if no crops are damaged in the process. You risk being seen and questioned, though. Not so sure about the GPR. That would involve equipment ... maybe a lot of equipment. I'll have to look into that one. My gut tells me you would need permission."

"Please check and let us know," Mel said.

"You don't really believe in that dowsing stuff, do you, Mel?" Al asked.

"I don't know. Some compelling evidence supports it."

"Mel, you're starting to sound like a lawyer," Al laughed.

"So I am. You'd better go then. And don't forget to send me a bill."

"I think we should talk about a retainer. But we'll worry about that later." Mel and Beau escorted Al Marcus to the door. "If anything comes up, give me a call."

"We will. Thanks a lot, Al. Hope to see you at the next Vintners meeting."

When Mel returned to the living room he joined Will and Karen in discussing all the information Marcus provided.

Karen said, "So I guess we have an attorney now."

"Yes, we do. Good suggestion, Will. Getting Al on board was the best thing we've done for ourselves so far."

"I think so too. Everybody say, 'We agree, Will.'"

From his vehicle parked in the bushes along the Gratztown Road two hundred feet from Mel's house, a smirking Charles Holtzman said, "We agree, Will."

***

Charles Holtzman found the spot on the Gratztown Road through trial and error when he discovered his receiver wouldn't work from the location Socks Smith suggested.

It wasn't perfect. He was hidden from Mel's house, but could be seen by anyone driving by on the Gratztown Road. He knew he couldn't spend a lot of time parked at the same spot without arousing suspicion so he worked out a schedule to be 'on duty.'

He also made drive-bys. A *lot* of drive-bys. He had about ten seconds of receiving time if he drove slowly past the house. It was hit and miss but this time it worked. He didn't hear all of Mel's phone conversation with Al Marcus but he caught the time they set for Al to make a house call. All he had to do was be at his spot at that time to be the fifth person attending the meeting. It paid off better than he could have ever hoped for. He now had all the information he needed to recover the coins and he had no inclination to 'follow the letter of the law' as his opponents would. *How stupid can they get?*

Since Socks Smith had explained to Charles the spot Dottie Hummel, Will, and Karen were milling around, and Charles already had general knowledge of the old Rhone property, he reasoned Dottie was there in response to the cemetery ad. All he needed to do now was pinpoint the location of the grave that contained the coins, then dig them up. He wasn't going to do the digging but he knew who would. *Socks should be sending his address soon. While they're fooling around being upright citizens, I have lots of time to come up with a plan.*

CHAPTER

TWENTY

The next day, as Lieutenant David Zimmerman stepped on Mel's porch, Beau stepped on his shoe with a dirty paw. When the immaculate dresser bent over to wipe his shoe with his handkerchief, Beau gave him a big lick across the face. The lieutenant turned his hanky inside out and wiped his face.

Witnessing the encounter through his large bay window Mel said, "Will, you'd better rescue Lieutenant Zimmerman from Beau."

"Sorry about that, Lieutenant," Will said as he held the door open.

"No problem. I guess it's better than being greeted with barks and growls. Why don't we all have a seat? I have some important information for you."

Karen asked, "Would you like something to drink, Lieutenant?"

"No thanks." He opened his notepad. "The information you gave on Charles Holtzman could be important. Nothing solid to connect him to the crime but we're looking into it. Can you give me a list of other Hoppe descendants like the one you gave for the Rhones?"

"Yes," Mel said. "We'll have it for you before you leave."

"We received the DNA report on the hairs we found here the day after the attack, and from the skin sample found on the window from the break-in. The person who attacked you, Mel, is the same person who broke into your house the second time. Knowing the same person committed the two incidents; we believe the second time this guy was here was for some other reason than to rob you. I think he could have planted a bug and tried to make it look like a robbery. I brought electronic eavesdropping detection equipment with me. I should run a check right away, if you don't mind."

"A bug? For what reason?" Mel asked.

"Information. As you told us, he didn't get much in the way of information on the treasure the first time around. A bug could be his second attempt. We'll see. Let's wait to say any more until after the test."

The power of suggestion had Mel, Will, and Karen scanning the living room from ceiling to floor, while Lieutenant Zimmerman walked to his car and retrieved an instrument about twelve inches square resembling a portable radio. On the front of the box were knobs, meters, small lights, and two antennae about four inches high. Attached to the box by a wire was a metal cylindrical probe about eight inches long and an inch in diameter.

The detective positioned the unit on the floor in the center of the living room. "This should tell us pretty quick if anything is here." Within seconds of him switching the unit on, it squawked. "See? Didn't take long. That tells us there is a transmitter present in this room and it's somewhere over there." He pointed to Mel's chair. "Now we flip this switch and use the probe to find it."

Lieutenant Zimmerman walked toward Mel, carrying the unit by its handle with the probe in his other hand.

"Do you want me to move?" Mel asked.

"No. You're fine." He moved the probe across Mel and then over the phone stand beside the chair. It emitted a high-pitched squeal. He got down on his hands and knees and looked under the phone stand. "And there it is." He took a pair of plastic gloves and a plastic bag from his suit pocket, pulled on the gloves, and removed the bug Socks Smith had planted. After examining the tiny black box with its miniature antenna, he flipped its switch off before sliding it into the bag. "Oh, the technology! I love being one step ahead of the bad guys."

"That's why Beau was so interested in that phone stand," said Mel. "He kept sniffing around there."

"I'm going to go through the rest of the house with this. I'll scan outside, and just for the heck of it I'll go over your vehicles too. Let's see if he planted more than one."

"Yes. By all means, Lieutenant," Mel said. "What about the phones?"

"This will pick up a wire tap." After the detective scanned the inside and outside of Mel's house and all three vehicles, he returned to the living room. "Looks like we got them all. He probably was in a hurry, thanks to your security system. Now you have to try and remember what you talked about of significance from the time of the break-in until now."

"Unbelievable. Just how powerful is that bug?" Will asked.

"Not too. This one isn't all that sophisticated. Probably has a range of two to three hundred feet at the most. I'll have it traced. But they're readily available. Doubt if it will tell us much. Have you noticed of late any vehicles parked within the range I mentioned?"

No one answered. "If we think of anything, we'll let you know," Mel said.

David Zimmerman went on, "We distributed the sketch of the man you encountered in the park and received no response. We then went door to door. A landlord on River Street in Millersburg identified the sketch as a tenant who skipped out on him. The tenant used the name Jeffrey Foster. We couldn't find anything on Jeffrey Foster. We then checked known aliases but didn't find him there either. The landlord gave us a description of his vehicle, but unfortunately he didn't get his license plate number.

"We checked the whole house for prints but it looks like he wiped the place clean. The good news is we did get lots of DNA from the drain traps. We're waiting for those results now. I'm betting it matches the previous two. This guy is pretty crafty, but we're closing in on him. We should have him ID-ed soon. Any questions so far?"

"What if he leaves the country?" Karen asked.

"We've notified Interpol and provided the sketch. If he did manage to get out of the country before we had the sketch, they'll find him. But I doubt he left. There's something here he wants that he didn't get yet … at least as far as we know."

"Lieutenant, there's something we need to tell you," Mel said. "But first, Will, please print out what we have on the Hoppe genealogy while I explain. Lieutenant, we think we know what the treasure is and where it is."

Lieutenant Zimmerman came to attention. "Please enlighten me."

"Well, first let me say that this is information of a sensitive nature. If it was to get out, there could be treasure hunting hysteria the likes of which we have never seen in this area. I'm afraid someone else could get hurt if that happens. At the same time, it's in everybody's best interest for you to know."

"Let me assure you. What takes place between you and me is police business. And the police never share information with anyone who doesn't need to know."

Speaking in the most general terms he could without withholding information, Mel explained what they knew about the treasure and how they knew it.

"I see what you mean, Mr. Rhone. My advice to you is to get an attorney."

"Already done. We've retained Al Marcus."

"About the only thing we can do right now in regards to protecting the treasure is run extra patrols in that area with instructions to investigate any suspicious activity in the fields. I believe the area you described can be seen from T-231, so that shouldn't be a problem. Another bit of advice: get those coins in your possession as soon as you can."

Will returned from the office and handed Lieutenant Zimmerman a copy of the Hoppe genealogy. "We're working on it, Lieutenant. We're working on it."

Walking toward the door, the lieutenant said, "In over twenty-five years of police work I have never seen or heard of anything like this. I wish you luck. You did the right thing by telling me."

As Will watched the policeman drive away he said, "Risky move, Grandpa. But I think you're right. You had to tell him."

"Now we have a problem," Karen said. "We mentioned the location of the coins any number of times since that bug was planted. We have to assume it was heard. And we have to assume that the only thing the bad guy needed *was* the location. Now I'm scared. I'm sure he won't petition the court for permission to dig."

"Make no mistake about it," Mel said, "we have to move on this. Karen, call your dowser friend and get him here as soon as possible. I'll call Al and tell him about this."

***

The female voice answering the phone was pleasant and professional. She identified herself as Ellen, wife and secretary of Asher J. Sankey, professional dowser.

"When will Mr. Sankey be back?" Karen asked.

"It's hard to say. I can take all the information he needs. Then I'll call you back with a quote. How did you hear about us?" Ellen Sankey asked.

"From your website."

"Okay. I'll need your name, phone number, and address; the

amount of land to be dowsed and its location; what it is you want to know; how soon you'll want this done; plus any other information you care to provide."

Karen answered all of Ellen Sankey's questions, stressing she would like the work to be expedited, then hung up the phone. In less than twenty minutes Ellen Sankey called back. Karen suspected Asher Sankey had been there all along.

"Ms. Holtzman. Mr. Sankey said he will do this right away but it will cost you five hundred dollars extra."

"Five hundred dollars! Why so much?"

"Because he is moving you to the top of the list. If it's as important as you say it is, Mr. Sankey feels you should be willing to pay for his expediency."

"Oh, all right," Karen relented. "What's the quote in total?"

"Based on the amount of land to be searched, and the detailed information you want on each grave, the cost will be three thousand three hundred dollars, plus traveling expenses."

Karen gasped, thought a moment, then asked, "How soon can he be here?"

"This Friday, June twenty-fifth, at noon. I should tell you that Mr. Sankey feels this could take more than a day. If it does, the expenses will be more. You are expected to pay the base amount in advance by cash or bank check, and the expenses in cash or personal check once he knows what they'll be. We don't take credit cards."

"Karen felt unsure if she should give approval without consulting her partners but said, "Okay." *Mel and Will are going to spit nails!*

"Ms. Holtzman, will you provide a meeting place and the kind of vehicle you will be driving?"

"Yes. At ten o'clock in front of the Gratz Historical Society on Market Street in Gratz. That's in Dauphin County. We'll be in a gray and red four-wheel-drive extended-cab pickup. Mel and Will Rhone will be with me."

"Okay. Mr. Sankey will see you then, but you'd better make it eleven o'clock. It's about a three-hour drive down there, and he's not an early riser. He'll be driving a black pickup with a cap. Thank you for you business."

As soon as she hung up the phone, Karen drove to Mel's house. She turned her head and grimaced as she handed Mel the information provided by Ellen Sankey, then told of their conversation. Mel said nothing, but swallowed hard.

"Mel, I know that's more than I first said it would be. I'll chip in."

"No, you won't. It's fine. We have to get this done."

***

Will slowed as he approached the new all-black pickup truck with an all-black cap parked in front of the Gratz Historical Society. Gold-leaf lettering on the door read ASHER J. SANKEY, and centered under that, DOWSER. Below that, Sankey's phone number. Sitting at the wheel was a dark-haired man with a mustache in his mid-thirties. Will stopped when his passenger window aligned with the driver's window of the black truck.

"Mr. Sankey, I'm Mel Rhone, that's my grandson, and back there's Karen Holtzman. Will you follow us?"

Asher Sankey gave a disinterested nod and reached for the ignition.

"He's young. I pictured him being older," said Karen.

Will commented, "Nice rig. Looks like the dowsing business is booming."

"You aren't going to heckle the whole time, are you, Will?" Karen asked, unhappy with his tone.

"No. No. I just like his truck," Will answered with a smirk.

Will turned left onto the Klingestown road, drove to T-231, and turned left again. After another mile he turned right onto the dirt access road that led to the field to be dowsed. He glanced in his rearview mirror to make sure Asher Sankey had followed.

"An overcautious Mel said, "Don't park near any of the suspected sites, Will. We wouldn't want to give Mr. Sankey any subtle clues."

Asher Sankey parked beside Will in the grassy area beside the field. He got out, opened the cap door, and slipped into a vest. In the vest he put the quart of bottled water he retrieved from a small ice chest, a handful of plastic flags of different colors (each a four-inch square attached to a rigid wire about a foot and a half long), and a pair of sunglasses. In a long, narrow pocket on the left side of the vest he slid six steel welding rods of three different lengths, the longest thirty inches, the shortest eighteen inches, each bent at ninety degrees four inches from one end. He then settled into a Philadelphia Phillies baseball cap.

"Oh, you're a Phillies fan too," Mel commented.

Asher Sankey said nothing.

As Will handed him a bank check, he said, "We suspect the grave is somewhere in this field. As Karen told your secretary, the field's about twenty acres or so. It starts at that fencerow down there that's the southern border and ends in the hollow over that little knoll that's the northern border. The width is from here— the western border—to that fencerow across the way the eastern border. I would ask that you walk west to east and back between the rows of corn. As you see it isn't very high yet, and it could be damaged if you tramp on it."

Asher Sankey said nothing.

As he walked out of earshot toward the southern fencerow, Will said, "I don't think we'll have to worry about him talking us to death."

When Sankey reached the starting point he removed two of the longest welding rods, held one in each hand at the short end, the long part pointing straight ahead, his elbows at ninety degrees tucked against his body and his forearms parallel to the ground. He aligned himself in the southwest corner of the rectangle. He then walked slowly east down the first row of field corn.

After an hour of walking the field back and forth between each row of corn, he stopped and stuck a red flag in the ground, walked over the spot several times, and then planted a yellow flag on one side of the red, and a blue on the other side of the red about six feet away from the yellow.

"What did he do that for?" asked Mel.

"Don't know. He's still about twenty-five feet from Luther Grace's spot. I'll go ask him," Will answered.

Will walked to Asher Sankey and asked, "Did you find something?"

Sankey never stopped walking, shrugged his shoulders, and said nothing.

"Oh. Well ... okay. I'll let you get back to work." Will return to his seat on the tailgate of his pickup.

"That was short and sweet," Karen said.

"No. That was just short. Anything but sweet. His silence is starting to freak me out. He has not said one word to us. Not one."

"Now, Will," Mel said. "He's just a quiet guy."

"Maybe he's a mute," Karen added.

"If he is, he should have told us that."

"Will, stop and think what you just said," Karen teased.

Will smiled and said, "Well, he should have gestured or wrote us a note, then."

"Will, why don't you serve us some of that iced cappuccino Karen made? There. In the thermos." Mel was trying to calm his agitated grandson.

Asher Sankey dowsed for another fifteen minutes, progressing toward the parked trucks.

"He's coming to Luther's spot now, Mel."

Sankey approached Luther Grace's spot, walked over it, and proceeded past it without ever breaking stride.

"Well, so much for Luther's memory," Will said.

Another hour brought Sankey even with the parked trucks and his three observers. He stuck a green flag in the ground at the edge of the field and walked toward his truck to retrieve another bottle of water.

"Sure is a hot one today, Mr. Sankey. Would you like a cup of iced cappuccino?" Karen asked.

Sankey barely shook his head and walked away without saying a word. Will's faced turned crimson.

"Just a minute, Mr. Sankey," Will said as he approached the dowser. "That's enough. I'll not stand by and watch you disrespect my friend and grandfather. You have not said one word to us even though we've attempted to be friendly to you. That's rude at best and I've had enough."

Asher Sankey was stunned. He removed his baseball cap and sunglasses, stood looking at Will a moment, walked back to his truck, opened the cap lid and tailgate, sat down, bobbed his head up and down several times, and said, "You're right, Mr. Rhone. I mean no disrespect to any of you. But you see, mine is a profession that is subject to a great deal of ridicule. I've been on the receiving end of merciless harassment and relentless skepticism. Even by the very people I'm trying to help sometimes. Over the years I've developed defense mechanisms, the best of which is silence. It's difficult to engage someone in debate if they don't speak. I'd rather have people think I'm an arrogant jerk than to endure their ridicule. No one has ever challenged it before. You seem like nice people. Please accept my apology."

Sankey's polite manner and sincerity disarmed Will. "I never thought of it that way. Your apology's accepted."

"Thank you. To answer your question, Ms. Holtzman, it *is* hot. I sometimes go through two gallons of water on a day like today. Yes, I would love some iced cappuccino. To answer *your* question, Mr. Rhone "

"Mel. Please call me Mel."

"Okay. Mel. Yes, I've been a Phillies fan since I can remember anything. When I was a kid I rigged a coat hanger for an antenna so I could listen to every game on the radio. I try to get to four or five games a year either in Philly or New York. They're doing real good this year. I'm hopeful." Looking at Will, Sankey said, "You're a Mr. Rhone too."

"Yes. My name's Will."

"I flagged that spot down there, Will, because something is buried there. Something large, not human. I suspect a cow, horse, or deer. I mark all things I find. It sometimes helps tell the story. I place a yellow flag at the head and a blue one at the foot ... well in this case ... the tail end. The red one is where I had my first hit. The green flag I just placed so I don't forget where I left off."

"Have you seen any signs of a grave site yet, Mr. Sankey?" Karen asked as she handed him his cappuccino.

"Thank you. Please. My friends call me A.J."

"Okay, A.J. My friends call me Karen."

"No. I've not seen any signs yet. This isn't ambiguous, though. There's either a grave there or there isn't. I don't get partial readings."

"How long have you been doing this kind of work?" she asked.

"Fifteen years. It was on my twenty-first birthday when I discovered I could do it. My family's well had dried up and after several unsuccessful attempts to find a new one my father was beside himself with frustration. I had read stories about dowsing for water so with nothing to lose I gave it a try. I cut a willow bough shaped like a tuning fork and started walking. I walked over this spot and the tip dipped down so hard it almost pulled from my grip. I couldn't believe what I was seeing. It was like someone tied an invisible string on the tip and pulled on it every time I walked over that spot. I kept going over it and tried with all my might to keep it from dipping. I couldn't. I showed my Dad and he had the driller try that spot. I guess I don't have to tell you what happened."

"You struck water," Will said.

"Not just any water. We struck an artesian well. Water came out of the ground like a Texas oil gusher. Some of the purest water in our area. The thing is still flowing just as strong as the day we found it. So I started my own dowsing business. It didn't take long to graduate to graves. I perfected my technique and I've been doing it ever since. Graves are ninety percent of my business now."

"But how does it work?" Karen asked.

"I don't know. I can't explain it. I just know it works. It's not black magic, witchcraft, or hocus-pocus, though. It's an improbable meshing of unknown forces in the ground and my body manifesting in a reaction through a piece of steel. Humans don't know everything about everything just yet. I see it as a gift from God. And I don't know why He gave it to me and not the next guy. There are lots of skeptics out there. When I run into them I invite them to follow me around a while and I'll change their minds. When I talk at all, that is. I've had no takers so far. You do have to be careful though … you the customer, I mean. There are shysters who claim to be dowsers but all they want to do is take your money. They make it bad for the genuine dowsers." Sankey gulped the last of his cappuccino. "I'd better get to work if I'm going to cover this field before dark."

He picked up the green flag and started walking. Another hour brought him within a few rows of corn of the spot Dottie Hummel named as the cemetery site.

"Grandpa, he's almost at Dottie's site," Will said low enough so Sankey couldn't hear.

Karen tensed as Sankey got closer. Three rows to go, two, one.

Will held his breath and then let out a sigh of disgust as Sankey passed over the exact spot where he was standing when Dottie made her claim. The dowser never stopped. One row past, two rows, three. Will hung his head.

He turned to Karen. "So much for …"

"Look Look at those wires swinging," Karen yelled.

A.J. Sankey retrieved a red flag from his vest and stuck it in the ground. He walked a few paces and planted another, and another, and then another. He moved perpendicular across the rows of corn now, carefully stepping over the young shoots and planting red flags as he went. After fifteen minutes of crisscrossing the area and planting red flags, he yelled, "Here's your cemetery. Come here, please."

"I can't believe it!" Will shook his head.

"Well, good ol' Dottie wasn't far off, was she?" Karen was elated as they quick-stepped toward the dowser.

"I'm going to finish the rest of the field to make sure nothing else is here and then come back and work this spot. I think I can get this done today." Sankey resumed his dowsing.

"Unbelievable!" Will said. "Karen, you're right. After all those years Dottie didn't miss it by much."

Mel surveyed the area. "I count twenty-three red flags. Didn't he say a red flag represented a hit? If so, that means twenty-three graves. I believe Mrs. Henry's list claimed twenty-one."

"Even if he just comes close to matching what's on the Henry list, I'll say I witnessed a ... well, I'm not sure what I witnessed," Will said.

Sankey spent an hour finishing the field, then walked back to Will and Karen at the grave site, Mel having retired to the shade of the nearest tree. Retrieving a pencil and tablet and one of the shortest rods from his vest, Sankey said, "This shouldn't take long. The graves are organized better than most. I think they're all oriented east to west, with the head facing east." Handing the tablet and pencil to Karen he added, "If you will help, it should speed things along."

"Okay. If you show me what to do."

"Will, if you would get me a handful of the white and orange flags from the box in the back of my truck I would appreciate it."

He turned to Karen. "Here's how this works. I'll determine the length of the body with the two rods I've been using. That will tell me if we have an adult or child. When I know that, I'll reposition the red flag over the mid-point of the body. Then with just one of the shorter rods I'll walk over the mid-point and if it turns clockwise it's a female, if counterclockwise it's a male. I'll then ask you to record that grave by using a short arrow pointing to the top of the page, that'll be east. The point of the arrow will be the head. At the base of the arrow mark an M for male, F for female, IM for infant male, or IF for infant female. Do that for each grave. I'll also be placing the flags, so not to worry if you mess up, you can fix it later. It looks like the cemetery is about twenty-five feet square with three rows of graves, so start in the upper left-hand corner of the page, and I'll start in the far left corner of the cemetery. Let's give it a try."

"Is this enough?" Will showed Sankey the flags.

"Yes. If you stay fairly close here, Will, I'll ask you to plant a white flag for a female and an orange for a male. Plant it beside the red one."

Sankey identified the first body as that of an adult male, the second an adult female. Using his fine-tuning procedure, and with the help of the recruited assistant dowsers, he moved quickly through the cemetery. When he got to the center of the second row of graves he stopped. With a puzzled look on his face he went back and forth over the grave of Magdalena Rhone several times, muttering to himself.

In frustration he said, "I don't know what's going on here … *something's* going on here. We'll have to come back to this one. Let's finish up."

When they finished, Karen tore off the tablet page she had recorded and handed I to Mel. He retrieved Mrs. Henry's cemetery list from his shirt pocket and studied both.

"Okay. What's going on here?" Sankey asked again, of no one in particular, as he removed his vest and reworked Maggie Rhone's grave. "This is definitely the grave of an adult female. *And ...* what else, I don't know. It could be that another body was buried on top of the first. I've seen it before. Yet that time the reading wasn't quite the same as now. I'm afraid I can't tell you anything more than that this is the grave of an adult female with someone or something buried on top of her. Please add her to your records with a question mark. I'm sorry about that."

"Sorry? Don't be sorry. I have a confession to make," Mel said. "We knew there was a cemetery in this field at one of two possible locations. I have a layout of it here. I know who is buried in thirteen of the graves. We just didn't know where the cemetery was. I must tell you, A.J., this is the most remarkable thing I've ever seen. You matched our list to the person. You found two graves that weren't listed, but I'm convinced now that the Henrys are the ones who missed them, for whatever reason."

"Aah ... yes. One more convert added to the ranks," A.J. said.

"No. *Three* more converts," Will added.

"Thank you. Now I have a confession. I knew you knew."

"You did?" asked Karen.

"Sure. Most of my customers know more than they let on and they never tell me until I'm finished. Human nature. I love it when there's an independent source like your list there."

Karen said, "Before you pull the flags, A.J., I'd like to get some photographs of the cemetery."

"I'll leave the flags, if you like."

"No. Take them, please. I'll mark the spot with this little number," Will said as he removed a handheld Global Positioning System unit from his pocket.

"A GPS unit. I've been meaning to get one of those," A.J. said. "Show me how it works."

Will stood over the grave of Maggie Rhone and turned the unit on.

"How accurate is it?" A.J. asked.

"Depends on the number of satellites you can pick up from this spot. Three's good, four's better. Looks like I can get a strong three here. That should put me within a few feet or better."

"That's really good. I need to invest in one of those."

Will recorded the coordinates from the GPS and said, "That should do it, A.J. I'll collect your flags for you. If you figure your expenses I'll cut you a check and you can be on your way."

"Yes, I have a three-hour drive ahead of me. But don't worry about the expenses. I'm waiving them. My way of saying I'm sorry about my rudeness. I'm glad it ended well. I would ask Karen if she would copy what she recorded from her page to my tablet. I keep a record of all my work. Also, add those coordinates if you will, please."

"Sure. Be glad to."

A.J. Sankey collected all his gear, shook hands with Will, Karen, and Mel, and crawled behind the wheel of his truck. He said from the open window, "I wish all the people I dealt with were as nice as you three. It was a pleasure. Maybe we can do this again sometime."

"Take care, A.J. Can you find your way back to the main road?" Will asked.

"Yes. Bye."

The three watched Sankey's truck meander toward T-231. They also watched as the police cruiser turned off T-231 and headed toward Sankey.

"Looks like we have company," Karen said.

The policeman waved Sankey to a stop through an opened window and pulled even with him. They spoke for a few minutes and then each continued in the direction he was headed.

Mel greeted the cruiser. "Hello, Officer Krull."

"Mr. Rhone. Doing a little grave searching?" Trooper Wilber Krull said without getting out of his vehicle.

"Yes, sir."

"Does that really work ... that dowsing?"

"It worked today. That much I can tell you."

"Amazing. Okay. Just saw the activity and thought I'd check it out."

Trooper Krull turned his vehicle and headed back to the main road.

"Well, at least we know they're watching the place," Will said.

"Yes. That's reassuring. Lieutenant Zimmerman must have got the word out," said Karen.

"What's next, Grandpa?"

"Let's find out what Al Marcus thinks about all this. I'll call him tonight. If he's free we'll meet tomorrow morning and come up with a strategy. But for now let's see if we can catch the end of the Phillies game. Karen, will you join us?"

"The Phillies game! How could I possibly say no?" Karen said with rolling eyes.

✳✳✳

Karen didn't sleep well. She found it impossible to stop thinking about the events of the day and the prospects they held. She thought about A.J. Sankey and the minor miracle she had witnessed. She tried to imagine what yet-to-be-discovered force enabled such a thing. She was relieved it had worked. She liked being the hero instead of the goat.

The alarm rang at seven a.m. She was asleep but had no idea for how long. Could have been hours or minutes. It didn't matter. She jumped out of bed and headed for the shower.

When she arrived at Mel's house both Will and Mel were up and having their morning cappuccino. Beau presented her with his usual gift as she entered the living room. "Oh … thank you, Beau. That's a very nice ball."

"Karen, we owe our success yesterday to you. You did the research, you found the guy, and you hired him. Most of all you believed it could work when Will and I were … well, let's say less than convinced."

Will added, "It was a most interesting day, that's for sure. My turn to eat crow, Holtzman. But we aren't home free yet. Grandpa, tell Karen what Al said."

"Yes. Al can't make it this morning, he has to be in court, but he gave us our marching orders. He felt it's time to meet with H. Dallas Fitzhugh of MAAC and try and strike a deal before we go for court approval. He said one of us, or two, or all three of us should approach him. Al felt if he himself were present it might put Mr. Fitzhugh on the defensive. I'd like you and Will to go see him. Will, I believe you have his contact information?"

"Yes. His office is in Philadelphia."

Karen asked, "Did Al have any suggestions on how we should go about this? I don't have any idea what to say."

"About the only thing he stressed was to be honest with him without giving him all the details. He said he wouldn't even tell him where you're from. It's going to be tricky—being honest yet not disclosing much. But I think if anybody can do it, you two can. He said to develop a strategy and practice what you're going to say. He reminded us again that this is risky but that it's our only real option. Try to get him to agree to signing a contract. If you do strike a deal, that's when Al will come in. Good luck. Will, call and make an appointment, please."

CHAPTER

TWENTY-ONE

The website of Leland Page intrigued Charles Holtzman. Page claimed that, with his souped-up pulse-induction metal detector, he could find a dime buried five feet deep. And he was for hire. Located in Silver Springs, Maryland, he was close enough for a day trip and far enough away so as not to be a nosey bother. He was just the person Charles was looking for. He sent Leland Page an email.

Early the next morning Page contacted Charles by phone.

"How much do you charge?" asked Charles.

"How large an area do I need to search?"

"About a fifty-foot square should do it."

"Three thousand will cover it. Cash up front. Expenses included."

"Three thousand! You're out of your mind."

"Hey, pal. You contacted me. That's my fee. If you don't like it find somebody else." Leland Page looked for the off button on his cell phone.

"Wait! Okay. Three thousand it is. How soon can you be here?"

"Wednesday of next week."

"Not quick enough. I need it done tonight."

"Tonight! No way. I have another job this morning. It would be dark by the time I got there."

"Good. It has to be done in the dark. I'm thinking two or three in the morning."

"No. Can't make it."

"I'll bet you could for and extra thousand," Charles said in a smug tone.

Silence on Page's end. Then he said, "You complain about three, now you offer me four?"

"Is it a deal or not?"

"Look. There's no cute stuff here, is there? I don't do illegal."

"No. Perfectly legal."

"Perfectly legal but you want it done at night?"

"That's right. I have my reasons and you don't need to know them. Is it a deal or not?"

"Forty-five hundred and it's a deal."

Charles turned red and clenched his teeth. "Deal."

"Okay. Give me directions."

"Do you have any advertising or identifying marking on your vehicle?"

"No."

"Then pick me up at my house. It's not far to the search area. You can drop me off when we're done and I'll pay you."

"You'll pay me up front … cash. Then I'll drop you off when I'm done."

Charles clenched his teeth again. "Alright … alright. Here're the directions."

CHAPTER

TWENTY-TWO

Will wasn't happy about the nine a.m. appointment with H. Dallas Fitzhugh but it was the best he could do. He was not a morning person and it meant that he would have to be on the road by five.

Karen, on the other hand, was the type that befuddled the matutinally challenged. As soon as her feet hit the floor she was coherent and happy, and all before any kind of caffeine fix.

This morning was different. Will spotted it right away. She was so positive and upbeat all of the time that even a slight deviation from the status quo stood out like an Amish buggy at a Corvette convention. As Will pulled out of Keith Holtzman's driveway, he told her to fasten her seatbelt, then asked if she felt okay.

"Yeah. I guess."

"That's not very convincing."

"Just contemplating love and life."

"In that order?"

"Yeah."

"That doesn't bring someone down most of the time."

"Well, I've taken some knocks in the love department."

"I'll listen if you talk."

"You're a nice guy."

"I am indeed."

That produced Karen's first smile of the morning. "Do you remember I told you I was almost married?"

"I do. No pun intended."

Second smile of the morning. Karen sipped tea from her travel mug. "Well, that doesn't begin to tell the story. My heart was so broken I thought I'd never recover and I'm not sure I have. That's why I moved back east."

"Go on."

"We had talked to the preacher and set a date. I had bought my gown. The invitations were sent. Reservations were made. Everything was in place. Then out of the blue he announced it was all off, he was in love with someone else."

"Just like that? You didn't see it coming?"

"No, I didn't."

"I'm sorry, Karen. That's a lousy deal. But it looks like you recovered. I mean, I don't know anybody more good-natured and well-adjusted than you."

"Recovered? I don't know. It took me a long time to get over it. Every once in a while I remember the pain. I then ask myself if it was my fault and what I did wrong. Then I start feeling bad. I'm afraid it left scars. I'm a little punchy about relationships now."

"Perfectly normal."

"Maybe. But how do I get myself straight? I mean straight enough to at least let my guard down a little."

"Objectively evaluate the situation you were in and tell yourself the truth. If you do, I think you'll see it was the fault of no one person."

"I'm not sure I'm prepared to hear it wasn't all his fault. But I'll try that. Right now I'm scared. I sometimes think the only way to avoid getting hurt again would be to just give up and forget about ever getting involved in a relationship."

"Well, that would do it. But why mow down the flowers with the weeds?" Will asked.

"Then how do I get comfortable in a loving relationship again?"

"Gain the knowledge of what a relationship is and what it is not, and what you can reasonably expect from it. Knowledge is the key."

"That all sounds so ... practical. Where's the romance?"

"Romance is a choice, not an automatic occurrence."

"Did you take psychology courses in college, Will?" Karen asked, somewhat taken aback by Will's insight.

"No. I'm just a student of the human condition. I've had a lot of time to observe the mistakes made by my friends and family in their relationships and I'll tell you this. Most people don't have a clue. I see them making mistake on top of mistake. Am I someone with special skills? No. I'm just a keen observer with an interest in the outcome."

"Well then, what happened in my situation?"

"I don't know. I don't know him and I've never seen you together. Apparently something wasn't right, though. I suspect neither of you took a good look at the other before you committed. What's his name by the way?"

"His name is, and now and forever will be, Ex."

Will laughed. "Well, maybe you and Ex didn't take the time to talk about what you expected from each other in a relationship, or what you wanted from life in general."

"No. We didn't. But we *were* attracted to each other."

"Physical attraction is important, but it's not enough. There *is* a practical side to love. A lot of time people will put more thought into buying a refrigerator than selecting a mate. Did you take the time to look at what kind of person Ex really was?"

"I thought I did. But obviously I didn't. I remember noticing we were opposite in a lot of things. And since opposites attract I thought that was okay. "

"Look, opposites attract is a clichéd myth. That's a perfect example of how just one misguided perception can get you into trouble. Opposites attract only for those looking for a temporary buzz, and it's usually just that—temporary. It's shallow if not down-right neurotic. If you build a life together on oppositions you end up with an adversarial relationship.

"Wanting the same things, having the same value system, feeling the same way about situations and events, and agreeing on how you as a couple should go about the business of conducting life will last forever. The three A's of a successful relationship are … agreement, agreement, agreement."

"Wouldn't that get kind of boring?"

"Another myth. You don't have to be in total locked-step in all things all the time, although that wouldn't hurt. But you should be basically the same kind of person. Two people contemplating a life together had better be moral equivalents or they're in for some hard times, if it works out at all. It's much easier to commit to a friend than an adversary. And if you're committed …"

"If you're committed you won't allow things to become boring," Karen finished Will's point.

"Exactly. The giving and taking of affection with a person you're committed to can't be boring."

"Did you ever wonder how things get so convoluted?" she asked.

"You mean other than listening to the convoluted information that's out there?"

"Yes."

"That's easy. Because sex is fun. Couples want to hear the song before they drop in the quarter. With just a superficial at-traction they'll hop in the sack. Then they're hooked on the sex and all they have is the *hope* things work out. Other than the physical, all too often the relationship is empty. Then they try to force it. It's like trying to build a house on a foundation of spaghetti."

Karen said, "You don't think sex is important … ? Wait! Don't answer that. I think I see how your mind is working here. Sex *is* important but only as part of the total relationship."

"You don't agree with that?" Will asked.

"I don't disagree with that. But there must be more out of whack than having sex too soon."

"That's a big part of it. But like I said, bad information. Much of what you hear about relationships is total nonsense. Instead of looking deeper with independent thought, *independent* thought, many people just accept what they hear from a variety of unqualified sources. Just because your Aunt Myrtle, or a clever TV commercial, or the afternoon soaps espouse a concept, it doesn't make it so."

"I don't have an Aunt Myrtle. So you're saying failed relationships are the fault of TV shows?" Karen asked.

"I'm saying opinions are formed from what's in the mass media in general, and *their* main objective is to sell … and titillation sells. They'll do what they feel they have to do to get the job done. It's all about ratings or how many books and magazines they can sell. Do you think they care anything about the social responsibility of getting it right? Bottom line is: for the most part the mass media is a lousy source for the truths of life."

"Not sure I agree with that. You may be right about the media's bottom line, but I, the consumer, feel I can separate reality from fiction."

"I'm sure you can … that's their argument, by the way. But they're very provocative in their presentation. It has a negative underlying effect on the human brain. If it's suggested to you from day one that all relationships live happily ever after without any more input than having rock-hard abs, then you'll give that credence whether you think you do or not. It fosters unrealistic expectations and distorts reality and *that* can cause problems. And nobody's exempt. Being aware of this, I still catch myself falling prey from time to time. The reality is relationships take input."

"Well, the media isn't going away. So what do you do?"

"You learn how to winnow."

"What?"

"You teach yourself how to separate the wheat from the chaff. You gain the knowledge necessary to make an informed decision so at least you give the thing a fighting chance. Most problems could be avoided by selecting the right person, and you can't magically make someone the right person like many try to do."

"And that's supposed to give you guarantees?"

"No. You know better. Relationships are a risk under the best of circumstances, but you *can* improve your odds with an intelligent selection process. Then the real work begins. After you get married. It doesn't end there. You would be surprised at the number of people who think marital bliss is automatic. It's not."

"Yeah. And at the end of the day you meet someone who just knocks your socks off and you fall head over heels in love even though the knowledge you took the time to gain says it's all wrong," Karen replied.

"Yet another myth. There is no Cupid who shoots an arrow into our butt cheeks rendering us incapable of rational thought. People choose who they'll love. Believe that if nothing else. Anyone choosing a relationship that their little voice, the subconscious, is telling them is wrong has deeper issues. Stop and think about it, Karen. Remove the love factor for a minute. No one would choose a friend or a business partner who is so diametrically opposite that nothing but friction exists between them, unless of course they have a neurosis."

"What do you have to back up your theories?" Karen asked, playing devil's advocate.

"Years of observing what makes one relationship work and another one fail. Reading what the people in the know have to say. And my own personal experiences with affairs of the heart.

"That's it?"

"Yes. But if you need something more concrete, look at the Amish community, where there's virtually no divorce. Why? They *choose* to love their spouse … not just tolerate them, but love them. They want the same things from life and agree on how to get it. And in the absence of the mass media they don't have a distorted view of the reality of a relationship.

"Granted, their fundamental belief system enters into it and that's fairly consistent throughout their community. But compare them to the non-Amish and tell me who has it right. This may be an oversimplified example, but it has merit. And it's more than just theory. I think it's common sense."

"But you can't just switch to being Amish."

"No. But we can learn from them."

"I guess." Karen thought a second and then said, "Apply *your* romantic affairs to what you're saying."

"Sure. I went with a woman for several months and we hit it off quite well. After a while it came out she didn't believe in God. I do. Two diametrically opposed positions that could have seeped into every aspect of a life together. She was a good person, but we were not moral equivalents. That doesn't mean she's immoral and I'm a saint. It's just a completely different belief system and the ramifications of that could have been disastrous. So even though I thought everything else was in order, I broke it off. And it broke my heart to do it, by the way."

"And you didn't wait until you were halfway down the aisle like Ex did."

"No. Anybody paying attention would never let it get that far."

"You don't think I was paying attention?"

"No, I don't think you were."

"Did you break them *all* off?" Karen pressed.

"Of course not. Even though a lot of people are clueless about relationships, many aren't. I always respected their decision to end it, my ego notwithstanding. The lesson here is it has to be right for both people or it's no good for either."

"Will you give me an example of that ... I mean when *they* broke it off?"

"I was very fond of a vegetarian and I had high hopes for the relationship. I'm not a vegetarian so she tried to convert me. When she saw she couldn't, she broke it off. Said she couldn't live with someone who ate meat. I had no problem with her eating whatever she wanted and I thought it was a trivial reason to end a good relationship. But she was right. It was important to her, so it was no good for either of us."

"What you say *does* make sense, Will. But what do I do about these funks that befall me every so often? They're a result of the past and I can't control the past."

"No, but you can understand the past. The funks will go away in time. You'll be okay. You're too sane not to be."

"I hope you're right."

"A good friend of mine, the wisest person I know in his own way, has a knack for reducing things to their lowest common denominator. About love and marriage he has a saying, 'Don't worry about it, there's a lid for every pot.' I think he's right. Somewhere out there is a lid just right for you. You'll love again."

"Speaking of which, you still haven't address the big one."

"What's the big one?"

"What *is* love?"

Will thought a long moment, then answered, "Haven't got a clue."

Laughing, Karen said, "All that and you don't have a clue!"

"I described what I think goes wrong, and what it takes to make it work, not what it *is*."

"Give it your best shot."

"You mean romantic love?"

"You know what I mean."

"Okay. I think it's physical, spiritual, biological, and delusional.

Physical, because it's sexual and affectionate. Spiritual, because I don't believe it exists without the existence of a Supreme Being. Biological, because of our inherent need to procreate. And delusional, because humans are eternally optimistic about it."

Still laughing, Karen said, "Wow! Are you always this philosophical in the morning? I didn't know you were this deep. I've never heard anybody say these things."

"Yeah, well, maybe you bring out the best in me."

"Readjusting her body toward Will, Karen asked, "And what about you and me?"

"What? What about you and me?"

"Do you think we want the same things and are moral equivalents?"

Surprised by the blunt question, Will faltered. "Ah ... I think you've probably formed an opinion about that already."

"I know what *I* think. I'm asking you what *you* think."

"Did I mention that a couple should be intellectual equivalents as well?"

"You're evading the question, Rhone."

Squirming in his seat, Will said, "I think ... I think "

"Will, have you developed a speech impediment?"

"I think ... so far so good," he managed to get out.

"See. There's one thing we agree on already."

Karen settled back in her seat. Will had somehow made her feel good about herself and she wouldn't forget that.

Will was just glad to hear Karen laugh again. He noticed it before. He loved to hear her laugh. "Now, will you please fasten your seatbelt?" he said.

***

Will drove by the center city office of MAAC and looked for a parking spot. Karen noticed they had their own underground parking garage. She read the sign aloud: "MAAC EMPLOYEES AND VISITORS ONLY."

"That sounds like us," Will said. He stopped at the guard station. "We have an appointment with Mr. Fitzhugh at nine."

A uniformed attendant holding a clipboard said, "Yes, sir. Fifth floor," then made a few pencil strokes on the board and added, "Sir, when you park please roll up your windows and lock your doors. Be sure to turn off your headlights. You'll need to check out when you leave. Elevators are to the right."

Karen read the directory by the elevator. "H. Dallas Fitzhugh – 5th Floor."

The elevator doors opened to a spacious circular room with a round receptionist's station in the center. In the station a well-dressed man and woman busied themselves answering the phones and typing on their keyboards. A large wooden plaque hanging over their heads proclaimed: *So neither he who plants nor he who waters is anything, but only God, who makes things grow.* – 1 Corinthians 3: 7.

The layout of the area gave the visitor the impression he was in the center of a hub. Will and Karen didn't walk to the receptionist's station immediately. They were fascinated by what was between the half dozen doors equally spaced around the perimeter of the room. From floor to ceiling, glass enclosures held shelves of farm and agricultural scenes in miniature. Arranged chronologically, from breaking the earth with a rock lashed to a stick to the latest super-tractors, the miniatures told the story of farming in America.

"Look at this, Will. I've never seen anything like this."

"And I doubt if you ever will."

"Aah … look at the little farmers in their tiny bib overalls, they're so cute," a delighted Karen said.

"I like the old hay baler."

"This is amazing. Can you imagine the time it took to do this?"

"No, I can't. Some of these pieces have to be handmade. I mean, where would one buy a miniature antique manure spreader?"

"Maybe we can look more later. It's almost nine o'clock." Karen led Will by the arm to the round reception area. "Hi. We have an appointment with Mr. Fitzhugh at nine—Will and Karen."

Pointing to the door that read "H. Dallas Fitzhugh" the male receptionist said, "Yes. Through that door, please. Mr. Fitzhugh will be with you shortly."

They followed the receptionist's instructions.

"Hi. Are you Mr. Fitzhugh's nine o'clock?" asked the secretary behind the desk in the small office-waiting room.

"Yes."

"Please have a seat. Can I get you a coffee or tea?"

"No, thank you. We're good," Will answered for both.

As Will and Karen sat down, a somewhat disheveled man in his mid-fifties entered from the reception area. He carried a brief-case and a stainless-steel travel mug with the words "Grandpa's Coffee" on the side. He held the Wall Street Journal under the same arm. From the way the secretary bristled with his entrance the two visitors knew this was H. Dallas Fitzhugh.

"Sorry I'm late, Doris. That construction on the Sure-Kill is getting more impossible every day." The Sure-Kill was the name its edgy travelers dubbed the Schuylkill Expressway, one of the busy main arteries to center-city Philadelphia. Turning to Will and Karen, Fitzhugh smiled. "Hi. I'm H. Dallas Fitzhugh. You're the mysterious Will and Karen, I presume? Can we get you anything?"

"No, thanks," they said in unison.

"Well, then ... c'mon in and take a seat."

The three entered an office with a large window and panoramic view of downtown Philadelphia. Fitzhugh removed his sports jacket, revealing a plaid shirt with tie and suspenders. He hung the jacket on a clothes tree and asked, "What do you think of my History of Farming in America diorama?"

Will answered, "It's magnificent!"

"How long did it take you to do it, Mr. Fitzhugh?" Karen asked.

"My whole life. I just keep adding things. When I run out of space I'll just buy a bigger office building," he said tongue in cheek. "And it's Dal, by the way. Call me Dal."

"Are you from Dallas?" Karen followed.

"Oh no. I was born right up here in Bucks County."

"Seems like an unusual name for a Northeasterner," Will commented.

Fitzhugh explained, "My Dad was a dreamer. He dreamed of traveling the world and visiting exotic cities. I mean, his idea of an exciting Saturday night was reading a travel brochure on Katmandu. But he was also a realist. He knew with a big family to feed and a farm to keep up and running he would never get to all the places he wanted to. So he named his kids after his favorite destinations. I have three sisters, Havana, Paris, and Miami, and four brothers, London, Zurich, Denver, and Sidney. We were always thankful he never wanted to go to Intercourse, P-A." He paused. "Sorry ... family joke."

Karen giggled.

Smiling, Will asked, "What's the H for?"

"Houston. Guess he figured while he was in Texas he might as well hit both places."

"Or maybe he thought he'd run out of kids to name before he saw everything."

Fitzhugh laughed. "Good one. I'll have to remember that one at the family reunion. You're all right, Will."

Two light taps on the door were followed by Doris entering and handing Dal Fitzhugh a folded piece of paper, which he glanced at quickly.

"Thanks, Doris," he said as she exited. "Okay. Let's get right to it. In most cases I wouldn't meet with anybody not willing to give their last names. But you said the magic words: 'We have a business proposition for you.' I'm intrigued. Let's hear it."

Karen said, "First of all, please excuse our vagueness. But I think that, as Will explains, you—as a businessman—will understand. Will."

"Dal, if we can come to an agreement, we all stand to make a lot of money. The 'we' are Karen here, my grandfather Mel, and myself. We have reason to believe there's a valuable treasure buried on your property ... and we know what it is and where it is. We've done our homework on you and we know that for you to reach the level of success that you have, you had to be a risk taker. We're asking you to take a chance on us."

"How valuable ... the treasure ... what's it worth?"

"In the millions."

Fitzhugh flinched. "Go on."

"Well, our intentions are to do this right and legal like. If we can form a partnership first, we will be as up front and honest with you as any business partner would be."

Dal said, "But any business partnership has a foundation built on trust. Why the need for mystery here?"

"It's complicated. That's why we need your help. Together we can be strong and totally legal. Apart, we become adversaries for sure."

"And you're sure this treasure is buried on MAAC land?"

"Yes."

"And that's all you're going to tell me?"

"Yes. For now."

"You're not giving me much to base an intelligent decision on. I mean, look at it from my perspective. Two strangers walk into my office and want me to agree to something without my knowing what the Sam Hill we're talking about."

"If we give you all the details now, you won't need us to recover the treasure. And that would break our hearts, since it's our families who put it there in the first place ... and for other personal reasons as well. Our only bargaining chip with you is the knowledge we have. And thank goodness that information is not widely known and would be difficult, if not impossible, to research by an outsider. It's as simple as that."

"I see. Well, that's an honest answer."

"We're taking a big chance here, Dal. Much more of a chance than you'll need to take. It's because of your reputation as a square-shooter that we're approaching you."

"And how would we form this partnership?"

"Through a legally binding contract. Our attorneys can work out the details."

"And you want no up-front money or anything else from me?"

"That's right. The only thing you're agreeing to is to be on our side when it comes time to recover the treasure and through any possible repercussions after we do."

"Repercussions? Interesting. Tell me about that."

"Others may ... no, others most likely *will* claim the treasure."

"I see. And what if there is no treasure?"

"Then nothing, or very little, is lost on your end."

"And recovering the treasure will have minimal impact to the land?"

"Yes."

"What's the split?"

"Eighty-twenty, our favor."

"And my twenty percent is still in the millions, you say?"

"That's right."

"Jumpin' Sam Hill! That's some treasure." Dal Fitzhugh sat back in his chair and rubbed his chin. "If I agree to this, I'll warn you both right now: I have the finest team of attorneys money can hire. You can't scam us. We'll catch you in any double-dealings."

"There'll be no double-dealings. Once we recover the treasure there'll be enough to worry about without worrying about each other. We must stay united in purpose."

"Good." Dal looked at the piece of paper Doris delivered.

"Now let me show you a little of what Dal Fitzhugh can do. As-suming you are the owner of the truck you drove here, your name is William Rhone and you live in RD Gratz, Pennsylvania. You are thirty-five years old; never married, never arrested, have an excellent credit rating, and are the owner and operator of Rhone's Woodworld, also in RD Gratz, and have the reputation of being an exceptional craftsman. Your father was William Senior, deceased, and your grandfather is Melchoir Rhone, presumably the Mel you mentioned. Pretty good for short notice. Say not?"

Karen and Will looked at each other. Chagrinned, Will an-swered, "Pretty darn good."

"Now it's your turn for understanding. Don't ask me how I know all this because I won't tell you. In my business I have to know who I'm dealing with. I have a lot of enemies. If it makes you feel any better, Karen, I have no idea who you are."

"Holtzman. Karen Holtzman," she said, seeing no point in hiding it now.

"If I can continue our little exploratory journey into the mind of Dal Fitzhugh, I'm guessing the treasure you speak of is buried on one of five possible tracts of land MAAC owns in your area. One is just outside of Harrisburg, one is near Halifax—so I'll eliminate those. That leaves the Killinger tract, the Van Norman tract, and the Henry tract. Total acreage of the three is seven hun-dred sixty-five, give or take a square yard or two. " He paused, then added, "You look surprised. Don't be. I'm a personal friend of every acre of land MAAC owns. I have to be."

"That's still a lot of land to search for treasure on, if you have no idea where it is or what you're looking for."

"Yes, it is. Don't get defensive, Will. I'm not trying to under-cut you here. I can tell by this information you are not a couple of shysters and are probably telling me the truth. I decided ten min-utes ago to accept your offer. I'd be a fool not to. But please. Tell me more about this. I'm intrigued."

"Sorry, Dal. You'll know everything eventually. But for now I'm going to follow the advice of our attorney." From Dal Fitzhugh's frown, Will guessed he was a man used to getting his own way.

"I'm going to need your contact information. You have a local attorney?" Fitzhugh asked.

"Yes. Al Marcus. We'll give you all our contact info before we leave."

"Al Marcus? That's not *the* Al Marcus, is it? ... formerly of Strawbridge Marcus Reinholdt here in the city?"

"I didn't know he was a *the*, but yes, that's him," Karen answered.

"Well, I'll be. So that's what happened to him. The famous Al Marcus. Good. I love working with the best."

Will said, "There is something else we would like to—"

"Will, I'm not sure Al would want us mentioning that right now." Karen stopped his mentioning the memorial just in time.

"No, I guess not. We'll talk about that later," Will said, surprised she had read his mind.

"Well, if you're not going to tell me more, I guess we're finished. You can swap contact info with Doris. Let's see what our lawyers can come up with."

"Thank you, Dal. After meeting you I feel better about this partnership."

"We'll be fine, Will. This sure is fun. I haven't been this excited since the hogs ate my pet frog. Tore poor old Jeremiah limb from limb, they did."

"Oh ... that's awful," Karen said.

"Are you going to tell us you wrote a song about him?" Will asked.

"Fitzhugh thought a moment, then laughed. "Another good one, Will. Nah, that wasn't my Jeremiah." He escorted Will and Karen to the door. Motioning with a pointed finger back and forth between himself and Will and Karen he said, "Doris, contact info," then added, "Give them each a bag of the toasted alfalfa sprouts for the road. One of MAAC's many experiments. See what you guys think of them."

Everyone said his or her good-byes and Will and Karen spent the next half hour absorbed in Fitzhugh's diorama before departing the building.

As Will maneuvered out of the city, Karen munched on the alfalfa sprouts. "These are good, Will. Do you want some?"

"Not right now."

"I can't believe he agreed to an eighty-twenty split. You're a good negotiator."

"He has nothing to lose, really. I have to admit, it was easier than I thought it would be. I almost blew it, though, by mentioning the memorial. Thanks for stopping me. Can you read my mind now?"

"Sure can," Karen replied.

"Well, good. Then you know when you're finished with your munchies I want you to give Grandpa a call and tell him the good news. Tell him we should meet with Al right away."

***

Will was healing. Since his grandmother's death a day had not passed that he didn't think of her. It affected him in all things. But after the meeting with Dallas Fitzhugh he felt more like the self-confident optimistic Will of old than at anytime since she died. He was experiencing a renewed clarity of thought. He had felt certain if he presented Fitzhugh with an everything-to-gain and nothing-to-lose scenario, he couldn't say no. Holding his own with the astute Fitzhugh felt good.

CHAPTER

TWENTY-THREE

When Al Marcus arrived at Mel's house, Will told him how Fitzhugh discovered the information about Will in less than a half hour. Also that Fitzhugh had accurately narrowed down the location of the treasure to three possible sites, the Henry tract being one of them. "He's sharp. I'll tell you that," Will added. "It's up to you now, Al."

"Ya done good," Al said to Will and Karen.

"Yeah. We should've gone for a ninety-ten split, I guess," Will said.

"No, you shouldn't have. First rule of negotiating … don't get greedy, it's give and take. You made the pot just sweet enough, so leave it at that. I'll contact the MAAC attorneys so we can feel each other out to get things started. I won't bore you with the details, but basically we'll go back and forth until we find a mutual comfort zone. Then we'll draw up a contract both sides can live with."

"Will you have to tell them a court petition will be involved before we dig?" Mel asked.

"Yes. But I don't have to mention it's for digging up a grave. They may deduce that, but again they won't know the exact location. I'll mention in the contract that telling details about the location of the treasure will not be disclosed until the contract is signed. Also, I'll assure them that said details are not in contradiction to the good faith of the contract."

"And they'll agree to that?" Karen asked.

"They should. I'll add a clause that gives them an out if they are not informed of all details to their satisfaction. Our job will be to see to it that they are informed to their satisfaction."

"I'm getting nervous, Al. How long is all this going to take?" Mel asked.

"I don't know. I'll inform MAAC that time is of the essence. After we all sign the contract I'll file the petition as soon as I can. Then, the wheels of justice turn slowly, as you know. It'll be my job to try and move it along. I have some options I can try. As soon as MAAC signs I'll talk to them about hiring around-the-clock security for the grave. Until then we'll just have to take a chance and leave it unguarded."

"Why wait?" Mel asked.

"We don't want to show them where the treasure is before we have their John Hancock, and guards would attract attention."

"We should have a plan before we go to court, shouldn't we?" Will asked.

"Oh yeah. We'll be well prepared. That's my job too."

"What are our chances of getting court approval … realistically?" a nervous Karen asked.

"Better than fifty-fifty, I'd say. There was a crime committed by someone pursuing the same treasure, and you're the victims. We'll have the landowner on board, and Mel and Will are descendants of the person buried in the grave in question. Plus, we're approaching the court with clean hands. All things in our favor. I'm optimistic."

"Then as soon as we get approval we can dig?" Karen asked.

"Yes. But we'll need a plan for that too. Certainly, we should be there, MAAC should be there, the police should be there, and maybe the judge will want the court represented. Plus we need a plan for what to do with this stuff when we get it. We'll need to get it in a secure location immediately." Al looked at the three concerned expressions facing him. "Well, don't look so glum. See?" Al pointed to his mouth. "Al Marcus is smiling … that's a good thing."

✳✳✳

The morning after the meeting with Al, Karen sat on her brother's porch steps staring at the unopened letter from Terryville School District. Four months ago she would have ripped it open before she closed the mailbox. She was feeling the strain of recent events. Months of work on the treasure now hinging on a signed contract and a court petition. Success for both looked good but there were no guarantees. The thought of someone beating them to the treasure made her anxious. Now this. She didn't want to face the decision to leave or stay. More accurately she couldn't accept the thought of leaving. She loosened the flap and removed the letter. After seeing the first word she returned the letter to the envelope without reading the rest.

"Congratulations …"

The weighty dilemma tired her and she did something she rarely did. Returned to bed in the middle of the morning. When she awoke for the second time that day it was early afternoon. She would do what had proved helpful in the past when she had thinking to do. Drive. Just drive to nowhere in particular. There was no shortage of back roads to nowhere in central Pennsylvania. She would get lost and like it.

"Maddy, I'm going for a ride. Don't know when I'll be back," she announced as she left the house.

After two hours of driving Karen was no closer to a decision to accept or reject the job offer on Long Island than when she had departed. *This shouldn't be that tough.* But she did feel better. The scenic rural landscape was therapeutic.

She didn't know exactly where she was but figured it must be somewhere in western Schuylkill County. She would try now to become un-lost, the sun sinking west. She saw someone ahead walking around an SUV. *I'll ask directions.* She slowed as she approached and then gunned the accelerator when she recognized Charles Holtzman. As she passed they looked each other in the eye. *He saw me.* As she watched Charles in the mirror, he stood watching her put distance between them. *What if he needs help? I can't do this.* She turned around, parked behind his vehicle, and walked toward her cousin.

"Karen. I thought that was you."

"Are you broke down, Charles?"

"No."

Karen then noticed the reason he was miles from nowhere. There were two black plastic bags of what looked liked garbage thrown in the underbrush beside the road and two more where they came from in the back of Charles's vehicle.

"Oh, I see. Just littering."

"Why pay a garbage man if I don't have to? You aren't going to report me, are you?"

Karen didn't respond. Then the idea struck her. *Since I'm here …*

"Charles. I'd like to ask you again as nicely as I can … blood to blood, if you like. Can I see what's in the trunk Grandma Holtzman gave you?"

"Must we go through that again? I told you before, just old stuff. Nothing you would be interested in."

"Wouldn't be interested?! It's my family too, Charles. Why don't you let me decide what I'd be interested in?"

"Yeah, well, maybe someday. Grab the end of the bag."

"I'm not helping you litter," Karen said as she glanced in Charles's vehicle. She noticed an electronic device lying on the passenger seat that could have been a receiver. Charles saw her looking.

Dragging the garbage bag by the tied end and supported by his Irish shillelagh, Charles flung the bag into the bushes. It landed on top of one of the bags he had already thrown there and busted open, spilling some of the contents.

What Karen saw next made her face flush and the hair on the back of her neck stand on end. She was shaken. *Missing hat … sample from a vendor … one of a kind,* raced through her memory. Again, Charles noticed.

"Rhone's Woodworld. So Will give you one of his shop hats?" she baited him.

"Yeah … yeah, I ran into him one day and he gave me one. I spilled something on it so I'm pitching it," Charles lied.

Socks Smith had thrown the hat in the box with the receiver on the day he swept his apartment clean and made a hasty retreat from the area. When Charles retrieved the receiver from Lebo's Storage, he threw the hat in is vehicle and later in the garbage.

Karen fought to remain calm and keep her voice steady. Charles wasn't fooled.

"Well, I must be going, Charles. I'll talk to you later." She moved toward her car and was about halfway to escaping when the report of Charles's pistol stopped her in her tracks.

"Leaving so soon, Karen? Why, I was just starting to enjoy your company. Tell me. What was it?"

"What was what?"

"What gave me away? The receiver? Or was it the hat? That idiot Socks!"

"I don't know what you're talking about."

"So now Charles is stupid. Is that what you're saying? You always did have an expressive face."

"So what are you going to do, Charles? Shoot me? Kill your own flesh and blood?"

"The thought occurred to me. But no. I have something more exciting in mind. Get in," Charles said, motioning to his vehicle.

"I'm not going anywhere with you."

Charles leveled the pistol slightly above Karen's head and pulled the trigger. Karen jumped and held her ears.

"Loud, isn't it?" Charles laughed. "Bet it makes a big hole, too. You wanted to see the contents of the trunk ... well; you're looking at one of the items. World War II vintage M1911A1 Colt .45 caliber semi-automatic, mint condition. Must have been our Grandpa Holtzman's. I'll either shoot you dead right here, Karen, or you can get in the vehicle. Your choice."

Karen considered her options.

"Don't look around. Nobody pays any attention to gunshots this far out in the sticks. Oh, and if you're thinking of running, I should tell you I've been practicing with this. I won't miss."

He's crazy. He'd do it. At gunpoint Karen walked toward her cousin's Toyota 4-Runner.

"Front," Charles motioned with the pistol. "Sit on the floor with your feet on the seat, your back facing forward. We wouldn't want anyone to see us together, would we? And I'll shoot you quick if you even think of reaching for the door."

Karen did as instructed. She stared at Charles as he drove. "How could you do it, Charles—kill an innocent woman; beat up an old man?"

"I'm afraid we'll have to blame that one on my accomplice. I told him not to hurt anyone."

"Well, aren't you noble. You know Mel would have worked with you. All you would've had to do was ask."

"I'm no good at sharing. You know that."

"You'll never get away with this, Charles. This can't end well for you. The police already suspect you."

"Shut up! The police have no idea I'm involved. You and your cronies suspect me, I heard you say it. The police don't."

"How do you—"

"Shut up! You always did have a big mouth. Don't say another word." Charles drove to his home and parked in front with the passenger door adjacent to his entrance walkway. "Don't move," he instructed Karen as he got out and walked around his vehicle. He looked around, then opened the passenger door. "Get out and get into the house quick. Stay low," he added, keeping the pistol trained on her. As they entered the house he yelled, "Socks! Get out here!"

Karen looked up at the man she had last seen in Riverfront Park.

"Socks, Karen. Karen, Socks. Oops, that's right. You two have already met," Charles chided.

"Well, well. If it isn't the attack dog's best friend. What's she doing here?" Smith said.

"She's here thanks to you and that stupid hat you stole. Now duct tape her to the chair and don't ask questions. We go tonight."

"Tonight? Thought you said there was too much moon until later in the week."

"Well, things have changed now, haven't they?"

"What are we going to do with her?"

"She's going to help you dig. Then … we'll see."

"Maybe she can entertain us while we wait till it's dark enough." Socks eyed Karen offensively.

"Knock it off. Just get the equipment loaded in your van. In *back* of the house, Socks."

Karen regarded her situation. She wished she had given Maddy a time she would return. There were no plans made with Will for the evening, so he wouldn't be expecting her either. *I won't be missed for hours.* She couldn't see Charles and his friend just turning her loose. *They'll kill me for sure.* Forced to confront her own mortality she felt things she had never felt before. Her emotions ran the gamut from rage to self-pity. *I'll never see another sunrise.* She had to find a way to escape. She would not give up. *My only weapon is my brain. Think.*

She recalled movies and TV shows when someone in her situation pitted one captor against the other. She wondered if it really worked. *It's worth a shot.* "How well do you know this guy, Charles?"

"Good enough."

"You must really trust him."

"No, I don't trust him as far as I can drop-kick him."

"Then he *could* turn on you."

"He's not that bright. But that's for me to worry about. Keep your mouth shut or I'll tape it shut."

Divide and conquer isn't going to be easy with Charles. Let's hope he's right and Socks isn't that smart. "Just tell me one thing, Charles. How did you ever know about the treasure in the first place?"

"I guess telling you that doesn't matter much now. Thank dear old Grandma Holtzman for that one. Didn't it ever occur to you that the reason I wouldn't show you the trunk is because it contained things I didn't want you to see?"

"No, it didn't. I thought you were just being your usual self … a colossal jerk."

"Yeah, right. Who's the jerk now?" Charles said as he tore a six-inch piece of duct tape from the roll and stuck it over Karen's mouth.

✳✳✳

"Just like we rehearsed, Socks. Turn off your lights and use the outline of the trees against the sky to keep you on the road," Charles said as Socks Smith turned off T-231.

Driving to the grave site with no headlights was not the only thing Charles and Socks had rehearsed. They had gone through several dry runs, which included finding an escape route should the road back to T-231 be blocked by anyone for any reason. They found they could access Mountain Road to the north by using several interconnecting farm roads. They had also experimented with hiding their digging activities at the site by parking Socks's van between the grave and T-231. They hid the van by covering it with a large camouflaged tarp that would also enable them to use small flashlights should they be needed. They discovered by doing this they could not be seen from T-231, even with binoculars. The waist-high corn helped.

Leland Page—the man with the metal detector Charles had hired—said he was getting a strong reading about four feet deep over the grave of Magdalena Rhone. They calculated that one man could dig a hole six feet long by four feet wide by five feet deep through the loose, plowed ground in about eight hours. Given the approximate eight hours of darkness in central Pennsylvania in July, they figured it would be close but they could make it. Now, with the help of another digger, they were sure of it.

"I want you to hobble her with that rope in the back."

"Hobble her?" Socks asked.

"Yeah. Tie a length of rope around her ankles just long enough so she can use her feet to dig but not long enough so she can run. And tie it tight." Charles ripped the duct tape from Karen's mouth.

"Ouch! You have such a nice, gentle touch with the ladies, Charles."

"Watch your mouth or I'll put it back."

With Karen hobbled, Socks and Charles draped the tarp over the van. Charles then handed a pointed, long-handled garden shovel to Karen. "I have a pick if you need it."

"We're not going to run into any skeletons, are we?" Socks asked.

"How should I know? Just start digging." Charles thrust a shovel at him.

"Forget it. I'm not helping you dig," Karen announced.

"Oh. The lady's in charge now. Knock it off, Karen. Who are you kidding? You're just as anxious to see what's down there as I am," Charles said. "Now dig and you won't get hurt. You too, Socks. Let's get moving. So much treasure and so little time and all that ... let's go."

Karen had to concede he was right. Even in her dire straits the thought of her being this close to finding the coins excited her. She was angry at herself for the thought. In a low voice, she started working on Socks as Charles busied himself at the back of the van.

"You know, you seem like an okay guy. Why would you want to be involved with the likes of Charles?"

"Who said I wanted to be? It's a business deal, that's all. I can't stand him."

"Do you really think he is going to let either one of us just walk away from this?" When Socks didn't respond she added, "It's too late for him but there's hope for you. Think about it."

"I have been thinking about it. How do you know I don't have a plan of my own?"

"I hope you—"

"A little less mouth and a lot more shovel over there ... let's go," Charles yelled.

Karen noticed she could nick the rope that bound her feet with the tip of the shovel as she slammed it down to get the next scoop of dirt. She had to be careful to execute the motion naturally so as not to draw attention to herself. The nylon rope was tough and she couldn't see if she was hitting the same spot each time, but she continued the routine of scoop, throw, and stab. If she could cut the rope she was certain she could outrun Socks to the hollow at the far side of the field and disappear into the thick brush and darkness.

She continued to drive the wedge between Charles and Socks deeper. "Look at him up there. We do all the work and he gets the treasure. Why do you put up with that?" Karen was careful to whisper. "Why don't you and I split it? We could team up and walk away with all of it. You're not such a bad-looking guy."

"Yeah. Like someone like you would have anything to do with someone like me. Do you think I'm that naïve?"

otield?

"Don't sell yourself short. What's wrong with doing the right thing and turning yourself in."

"Never. I'm never going back to prison. I told you I have a plan. Just be quiet and watch."

After over two hours of digging Socks and Karen had reached a depth of almost two feet. Charles retrieved from the van the VLF metal detector he had bought.

"Look out. This thing will detect up to a foot deep," he said as he scanned the bottom of the hole. "Nothing yet. Keep digging."

"How about a break and a drink of water?" Karen asked.

Charles threw her a liter of bottled water. "You got five minutes."

Blisters were forming on Karen's hands and her back hurt. The thought of cutting through the rope and freedom kept her going. After every shovelful of dirt she threw from the hole she still stabbed at the nylon rope. She noticed some fraying but the rope continued to hold tight.

Charles scanned the bottom of the hole every few inches. The metal detector remained silent.

Karen and Socks dug for over four hours. When Charles checked at the four-foot level it was after 2:00 a.m. The detector let out a beep.

"There! Did you hear that? We're getting close. Has to be less than a foot now. Keep digging," Charles prodded.

Another six inches of dirt were removed in record time, due in large part to an exhorting Charles. Karen's shovel struck first. The hollow *thud* brought all three to attention.

✳✳✳

Since 5:00 p.m. Will had been trying to contact Karen to tell her the good news. Al Marcus and Dal Fitzhugh's lawyers had come to an agreement on the terms of the treasure partnership. Thanks to facsimile technology it was a done deal. He also wanted to tell her that Detective Zimmerman had called earlier with the news that a DNA match had been found in the police databank and Socrates Smith was identified as the perpetrator. The detective felt certain that tracking him down was just a matter of time.

At 9:00 p.m. a worried Will told the Holtzmans to call as soon as she returned.

With no word from anyone, by midnight he was frantic. For her not to call if she would be late was so out of character that Will knew something was wrong. He called everyone he could think of that may have had knowledge of Karen's whereabouts, including all the area hospitals. When that failed he drove around looking for her. He knew it was a shot in the dark but he had to do something. He checked everywhere he knew she frequented and even places she didn't.

Karen had shown him where Charles Holtzman lived. He drove by but saw only his SUV parked at the unlit house. He then drove on T-231 to the cemetery site. Nothing unusual. Charles's camouflaged tarp had worked. He returned to Mel's house to see if he had heard anything from Karen or Keith and Maddy, though he was certain his grandfather would have contacted him by cell if he had. *Maybe I was in a dead spot.* Mel had no news and another call to Keith produced nothing.

Will called Detective Zimmerman to report Karen missing. When the duty officer informed him that the detective wasn't there, Will insisted that he pass on to him as soon as possible a message to call Will Rhone. He told the duty officer why it was urgent. The officer suggested Will give him all the information he could on Karen so he could get a "be on the lookout for" to all the troopers on duty. Will noted the time. Just after 1:00 a.m. He grabbed his cell phone and got back in his truck.

***

Karen and Socks took great care in removing the soil around the old stoneware jug. Charles lit the area with his flashlight. As they worked they uncovered the side of a second jug.

"Just work on one at a time. When you free it, hand it up," Charles ordered.

When all the dirt had been removed around the jug, Socks grabbed the handle to heave it out of the hole. With the full weight of the coins now on the deteriorating stoneware the handle broke off and the bottom fell out. All three stared at the mountain of Continental Dollars.

Charles began to holler and laugh at the same time. "I knew it! I knew it! I knew they were there! Give me some."

Socks handed him a handful of coins. As he studied them, Karen picked up one of the dollars. The weighty coin felt good in her hand.

"Look at the condition ... they're like new!" an animated Charles said. "I was worried about that."

"There's hundreds of them ... thousands. Where are we going to put them?" Socks asked.

"What do you think the duffels are for?" Charles had bought a dozen of the canvas duffel bags along with the camouflaged tarp at the army surplus store in Harrisburg. Throwing one of the bags at Socks he said, "Let's go. We can look at them later." Ironically, those were almost the same words Rudi had used when he and Robert recovered the coins over two hundred years earlier.

"Should we shovel them in?" Socks asked.

"No! One of you hold the bag open and the other *gently* scoop them up with your hands and *gently* put them in the bag. And get them all. Why do I have to tell you everything?"

"Hey, there's not a lot of room to work down here, Chuck," Socks complained.

"Find a way. Let's get going."

Karen held the duffel and Socks scooped.

When the dirt around the second jug had been removed, Charles said, "Listen, Socks. Get your shovel under the bottom and pry it loose, carefully. Then lay it on its side and work it into the duffel. Then hand the duffel to me."

This method kept the next five jugs intact. After the sixth duffel was in the van Charles scanned the excavated hole with his metal detector, as he did after every jug was handed to the surface. The seventh jug was just beside the area excavated by Karen and Socks. It still had four feet of soil covering its top but could be seen from inside the hole.

Charles said, "Just clear around it as best you can from the side. Then smash the jug with your shovel and scoop the coins into the duffel again. We don't have time to fool around with it. It'll be dawn soon."

After Karen and Socks had done as instructed and handed the seventh duffel to the surface, Charles again scanned the site with his detector, this time without getting a reading. "That's it. We got them all." He then put the last duffel in the van.

Charles had planned to shoot both diggers while they were helpless in the pit. But he hesitated when he couldn't recall if he had touched the shovels. *I can't leave my prints here and I'll never get out of the hole if I have to go after them.*

"Throw the shovels up, Socks."

Socks didn't bite. "No. Just grab the handle and help us out."

Charles pulled both Socks and Karen to the surface and said, pointing, "Duct tape her to one of those trees in that fence row. And tape her mouth shut too." He then retreated to the back of the van, crawled in, and opened the sliding side door. He chambered a round in his antique Colt, hunkered down, and waited.

As Socks taped Karen's hands together behind her back and around a small tree he whispered, "Now. Watch what happens next. I told you I have a plan." As he walked away Socks reached in his pocket and found the pistol grip of his 9mm Beretta.

For the first time since she was abducted Karen felt a glimmer of hope. *Maybe I did get to him.* As Socks neared the van she could only make out his dark silhouette. When he was ten feet from the van Socks removed the pistol from his pocket and held it behind

his back. He flicked the safety catch to the fire position. He didn't
see Charles lying in wait.

Charles watched as Socks approached the side door. He leveled
his pistol at head height. When Socks was in the opening he pulled
the trigger. The noise of the report at point-blank range and the bullet striking his head caused Socks to leap off his feet, flinging his
pistol into the rows of corn. He slumped to the ground. Charles
watched Socks a few seconds in the moonlight as black liquid drained
over his face. Smith twitched a few times and then was still.

Charles hoped firing his pistol from inside the van would limit
the distance the report would travel. He knew wildlife conserva-
tion officers from the Pennsylvania Game Commission regularly
patrolled this area looking for deer poachers. Hearing a shot at
this time of the morning would be sure to bring them running.
He would have to make the second shot without the muffling
effect of the van and then would have to get out of the area fast.
He walked toward Karen.

She could tell by the way the dark image moving toward her
limped that the gunplay did not turn out as she had hoped.

Charles stood in front of her. "Well. Just look at the golden
girl of the Holtzman family. Not looking down your nose at Charles
now, are you? You always thought you were so much better than
me. Didn't you?" He thought a moment. "Well, for that matter
the whole family always thought you were better than me."

Karen's wide eyes pleaded as she shook her head.

Charles continued talking himself into doing what he was
about to do. "Just look at you now. I outsmarted you *and* your
buddies and I'm going to survive this and you're not. And you
know the best part? This isn't going to bother me one little bit."

Charles moved back a step and pointed his pistol at Karen's
head.

CHAPTER

TWENTY-FOUR

Will had been driving around aimlessly for hours. Every fifteen minutes he called either Keith or Mel. They had heard nothing.

It was after 4:00 a.m. when Detective Zimmerman reached Will on his cell phone. A trooper had found Karen's car, but there was no sign of Karen. The detective gave him directions to the car's location and asked if he would meet him there.

"Mr. Rhone. Thanks for coming. I'll tell you what we think is going on here but first I have some questions. Do you think Ms. Holtzman is the type to just wander off on her own after she'd parked here?"

"Definitely not."

"I didn't think so." Lighting it with the beam of his flashlight, the detective handed Will a clear plastic bag. "Is this the hat you reported missing after the second break-in at your grandfather's house?"

"That's it!"

"Did Ms. Holtzman know about the hat?"

"Yes, she did."

"And you're sure there's only one of these?"

"That's right. It's a sample from a vendor. Where'd you find it?"

"We found it in that garbage over there. The vegetation under the bags is still fresh so it was just put there. They're going through the rest of the garbage now. Maybe we'll catch a break and find some mail, but as far as I'm concerned I don't need it. It doesn't look like she was forced off the road. No sign of a struggle, no blood, no nothing. It looks to me like she stopped here of her own free will, which tells me she most likely knew the person.

"So I think she was driving by here for whatever reason, saw whoever disposing of his garbage, stopped for whatever reason, saw the hat, and confronted the person—and consequently she got abducted, or God forbid … worse. We know it was Smith who did the deed both times at your grandfather's. We know it was Smith your dog tried to attack, which means Ms. Holtzman knows what he looks like, and I'm sure she would never stop for him."

"Charles Holtzman!" Will exclaimed.

"Exactly. That's what we figure. I haven't told you because I just found out myself late yesterday, but after we ID-ed Mr. Smith we checked into his prison time. Guess who served time with him in the same cell block?"

"Charles!"

"Right again. I have a search warrant and some backup coming and as soon as they get here we're going to pay Mr. Holtzman a visit. You can come along if you like, but stay out of the way. Don't know what we'll find there."

***

As Detective Zimmerman and three troopers searched Charles Holtzman's house, Will waited in the driveway at a safe distance. As the police lieutenant hurried from the house, Will saw an urgency in his step. He gestured to Will to join him.

"Nobody home. We found some balled up duct tape that could have been used on Ms. Holtzman," Detective Zimmerman said as he looked skyward. "The sun's coming up. While they finish up here let's go for a ride. I have a bad feeling."

***

Karen closed her eyes. *Lord, I commend my soul to your loving care. Please watch over—*

For the rest of her life she would never forget the next sound she heard. It was composed of three distinct tones. The dull *thunk* made by knuckling the bottom of a fresh baked loaf of bread, the high-pitched reverberation of metal like a struck tuning fork, and the cracking of a peanut when squeezed between the thumb and forefinger.

Charles dropped on impact.

With her would-be killer now on the ground, Karen faced a bleeding Socks Smith. He staggered, looked down, and delivered another blow to Charles's head with the long-handled garden shovel.

Charles Holtzman was dead.

Smith reached down and picked up the pistol Charles had held just moments before. The two stood facing each other for a few seconds, then Socks walked up to Karen. She was sure she was next. Instead, Socks reached to her face and slowly removed the duct tape covering her mouth.

"You scream and I'll put it back," he said.

Karen gasped a gulp of air. "I won't. I thought he killed you. You're hurt."

Socks ran his fingers over the long bloody groove in his forehead and said, "He tried. The bullet just creased me. I don't feel so good, though. My ears are ringing." He slumped to his knees.

"Let me loose and I'll help you," Karen said.

Smith sat down trying to regain control of himself. After a minute, with the aid of the shovel, he struggled to his feet. "No. I can't do that."

"Are you going to kill me?"

"No. I'm not going to kill you. But I'm not turning you loose either."

"Look. Just let me loose and I'll help you. Then you can drive away a very rich man."

"No. I have to get out of here. It's getting light. You'll be alright here for a while." Smith walked toward the van.

Karen called after him, "Thank you for my life."

Socks didn't stop or look back but acknowledged with his hand.

"Before you go, tell me something."

Smith stopped and turned.

"Why? Why are you letting me live?"

"Because I like you, okay? I like your fire. And because nobody every told me the things you did. I know you didn't mean it, but it was nice to hear, anyway." Smith walked a few more steps and turned again. "I want you to know something else. I never meant for her to die … the old lady … it was an accident."

Karen didn't respond. She watched as Smith crawled into the van and drove down the farm road toward T-231.

She fought against the duct tape around her wrists. *Impossible!* She worked her hands down the tree until she was in a sitting position. *I'm alive. I can't believe it. I'm alive.*

She noticed things like the cool dawn breezes mixing with the warmer air rising from the ground, the first chirp of an awakening bird, the surprised expression on her dead cousin's distorted face. And she noticed she noticed. She had heard that anyone surviving a near-death experience was never quite the same in how they thereafter perceived life. She now knew it was true.

She marveled how the rotation of the earth revealed itself as the sunlight crept down Short Mountain to the south. *Sunrise! Thank you, Lord. Oh thank you.*

She wept openly.

***

In a little less than an hour Socks Smith was on I-83 south. *Another hour or so and I'll be in Maryland.* He had cleaned the blood off his face as best he could. The wound continued to ooze and he periodically blotted his forehead. He was dizzy and sick in the stomach. *Drive the speed limit, don't swerve, don't attract attention.*

As he drove he formulated a plan. He would lay low in Baltimore until things cooled down, as he had successfully done in New York City. *Rent some cheap digs, stash the coins, and ditch the van as soon as possible. Worry about unloading the coins later ... much later.*

He would sell the coins one at a time to maintain a cash flow until he found a fence. *Oh, mister coin dealer ... my dear old grandma left me this coin ... is it worth anything? This should be fun.* Then, when the time was right, he'd sell them all at once. He knew he would have to sell at a discount, but they should still bring him millions.

He straightened slightly when he saw the patrol car approaching in the passing lane as he glanced in the rearview mirror. *Act natural. Don't respond.* He hid his wound by pretending to scratch his head. The police cruiser pulled even, hesitated, and then slowly passed. He breathed relief. The cruiser settled in the driving lane and held its position a few hundred yards directly in front of Smith. *Coming into York. Once I get through York the state line isn't far.*

When Smith saw the second cruiser approaching from the rear he tried to convince himself it was just a coincident. *This can't be happening. They couldn't have made me this quick.* He knew better when a third marked car pulled even with the second and blocked all oncoming traffic behind them. *They're boxing me in. Shrewsbury two miles. The last exit in Pennsylvania. I got to get off the interstate and make a run for it.*

As he approached the Shrewsbury exit he could make out a line of police cars, lights spinning and flashing, blocking both lanes of I-83 as well as the exit ramp. All traffic was being hustled around the blockade on the berm. Now, the only vehicle in front of him still moving was the cruiser he had been following. It plugged the hole on the berm. Behind him the two police units had stopped all southbound traffic. *I'm trapped!*

On the right flank of the solid line of coruscating vehicles he saw an opening. If he could bust through the gap between the last car and the tree line he just might make it to the exit ramp. He didn't hesitate. He stomped down hard on the gas pedal and took aim. As soon as the wheels were on soft ground the vehicle lost momentum. The van slammed into the police car on the left and a tree on the right, wedging it to a stop. Smith raced the engine but the best the wheels could do was spin in place. He stared straight ahead for a moment, then picked up the old Colt .45 on the seat beside him. *I'm not going back to prison.*

***

Lieutenant Zimmerman's hunch was right. He and Will discovered Karen and the gruesome scene at the grave site just minutes after Smith fled. Their first priority was to get Karen medical attention.

The routine at the Dauphin County Hospital was becoming all too familiar to Will. Four months earlier with his grandmother and grandfather, and now with Karen. The receptionist told him he and Mel could go straight to her room and join Karen's other visitors.

Keith, Maddy, and Jason were seated around Karen. Her bed was inclined to a conversational position. Other than an IV tube attached to her arm, she looked good.

Will took her hand, leaned down, and kissed her on the forehead. "I was crazy with worry. You scared me bad. Do you know that, Holtzman?"

"I would have chosen not to," she said.

"How are you feeling?" Mel asked.

"I'm good. Doctors say I can go home tomorrow. Can someone pick me up?"

Everyone volunteered.

Will asked, "What are they giving as a reason for keeping you overnight?"

"Observation. They say I'm dehydrated and exhausted. I have some abrasions on my wrists, ankles, and face. But other than that I'm good to go. Oh … and blisters. See?" She proudly displayed her palms.

"Good. I wasn't so sure this morning. You weren't too with it. It's amazing you remembered Smith's license plate number," Will said.

"So you haven't talked to the police since this morning?" asked Mel.

"No. I told Will and Detective Zimmerman what I could before they whisked me off in the ambulance."

"Then you haven't heard?"

"Heard what?"

Will answered. "Smith is dead. He was stopped at a roadblock near the Maryland border early this morning and decided to shoot it out with the police. He lost."

"Smith saved my life. Charles was going to kill me. Did I tell you that? He actually was going to kill me." Karen shook her head in ambivalence. "What about the coins?"

Will said, "They recovered seven duffel bags. Were there more than that?"

"No. The coins were in seven old jugs. We put one jug per duffel. Two of the jugs were broken, though. I saw the coins, Will. There must be thousands of them. We were right. We were right all along. Where are they now?"

"The police will keep them under lock and key until this all can be sorted out. If I knew your life would be threatened I would have never—"

"Will, how could you have known? Don't beat yourself up over this. If anyone is to blame, I am. I should have never stopped for Charles. The good guys won here. That's the bottom line."

Will lowered his head and nodded. "Thank God you're alright. Now … tell us everything that happened."

Karen told the whole story as well as what took her to the sticks in the first place; her indecision on whether or not to accept the teaching job on Long Island. "I can tell you all this right now. I'm not accepting the job. The people that matter to me the most aren't on Long Island. I'll wait for something to turn up here."

Will tried not to show his delight. "Whatever your decision, we accept it."

"So, what's next?" Karen asked.

"Grandpa will explain that, but first look at this." Will dropped the metal object in Karen's hand.

"What is it?"

"Grandpa said it was an old barrette. I found it at the grave site. You must have dug it up."

"I looks like it was inlaid with something in the shape of a flower of some kind."

"That's what we thought too." Will stuck the barrette in his pocket. "Grandpa, tell Karen what's next."

"We have a meeting with Al Marcus set up for the day after tomorrow, 10:00 a.m. sharp at my place. Can you make it?"

Karen grinned. "The proverbial wild horses couldn't keep me away."

✳✳✳

"Well, well. Can this case get any more exciting? Do you have any more surprises in store for ol' Al?" Al Marcus said as he entered Mel's living room. Everyone smiled. No one responded. "Glad to see you're okay, Karen. Quite an ordeal."

"Thank you. You don't think I'll get arrested for digging up a grave site without court approval, do you?" She was only half joking.

"Nope. You were under duress."

"So now what happens?" Mel asked.

"This changes everything. Obviously we won't file a petition to dig up the grave. Now we file for ownership. It's called an 'In

Re:' petition. We'll claim Karen is the finder. Remember what I told you about the Finders-Keepers law? What will most likely happen then is Uncle Sam will file preliminary objections as to venue and jurisdiction because he'll want one of his courts to hear the case. Then oral arguments will be scheduled in front of a three-judge panel to resolve those issues.

"Time is of the essence now. We need to file for ownership before the state and feds figure out what the coins are and how much they're worth. I should be able to file today."

"How will the state and feds know you filed for ownership?" Will asked.

"I'll tell them. I'll have to inform any possible claimant when I file the petition, so they'll know something's up."

"You have to inform any possible claimant?" Will was incredulous.

"Yes."

"Do you have to inform all descendants too?" Karen asked.

"No. Claiming Finders-Keepers eliminates everyone except the state and feds. They'll use other legal means to claim ownership."

"What will these oral arguments tells us?"

"Venue and jurisdiction. Legal stuff. Basically what oral arguments tell us is where and how we'll proceed—in other words, who can do what and by what law, and what court this will be heard in, state or federal. As I said, Samuel will try to get this in federal court. We want our petition heard in Dauphin County. The state will be on our side with this."

"This won't give us ownership?" Mel asked.

"No. Once all the procedural issues are settled then we go before a judge who will determine ownership. This is just the first step. But it's a crucial first step. If this goes to federal court, I think we lose."

"How long is all this going to take?" Karen asked.

"Unless something dramatic happens it's going to take a while. The oral arguments could happen as soon as October. But the rest … be prepared for the long haul."

"So it will be us and the state and the federal governments in front of this three-judge panel to hear the oral arguments?" Mel asked.

"That's right. All three entities will have a chance to make their case. We'll go first, assuming I'm the first to file, which I think I will be. The judges will ask questions as we go … well, at least one of them will. More on that later."

"And you want all three of us present in court?" Mel followed.

"And Dallas Fitzhugh. As soon as I heard what happened, the first thing I did was set up a conference call with Fitzhugh and his attorneys. Told them the whole story. They thought what happened might have changed our position. They were delighted we're going to honor the partnership and they wouldn't have to fight us on that. Then we discussed strategy, some of which I just shared with you. One of MAAC's attorneys will assist me in court.

"Now, what I need from you are copies of everything you have on the coin. How you knew about it, the steps you've taken, your research, everything. And I need it ASAP. So get yourselves organized. I'll take care of getting all the police reports.

"Things you should know about: how to act, how you should dress, and some things to expect on court day. First and foremost, behave. Decorum always. I'm not really worried about that with you three, but I have to say it. No interrupting the proceedings. Speak only to me and then only at a whisper. As a matter of fact I'd much rather if you have questions or comments that you write them down and hand them to me … discreetly. The judges may ask you questions directly, or they may not. If they do, answer with respect. It's always 'Your Honor.' Watch your tone and never cop an attitude. Everybody say 'We understand, Al.'"

"We understand, Al," the three said in unison.

"Dress conservatively. Nice clothes, but Mel and Will, no suit and tie. We're just regular folk and we want to convey that. Fresh haircuts. Karen, wear your hair just like you have it. Don't put it up. We'll go over everything again once I get a date. A lot of things will be said that you don't understand. Don't worry about it. I'll explain it after the fact."

Al shifted his body into his something-profound-is-coming position. "On to the panel of judges. You need to be prepared for this. I don't know the judges we'll draw yet but I can tell almost with certainty they will be of a predictable temperament in court, no matter who they are. Don't ask me why. I used to think it was just coincidence. I now believe it's by design.

"I have names for them. There's the Owl, who is silent and wise. He seems to know what everybody is thinking. He doesn't ask many questions and watches you intently.

"Next is the Noticeably Absent. He doesn't even seem to be in the room. He looks like he'd rather be anywhere but where he is. He asks no questions and rarely looks up from his notes.

"Then there's the Ramrod. The dominant one. He runs the show and asks the questions. He wears a scowl and is always in a foul mood. He appears to be a self-promoting egomaniac and you'd think the whole proceedings were about him. He speaks to you in a belittling tone and acts as though he doesn't believe anything you say.

"And with all that they still somehow always manage to come to the right decision."

"Will they make a decision the same day as they hear the case?" Karen asked.

"No. They'll say they will take the matter under advisement and issue a written judgment within thirty days."

With that Beau announced the arrival of a visitor in his usual less-than-subtle way. Everybody flinched.

✳✳✳

"Who is it, boy? We have a visitor?" Mel and Beau both peeked out the window closest to Mel's Easy-Lounger, Beau with his tail wagging and front feet on the sill. "Karen, I think it's your Uncle Gene."

"Charles' father?" Will asked.

"Yes, that's him," Karen said as Eugene Holtzman walked across the porch. Karen invited her uncle in and made the introductions.

"Sorry to interrupt. Keith said I'd find you here."

"That's okay," Karen said.

"If you'll excuse me, I really should run," Al Marcus said.

"No. Please, Mr. Marcus. This will only take a minute."

Al took a seat.

"Uncle Gene, I'm so sorry about all this."

"So am I. Nobody knows better than you, Charles always had a way of finding trouble … even as a kid. It was bound to catch up with him sooner or later. I'm just thankful he didn't hurt you."

"I'm fine. Can I get you anything?"

"No, thanks. I'll get to the point and then be gone."

"How's Aunt Miriam?"

"She's devastated, of course. But she's not surprised Charles met his end this way. Not really. As parents we have to live with the question 'what did we do wrong?'"

"You didn't do anything wrong. If I can help in any way, just ask."

"Thanks, but we'll be okay … eventually."

Mel said, "Have a seat, Gene."

"No, thanks. I can't put into words how sorry I am about Polly."

"Thank you very much."

Gene Holtzman turned back to Karen. "Your Aunt Miriam and I have been going through Charles' things. I already talked to your dad and Keith about this, and they agree with our decision. We'd like you to have the trunk Mom gave him. I was angry when

I found out she did that, but you know she always saw some good in Charles. Or at least she thought she did."

"Thank you. I'll accept it. You know Charles wouldn't even let me see the trunk."

"Yes and I'll show you why, if someone will help me bring it in."

"You have it with you?"

"Yes."

Will helped Karen's uncle retrieve the old trunk. Once it was inside, Gene Holtzman opened the trunk and handed Karen the letter written by Philip Hoppe Jr. to John Jacob Holtzman.

"This is what started it all, Karen. It never even occurred to Charles to include any other family member in helping him pursue this. His mind didn't worked that way—always making the wrong decisions. When you're finished with that, look at the papers in the Bible. Rudolph Hoppe tells the story of the coins. It's in German, but there's also a translation. Now you can see why Charles didn't want you in there. If I'd taken the time to look through the trunk when I had the chance, maybe none of this would have happened. I'll have to live with that."

When Karen finished reading the letter and the story Rudi had written, she passed them around the room. She also passed around the Continental Dollar her uncle handed her.

As Al Marcus read them, it was all he could do to contain his delight. He was glad he had stayed. He had in his hands hard evidence of the coins' arduous journey written by the primary participant. As a bonus, Philip Hoppe Jr.'s letter would help show what triggered the chain of events that led to the present-day situation. *Get these documents authenticated and we're in business.*

"Uncle Gene, this coin is worth a lot of money. I want you to have it," Karen said.

"No. I don't want anything to do with any of this." Karen nodded understanding. "The only thing I ask, Karen, is that you keep the trunk in the family."

"You can count on it." Karen escorted her uncle out of the house and to the edge of the porch.

"You don't have to feel obligated to attend the funeral, you know."

"I know. But I'll be there anyway. Tell Aunt Miriam … well, tell her I'm very sorry."

"I will."

"Take care, Uncle Gene."

Karen watched as her uncle drove away. When she entered the house she noticed the atmosphere had changed in spite of the obvious advantage of having the trunk in their possession. Gene Holtzman's pain had turned the mood to that of somber understanding.

CHAPTER

TWENTY-FIVE

"This is Lincoln Naugle from MAAC. He'll be assisting me in court. Linc, this is Mel and Will Rhone and Karen Holtzman. And Mel, this is Dallas Fitzhugh. Will, Karen, and Dal are already old friends," Al Marcus said as the two attorneys plus one entered the consultation room at the Dauphin County Courthouse. Hands were shaken all around.

"We have a few minutes before we need to go into the courtroom, so let's go over a few things. We've drawn three good judges, all very astute. Two women, one man. Remember the titles I gave the judges? I predict Daniel Jay will be the Ramrod. He'll be the one in charge. Intelligent. No nonsense. History buff. He authenticates documents for the courts. Prides himself in being a descendant of Founding Father John Jay. Twitches his cheek muscle when he thinks he's gotcha. Don't take his posturing personally.

"Sallie Anna will be the Owl. Down to earth. Very sharp. Claims she's retiring at the end of the year. She's been saying that for ten years. We'll not hear much from her but believe me ... nothing gets by her.

"The Noticeably Absent will be Jennifer Leigh. Knows the law inside and out. You'll swear she's playing tic-tac-toe on her notepad. Not so. She's presided over some of the most complex cases I've seen and reached the correct decision every time.

"Bottom line: I'm happy with the assignment."

Mel said, "Al, you grilled us to no end. Are we ready?"

"You're ready. Linc, do you have anything?"

"We're ready. No need to grill Dal. He's an old pro at this kind of thing." Linc held up a piece of paper. "*But ...* I'm concerned about this letter in the government's discovery. We didn't have this, and I think we would all agree it's compelling evidence that a crime was committed, and probably murder. I'm afraid it's going to look like we purposely omitted it from our discovery."

"I'm sorry I missed it," Karen said.

"Different name," Al said. "How could you have known? You're only one person. We just don't have the resources Uncle has. We'll deal with it by telling the truth—you missed it, plain and simple. Besides, it *suggests* a crime may have been committed. No hard evidence there, so that's what we'll sell. Oh ... one more thing. Usually in argument everybody sits in the gallery. Not today. We'll sit at tables. I think because there's so many of us. They probably want to know who's on whose side."

The bailiff knocked twice and said through the door, "Time to go."

✳✳✳

"Hear ye, hear ye, hear ye," the bailiff chanted. "The Commonwealth of Pennsylvania, County of Dauphin, Court of Common Pleas, October 2004, Session of Civil Argument Court is now in session. The Honorable Judges Sallie Anna, Daniel Jay, and Jennifer Leigh presiding. All rise."

The three entities were at three tables in front of the judge's bench. Facing the bench on the right was the Commonwealth of Pennsylvania; on the left, the partnership; and in the middle, the Government of the United States.

At the partnership's table Al Marcus stood between Mel and Lincoln Naugle on one side and Will, Karen, and Dallas Fitzhugh were on the other.

Judge Jay spoke first. "Be seated. We are convened in the matter of preliminary objections resulting from a petition for ownership filed by Alistair Marcus representing the partnership of Melchoir Rhone, William Rhone, Karen Holtzman, and H. Dallas Fitzhugh, which will hereafter be referred to as the Partnership, in reference to a cache of coins recovered from a grave site in Lykens Township, Dauphin County, Pennsylvania. The coins, known as the Continental Dollar, are currently in the protective custody of the Pennsylvania State Police and will remain there until the matter of ownership is decided. The coins, totaling 8,634, are identified as follows: 5,812 pewter, 2,756 brass, and 66 silver. Two independent research organizations have deemed the coins authentic.

"All parties will have the opportunity to present their case to their satisfaction. That being said, I would ask that you be as concise as possible in your argument. There is no reason this case should have to go into the second day if all parties remain cognizant of the length of their presentation. The Panel will stop any argument we feel is excessive in length.

"The Panel will ask questions as we proceed. If you have questions of each other, ask them through the Panel and not directly of each other.

"Before we begin I would like to advise counsel that while we will proceed in a somewhat informal manner you will be expected to adhere to the courtroom decorum of which you are accustomed and at all times show the respect worthy of this Court.

"Mr. Marcus, you will argue first, then the Government, then the Commonwealth. Please begin."

Al Marcus stood. "Thank you, Your Honor. I am Alistair Marcus and my co-counsel is Lincoln Naugle. We are representing the Partnership, as previously stated.

"I would like to point out to the court that the land where the coins were recovered is owned and maintained by Mid-Atlantic Agricultural Conglomerate and that H. Dallas Fitzhugh, a member of the Partnership, is the CEO of that corporation."

"So noted," Judge Jay said. "Continue."

Al Marcus spoke for almost half an hour, referencing his notes only once. His strategy was to present the court with every detail of the ordeal his clients had endured. He was articulate and professional, eloquently weaving the story into a coherent argument that could only be rightfully concluded by ruling in favor of the four people he represented. To bolster his case he interjected, with precision timing, the Franklin letters Karen had discovered, the Philip Hoppe Jr. letter, and the Rudolph Hoppe story found in the Holtzman trunk. He believed highlighting the law at this stage would serve him better than being negative toward his two opponents. He'd have plenty of opportunity for that.

"Objection, Your Honor. Should this be allowed? Mr. Marcus argues as though he is going for ownership rather than venue," John Van Kamp said.

"Your Honor, we believe it is imperative that the Panel have the opportunity to hear all the facts surrounding this case," Marcus responded.

"Yes, yes. Go on, Mr. Marcus," Judge Jay said.

Marcus then concluded this part of his argument by pointing out that although Karen Holtzman was forced to participate in the illegal recovery of the coins, she was now the only surviving finder and should be considered the finder of record. Given the fact that she was kidnapped and under the duress of her life being threatened, she could not and should not be held accountable for any wrongdoing, and consequently that should not become an issue at these proceedings. He wanted to nip that potential bugaboo in the bud.

Judge Jennifer Leigh yawned. Court was recessed for lunch.

After lunch, as prearranged, Lincoln Naugle addressed the court. He told the court of prior cases with similar circumstances that had resulted in decisions he hoped would be mirrored in the case at hand. Dallas Fitzhugh was right. Naugle was a competent attorney. When he finished Marcus again tried to addressed the court.

Judge Jay stopped him. "Mr. Marcus, I've already allowed you more time than usual."

"I know, Your Honor. Thank you. But if you'll indulge me, I'll be very brief."

"You have one minute."

"Thank you, Your Honor. In the question of venue, we believe the facts presented by Mr. Naugle and myself will show that this is clearly a Pennsylvania issue and should be heard in this court. No federal question is to be decided in the matter of rightful ownership. Also, as the first to file in this court, it is prejudicial we should be heard in the court of record."

"Very well, Mr. Marcus. Are you finished now?"

"Yes. For now, Your Honor." During his presentation the judges had asked few questions. Marcus knew that was to come.

Looking at the United States Government's table, Judge Jay said, "You're next."

"Thank you, Your Honor. The Government believes—"

"Who are you?" Judge Anna interrupted.

"I'm sorry, Your Honor. I'm John Van Kamp and my colleague is Dennis Clark. We are representing the Government of the United States."

"Continue."

"The Government believes the coins were clearly at one time the property of the United States Government, stolen from the United State Government, and therefore the Government has a superior ownership interest making this a state vs. federal issue to be heard in federal court."

The Government argued, using the Franklin letters as proof, that the coins were commissioned for minting by a representative of the United States Government, Benjamin Franklin, and therefore were now the property of the United States Government.

As proof a crime had been committed while the coins were in transit to Franklin—most likely murder as well as theft—they referenced the letter Lincoln Naugle was concerned about before court convened. John Van Kamp read it aloud.

To The Honorable Benjamin Franklin, et al.
Philadelphia, Pennsylvania

Dear Sir,

While it is my understanding you are not in the Country at this writing it is my fervent hope that your assigns will respond to this letter in your stead. As the legal representative of Elijah Birchfield of New York City and him taken sick of recent weeks I am writing in the matter of shipment of the commodity mentioned in his letter of September 2, 1776, addressed to you.

It is with deep concern and sadness I must report to you that the two men in the employ of Mr. Birchfield assigned to make delivery of the commodity to your place have not returned. We have estimated the trip to Philadelphia and the return to New York City should take in total no more than fourteen days; that time taking into account unforeseen delays. Being they departed New York City December 20, 1776, and no word being received of their disposition, neither from you nor them, and both men having the complete trust of Mr. Birchfield, I must conclude they and the afore-

mentioned shipment have met with an undesirable fate. If you can
confirm or deny receipt of the shipment or provide information
contrary to our suspicions, please do so at your earliest possible con-
venience.

Your Humble Servant,
Josiah Werth, Attorney
New York City, New York
January 21, 1777

"Your Honor, no response to this letter could be found. As a
matter of fact no mention of the coins could be found by Benjamin Franklin or anyone else after the date of this document.
When this letter is taken in context with the report of Captain
Samuel Rickert—exhibit D—we believe the only logical conclusion that can be reached is that Rudolph Hoppe and Johan Conrad
Mueller murdered the two men and made off with the coins."

"Objection, Your Honor. How is this going to venue?" Al
Marcus said.

"Your Honor, if Mr. Marcus can restrain from interrupting,
that question will be answered"

"Objection overruled. Continue Mr. Van Kamp," Judge Jay
responded.

"We believe that conclusion is supported by Rudolph Hoppe's
own account—exhibit A—of the events that brought the coins
into his possession. We believe Hoppe's account in corroboration
with Captain Rickert's report leaves no doubt that Hoppe was the
second man Rickert saw the morning of December 26, 1776. We
further believe that Hoppe's account of these events was skewed
by him in an attempt to absolve him of any wrongdoing in the
eyes of his family and descendants.

"In conclusion, Your Honor, we believe the Werth letter shows
beyond a reasonable doubt that the coins where stolen from the

United States Government, clearly indicating that this a federal matter and should be heard in federal court."

"What you're asking the Panel to do, Mr. Van Kamp, is to pick and choose what parts of Hoppe's account we should believe or disbelieve in respect to how it advances or hurts the Government's case. Is that correct?" Judge Jay said with a twitching cheek.

"No, Your Honor … I mean, yes." Van Kamp took a moment to collect himself. "Your Honor, we believe human nature dictated what Rudolph Hoppe chose to reveal in his account, making it possible for parts to be true and parts fabricated."

"With no regard that his account in whole just may be the truth?" Judge Jay replied.

John Van Kamp did not respond.

"Does the Government have anything else, Mr. Van Kamp?"

"Yes, Your Honor. We are disturbed by the fact that the Werth letter was not part of the discovery submitted by Mr. Marcus. The Government does not want to believe that the omission of such a damaging piece of evidence to his argument was intentional, jeopardizing his good faith."

"How do you respond, Mr. Marcus?"

"Your Honor, neither I nor my clients were aware of the Werth letter prior to its being submitted by the Government. I would remind Mr. Van Kamp and the court that the discovery submitted by us—with the exception of the Philip Hoppe Jr. letter and the Rudolph Hoppe account—was gleaned by one person in just two partial days of research. It is entirely believable that a document written by a person not known to the researcher at the time could be missed, and in fact that is what happened.

"We would also like to suggest that the conclusion the Government draws from the Werth letter is nothing more than speculation. There is no evidence that links Hoppe or Mueller to the disappearance of the two men mentioned. In fact, as the Government conceded, no response to the letter or any evidence that the two men were murdered, was ever found. We have no way of knowing for certain the men didn't surface at a later date."

"Duly noted, Mr. Marcus," said Judge Jay. "Mr. Van Kamp, do you have anything else?"

"Nothing, sir, other than to point out to the court that the Government is basing its case on the preponderance of the evidence in regards to the submission of the Werth letter in conjunction with the other exhibits."

Judge Jay said, "Very well. Now, I just know the Commonwealth of Pennsylvania would like to be heard. Commonwealth, what say you?"

"Thank you, Your Honor. My name is Lawrence Covert. My colleague is Thomas Hartman. We are representing the Commonwealth of Pennsylvania.

"As to venue, in addition to the objections noted by Mr. Marcus, we object to a federal venue on the grounds that there is no diverse jurisdiction in question here. Also, superior ownership cannot apply in this case. The Government can no more claim superior ownership here than they can to any U.S. coin of numismatic value held in the private sector. This is a Dauphin County, Pennsylvania, issue and should remain in this court."

The state's argument was straightforward. The coins were bound for Pennsylvania, buried in Pennsylvania, and found in Pennsylvania, so the argument for ownership should be heard in state, not federal, court. In addition, they reasoned, if indeed a crime had been committed, precedence dictated Pennsylvania Forfeiture laws would apply, again to be heard in state court. Covert's argument lasted all of fifteen minutes.

When the Commonwealth concluded, the Panel asked questions and asked for points to be clarified. In light of the Panel's outwardly disinterested demeanor, based on the poignancy of their questions the causal observer would find it remarkable they retained as much information as they did.

When it came to the Government's turn Al Marcus settled in, prepared to enjoy the Panel's drubbing of his principal opponent. He was disappointed and concerned when they didn't.

Marcus was next.

Judge Jay said, "Mr. Marcus, you present a compelling case, but one thing concerns me more than any other. Rudolph Hoppe is vague at best when he speaks of how he and Robert Rhone made an attempt to return the coins to their rightful owner, which would absolve them of any wrongdoing and make the issue of venue crystal clear. Can you offer anything that would help me decide whether or not he is telling the truth on that point?"

"Your Honor, Hoppe's account of events are substantiated by the exhibits submitted. Based on that, we believe all points in his account tend to be truthful. No reason we shouldn't, and no evidence to the contrary has been brought to the attention of this court."

"So, based on *lack* of evidence to the contrary, you are asking me to take a leap of faith and believe *everything* the man said?" Before Marcus could respond, Judge Jay added in a low voice with his cheek twitching, "You sound a little like Mr. Van Kamp in reverse. He asks me to pick and choose and you ask me to give Mr. Hoppe carte blanche."

Al Marcus didn't respond.

"Furthermore, Mr. Marcus, if the Hoppe account is to be believed in its entirety, doesn't that bode well for the Government's case? I mean, Hoppe himself said he and Major Mueller buried the coins in *New Jersey*. And then he and Robert Rhone recovered the coins in *New Jersey*."

Marcus wasn't rattled. "Your Honor, if you believe the Hoppe account in its entirety, then you must believe he and Rhone made an attempt to return the coins to their rightful owner regardless of the circumstances that led to the coins being in their possession in the first place. The fact still remains that the coins were buried in a grave in Dauphin County, Pennsylvania, and spent the last two

hundred sixteen years in that grave until they were recovered recently ... in *Dauphin County, Pennsylvania*. Not one shred of solid
evidence has been submitted that links Hoppe or Rhone to a crime,
or Major Mueller for that matter. For all we know the two men making the delivery as mentioned in the Werth letter stole the coins and
Mueller stumbled onto their hiding place. And we believe that that
fact alone nullifies the Government's claim of superior ownership,
which in turn nullifies their argument for change of venue."

Al Marcus felt he won that little skirmish, but he still had an
ugly feeling in the pit of his stomach.

✳✳✳

At Harrisburg International Airport a man hurried off the
plane with his briefcase—the only thing he had brought with him.
He wasn't dressed for autumn in Pennsylvania and he responded
to the crisp air with a shudder as he hustled out of the terminal
and hopped into the nearest cab.

"Dauphin County Courthouse, please. And hurry!"

✳✳✳

Judge Jay was prepared to close the proceedings when a bailiff
entered the rear of the courtroom through the large double doors
and went straight to Lincoln Naugle. He bent down and whispered in his ear. Naugle jumped to his feet and followed the bailiff
out through the double doors. When he returned two minutes
later he sat, leaned over to Al Marcus, and said, "Get a recess."

"Your Honor, before court's adjourned we request a fifteen-
minute recess."

"What on earth for, Mr. Marcus?" The Ramrod asked.

"I don't know, Your Honor. My colleague thinks it necessary."

Judge Jay scowled. "Alright. You have ten minutes. Court will
recess until 3 pm ... *sharp*."

When the gavel came down, Marcus said to the four-member
partnership, "You all might as well stay put. I don't know what's
up but it shouldn't take long. Unless you have business, of course."

Ten minutes later Marcus and Naugle entered the courtroom. Marcus remained standing after the proceedings were reopened. Will noticed he was repressing a smile.

"Your Honor, we have just received some new information in our case. I would like to present it at this time."

John Van Kamp stood. "Objection, Your Honor. Isn't it a little late for discovery?"

Lawrence Covert was also on his feet.

Before anyone could speak Al Marcus said, "Your Honor, if you allow this, the relevance and circumstances involved will become self-evident. We didn't know about this ourselves until ten minutes ago."

Judge Jay said, "Objection overruled. I'll allow it, Mr. Marcus."

"Thank you, Your Honor. I would like to submit this letter as exhibit F." Marcus handed a letter encased in a clear plastic sheath to the bailiff, who in turn handed it to Judge Jay.

Lincoln Naugle stood and said, "Your Honor, I have copies of this letter for the Commonwealth and the Government as well as the Panel. May I present them now?"

Judge Jay gestured in the affirmative with his hand. Naugle handed the copies to the bailiff, who passed them out.

"If I may, Your Honor, I would like to read this letter to the court," Marcus said.

"Please do," Judge Jay said as he looked over the original.

This is what he read.

To My Esteemed Friend John Klingman, Overseer of the Poor
Upper Paxton Township, Dauphin County, Pennsylvania

Greetings
   Received yours on behalf of your constituents Messrs. Robert
Rhone and Rudolph Hoppe on Tuesday last along with the coin in
question. I will not speculate from where Messrs. Rhone and Hoppe
obtained the coin but I have endeavored at your request to estab-

lish its value unfortunately with no success. I have no personal knowledge of such a coin being minted at any time for the Government of the United States or for any of the Colonies for that matter, even though information on the coin itself suggests otherwise. However, finding it intriguing I sought further assistance from my colleagues with knowledge of currency, two of which are members of the present Congress. They too were baffled by the coin. Therefore it stands to reason without any knowledge of said mintage there can be no knowledge of any quantity missing or stolen. Please accept my apology and know I did my best for you.

I can tell you this, however, with all the assurances of my Office and Position and that of my colleagues as well. The coin has no value as legal tender in the United States of America and I would caution against any attempt to use it as such. It is our collective ruling that you are free to keep the coin and do with it as you wish. I would suggest if you have any quantity of coins you could do your best by reforging them into something useful. I regret having to report in opposition of your favor but I trust I have been of some assistance in this matter. I am herein returning the coin and will consider this matter closed.

I Remain Your Obedient and Humble Servant,
David Rittenhouse, Treasurer
Commonwealth of Pennsylvania
Philadelphia 14th Day of September 1785

"Fascinating," Judge Jay said under his breath.

John Van Kamp jumped to his feet. "Your Honor, the Government adamantly objects. How do we know this letter is authentic? And how did it magically appear at the eleventh hour? This should not be allowed."

"Your Honor, if the court would allow I can call the person

who delivered the letter and it can be explained," Al Marcus said before the judge could respond.

Lawrence Covert was on his feet again. "Objection, Your Honor. Mr. Marcus knows full well there can be no witnesses at these proceedings."

Judge Jay's mouth was moving but no sound was emitted.

"Well, you two seem to have all the questions. Just trying to help out," Marcus responded.

Lincoln Naugle stood beside Al Marcus. "Your Honor—"

Judge Jay banged his gavel. "That's enough! Sit down. All of you. There will be order in this court."

Mel, Will, and Karen were stunned by the intensity of the sudden flurry. Dal Fitzhugh took it in stride.

"I want to see all of you in chambers. Right now." Judge Jay said.

The Partnership got to their feet.

"Not you," the judge said. "Mr. Marcus, bring the person who gave you this letter. I need to know what's going on here."

Al Marcus and guest were the last to enter the Judge's chamber.

"I don't expect to see an outbreak like that again," Judge Jay frowned at counsel, shifting his eyes in turn to all six. "Now here's how it's going to be. I or my colleagues speak. You speak when I ask you to. Otherwise you listen. Are we clear on that?" he said, still frowning. "Now. Where did this letter come from?"

"I brought it, Your Honor."

"And who are you?"

"My name is Delbert Rhone."

Sixty-five-year-old Delbert Rhone had all-white hair and a neatly groomed matching beard. He resembled the mature Ernest Hemingway. He carried himself with assurance and an air of professionalism. Arched across the athletic gray t-shirt he was wearing were the words "Aggies Football" in maroon letters. His attire was completed with khaki pants, white socks, and sneakers. It was apparent he didn't waste much time dressing for the trip.

"Mr. Rhone just got off a plane from Austin, Texas. He—"

"Mr. Marcus! Did you hear what I just said about speaking out of turn?"

"Yes, sir. I'm sorry."

"Alright, Mr. Rhone. I can't wait to hear this. Tell me the story."

"Well, early this morning I called Troutman Brothers Meats in Klingerstown to place an order. They have really great ring bologna."

Judge Jay looked at the ceiling. His colleagues snickered. "Go on, Mr. Rhone," Daniel Jay said as he pinched the bridge of his nose.

"Yes, well, anyway, the clerk at Troutman's and I were chatting and I mentioned my connection to Mel Rhone. That's all it took. He told me the whole story of the coins and what happened to Mrs. Rhone and Ms. Holtzman. He said in fact the case was going to court later today. I figured it was in response to an In Re:, based on what he told me. That's when I remembered the letter."

Judge Jay asked, "Are you and Mel Rhone related?"

"We're distant cousins. We share an ancestor."

Judge Leigh said, "Mr. Rhone, start from the beginning, please. How do you know any of Mr. Marcus' clients?"

"I have spoken to Mel Rhone and Karen Holtzman by phone and corresponded with Mel by email. The other two I have never had contact with."

"And how did you meet Mel Rhone?"

"He wrote to me. We then made contact online."

"And what was the nature of your contact with Mel Rhone and Karen Holtzman?"

"Genealogy. That's it. To make a long story short, Mel Rhone contacted me after he learned I had in my possession the family Bible of Robert Rhone. He's the ancestor we share. Subsequently we exchanged a lot of family information. I spoke with Karen Holtzman when we were making arrangements to have the family information in the Bible duplicated and copies sent to Mel. Which we eventually did. Ms. Holtzman said she was helping Mel Rhone."

"Okay. Tell us about this morning," Judge Jay said.

"Well, it was a little after 7:00 a.m. my time … when I called Troutman's. After the clerk told me the story he said the case would be heard today at 11:00 a.m. your time. He double-checked the time in the local paper for me. I knew I couldn't make it by then but figured I could make it before court adjourned if I got a good flight. I did and here I am."

Judge Anna spoke. "Mr. Rhone, I find some things troubling with your explanation. Why would you make the connection that this letter was of importance in this case to the point of hand-delivering it from Texas? And how do you know the term 'In Re:'?"

"I'm a retired attorney, Your Honor. I knew in a question of ownership the letter would be crucial. And certainly with the high estimated value of the coins I thought hand-delivering it was the least I could do. Until this morning when I heard what happened here, the letter held little meaning for me other that it was a nice historical document with a famous signature."

"Why didn't you provide this information to Mel Rhone when you were exchanging historical information the first time around?" Judge Anna continued.

"The only knowledge I had at that time was Mel was interested in *genealogical* information. The letter provides none of that, so I didn't think he would be interested. As I said, I didn't attach much meaning to the letter in and of itself."

"You never heard any family stories of a buried treasure?"

"No."

"And you never discussed a Rhone treasure with Mel Rhone?"

"No, Your Honor. Never. The subject just never came up. Our initial contact was almost two years ago. I won't speculate why, but for whatever reason Mel just never brought it up. Filling in family gaps and the Bible information was his main concern. Ms. Holtzman never told me about the death of Mrs. Rhone either. I didn't learn that until this morning. You'll have to ask them why they didn't mention those things. I don't know."

"I see," Judge Anna said, then looked to the other judges.

"Mr. Rhone, would you tell us how you came into the possession of this letter?" Judge Jay resumed the questioning.

"It was in the Bible."

"The Rhone family Bible you mentioned?"

"Yes. I framed the letter a few years ago and it's been hanging in my den until this morning."

"And how did you come to possess the Bible?"

"It was passed on from one generation of my family to the next."

"So to your knowledge the Bible has never been out of the possession of your line of the Rhone family?"

"That's correct."

Judge Jay asked, "Do the Panel members have any more questions of Mr. Rhone?"

"Yes, I do, Judge Jay," Judge Leigh said. "Seeing that Robert Rhone lived in Pennsylvania, how did the Bible end up in Texas?"

"My grandfather moved to Texas from Pennsylvania many years ago. He brought the Bible with him."

Judge Leigh nodded.

"Is that it?" Judge Jay asked.

No one responded.

"Okay. Thank you, Mr. Rhone. You may go."

After Delbert Rhone left the room, Judge Jay looked at the six attorneys for a moment, then said, "I don't think I have to tell you what this letter means."

Al Marcus and Lincoln Naugle were the only ones smiling.

"Your Honor, may I speak?" asked John Van Kamp.

"You may."

"I would like to request that this letter be authenticated."

"Nothing like accentuating the obvious. Okay. So noted, Mr. Van Kamp. But I can tell you this off the record. I've been authenticating old documents for many years and it looks authentic to me. Does anyone have anything else to say?"

The room was silent.

"The six of you, back to court. I'd like to speak to the Panel alone."

Three minutes later the Panel returned to the courtroom.

After he reconvened, Judge Jay said, "In light of the letter just submitted as exhibit F and pending authentication of same, it is the Panel's unanimous recommendation that the arguments continue for a period of thirty days and the Partnership, the Commonwealth of Pennsylvania, and the United States Government resolve this matter among themselves by the end of those thirty days. You will submit your resolution in writing to this court."

Judge Daniel Jay brought down his gavel.

CHAPTER

TWENTY-SIX

It was mid-morning the day before Thanksgiving 2004. Most of the colorful leaves had fallen from the trees. Just the brown ones of the oak family still clung on; they were always the last to fall. The kaleidoscope was gone for another year. The sun was out and it was bright but there was a winter sting to the air. A slight breeze was blowing over the knoll in the open field.

Will and Karen stood inside the twenty-five-foot-square wrought-iron fence facing the massive slab of light blue marble positioned upright in the center. Row after row of tan dried cornstalks, with their ears turned groundward, surrounded the fence on three sides. The stalks rattled with the slightest puff of wind. The small groomed island looked very much out of place in the sea of tan.

The stone was six feet high, two feet thick, and four feet across. The finish was all natural except for a two-foot-square faceted area attached with a bronze plaque. The plaque had a slight backward tilt and contained fifteen names—thirteen from the Henry list and two from Robert Rhone's Bible—underneath the words *Rhone and Hoppe Family Cemetery*. Below the names it stated, *There are eight unidentified people here interred – four adults and four infants.*

"It's so beautiful," Karen said.

"Much more than I expected. Fitzhugh does things right," Will responded.

"And he just donated the land and paid for the stone?"

"Yep. It'll be here and open to the public for all time. And his people will maintain it too. He said had he known there was a cemetery here he never would have cultivated this spot."

"How did they get the grass to grow so fast?"

"They didn't. They just laid turf sod."

"All those years and now it's sacred ground again."

"Yes. Grandpa's more excited about this than the coins."

"Has he seen it yet?"

"He's coming later today. Can you guess with who?"

"Not Mrs. Adams!" Karen exclaimed.

"You got it."

"Told you he'd miss her when she wasn't around."

"Did you notice Grandpa is much more at ease now?"

"I did notice that."

"It's like he needed to see Grandma's death avenged. Truth be known, so did I."

"I'm glad it's over, too," Karen said.

"And I'm glad it turned out like it did. Your suggestion to offer some coins to the Government and State as incentive to settle this was nothing short of brilliant."

"Brilliant? I don't know about that. Like Al said, after the letter was authenticated they knew it was pointless to take it any further. I mean, there it was in black and white. Proof Robert and Rudolph tried to return the coins and proof they were given ownership. And signed by a government official no less." Karen thought a moment. "You don't think a hundred coins each was too many?"

"It worked, didn't it? I think it was just right. It may have been pointless for them to try, but they still could have dragged this out."

"I'm just happy they accepted."

"Giving Delbert Rhone a dozen was a nice touch, too," Will added.

"Well, it was the Rittenhouse letter that turned the tide for us. He earned them."

"Yes, he did. I hope he doesn't blow it all on ring bologna."

After gently poking his solar plexus, Karen said, "Talk about a nice touch. You paying for Jason's education is the nicest touch of all time. Keith and Maddy are ecstatic."

"He gave us another pivotal moment, Karen. Least I could do."

"It's so ironic, isn't it?"

"What's that?"

"The Rittenhouse letter. I mean, at the time it must have devastated Robert and Rudolph. Yet that very letter had the exact opposite effect on us."

"It is ironic," Will replied.

"So what happens with the coins now?"

"Al's looking for an auction house that will manage the disbursement for us. He said it could take fifteen or more years to sell them all. Have to be careful not to flood the market and drive down the price. Bottom line is we're very rich," Will answered.

"What will you do now, rich guy?"

"I've been kicking around some ideas. The first thing I'm going to do is sell the business to Ed Klinger. He's very excited about it. How about you?"

"I've been thinking, too. We've been so fortunate, I want to find some way to give back. I think the idea you had to set up a trust fund in Polly's name was great. I want to give some of my share to that."

"Al's working on that too. We're going to give full college scholarships to outstanding high school students who plan to major in history. He said we should be able to award a couple by next year. Should be able to add more scholarships as we go. It'll be interesting."

"How will you determine who gets the scholarships?"

"We've been thinking about a combination of high school records and an essay contest. Grandpa and I would like you to be on the board and help us with those kinds of decisions. Will you do it?"

"I'm honored. Of course I will."

"Great." Will paused and looked at the stone for a second. "Have you been getting calls from investment brokers since the *USA Today* article?"

"Have I ever! I'm thinking about getting an unpublished number," Karen replied.

"Do it. We're going to."

"I'm not sure I like being famous."

"Now you know what every celebrity goes through. But I'll tell you this. I'd rather be rich and harassed than poor and anonymous."

Karen laughed. "I guess so. But you were never poor."

"Okay. How about, I'd rather be rich and harassed than moderately well off and anonymous."

"That's better."

"I'd like to ask you something else, but first I have something for you."

"What?"

Will reached into his pocket and handed Karen a small black velvet pouch with tie strings. "Open it."

"Oh, Will. It's beautiful. Is this the same barrette you showed me in the hospital?"

"Yes. We took it to a jeweler to find out more about it. He confirmed it was silver and said if it's from the eighteenth century it was most likely inlaid with mother-of-pearl. He said he could restore it close to the original. So we told him to do it. Grandpa and I want you to have it."

"Oh no. I couldn't possibly. That probably was Magdalena Rhone's."

"After what you went through, you can and you will, with one request though."

"What?"

"You wear it for us every once in awhile."

"Okay. I'll do that. Thank you so much. I'll treasure it forever."

"Is that a tear I see?"

"No. Something blew in my eye. Anyway. You said you wanted to ask me something." Karen rubbed her eye.

"Oh yes. Well, we never have to work again … in the traditional sense, anyway. But that's not acceptable to me and I know it's not acceptable to you. So I've been thinking. We go into business. We take on really tough genealogical cases. The ones nobody has been able to solve. The ones where the outcome has significance. We pick and choose what we'll tackle and it'll have to be for a good cause. Grandpa will be our consultant and provide our home base of operations. We do the legwork. And we'll only charge our clients for expenses and a donation to a charity. We'll call it *Rhone Genealogical Investigations … RGI*. What do you think?"

"Like sleuths of the family tree. Gumshoes of the bloodline."

"You got it," Will said, smiling from ear to ear.

"And we've already made a name for ourselves, haven't we?"

"Exactly."

"Have you talked to Mel about this?"

"Yes. He loves the idea."

"So do I. You're on. But there is one thing that'll have to change."

"What?"

"You said Rhone Genealogical Investigations. Don't you mean Rhone and *Holtzman* Genealogical Investigations?"

"No, I don't."

Karen looked puzzled.

"Marry me. I love you more than you could possibly imagine."

EPILOGUE

Alistair Marcus, et. al.
Daniel Jay, Judge
Court of Common Pleas

Dear Mr. Marcus,

I am writing you in an unofficial and informal capacity. First of all, congratulations on your settlement of the issue heard before my panel last fall; I believe Justis was served. I must say it was one of the most intriguing cases I have ever adjudicated, more for the historical than the monitory significance, although that was indeed substantial. In brief, I would like to share with you some of my thoughts on the case.

As I'm sure you are aware, I am a student of American History. As such, I found the Rittenhouse letter of particular interest because of the predicament it placed Mr. Rittenhouse (whom as you know was to became the first Director of the US Mint) when he was questioned on the Continental Dollar by Rhone and Hoppe. I am certain he knew about the existence of the coin either directly or indirectly, but due to the clandestine manor in which it was minted, its subsequent failure, and I'm sure his desire to keep it all very hush-hush, had no choice but to disavow its existence. You could almost see him squirming in his seat, suggesting (when I'm sure he would have rather commanded), that Rhone and Hoppe melt down the coin[s] they had. If only we knew what transpired behind closed doors when the coin showed up on his desk. It makes one wonder if he consorted with Ben Franklin himself.

The conundrum he found himself in left Rittenhouse few options, if any. He could not pursue how Rhone and Hoppe came to possess the coin, and risk drawing attention, so he did the only thing he could and close the matter as quickly and quietly as possible. As it turned out it was the right decision from his perspective as Rhone and Hoppe did the next best thing to destroying the coins by burying them. Fascinating.

The inter-workings and nuances of history often become obscure making a find of this magnitude rare indeed. I am pleased I had the opportunity to witness it first hand. Please pass on my best regards to your clients in this case.

Wishing you the best,
Daniel Jay

CONTINENTAL DOLLAR FACTS

- Although called the Continental Dollar its intended value remains unclear. It was the first silver dollar-sized coin proposed for the United States.

- It is widely believed Benjamin Franklin was the designer and Elisha Gallaudet was the engraver of the Continental Dollar. The mint[s] used to produce the coinage is unknown.

- Five different dies are known to have been used in minting the Continental Dollar; three spellings of CURRENCY, with and without EG FECIT, all in different combinations of brass, pewter, and silver. This suggests more than one mint was utilized in their production.

- In October of 2003 a silver Continental Dollar in EF (Extremely Fine) condition sold at auction for $425,500. In January of 2005 another silver in VF (Very Fine) condition sold at auction for $345,000. These are the only two silver Continental Dollars known to exist.

Obverse   Reverse

- The value of other varieties of the Continental Dollar in brass and pewter range from $19,000 to $80,000 each in VF to EF condition.

- Many counterfeits are known to exist and authentication is recommended before purchasing a Continental Dollar.

- Although it is believed between six and ten thousand Continental Dollars were minted, less than one hundred are known to exist. The disposition of the balance remains a mystery.

- Franklin borrowed the sun with rays icon, the interlocking rings, and the WE ARE ONE icons from the Continental Dollar to design the Fugio Cent minted in 1787/88. He also used a sundial and the words MIND YOUR BUSINESS for the coin but changed their design. The Fugio Cent, also called the Franklin Cent, was minted in copper, and was the first *authorized* coin minted for the United States.

- It wasn't until 1794 that the first officially minted silver dollar was released for general circulation in the United States. No design aspects from the Continental Dollar were used in its production.

Recommended Reading & Resources

Books

Fischer, David Hackett, *Washington's Crossing*. New York: Oxford University Press, 2004.

Guth, Ron. *Coin Collecting for Dummies*. Hoboken, NJ: Wiley Publishing, Inc., 2001.

Helm, Matthew, L. and Helm, April Leigh. *Genealogy Online for Dummies*. Hoboken, NJ: Wiley Publishing, Inc., 2004. 4th Edition.

Humes, James C., *The Wit and Wisdom of Benjamin Franklin*. New York: Gramercy Books, 2001.

McCullough, David. *1776*. New York: Simon & Schuster. 2005.

DVD's

The American Revolution; The History Channel, 1994.

Benjamin Franklin: Citizen of the World; Biography, 2006.

Family Tree; The History Channel, 2006.

Liberty! The American Revolution; PBS, 1997.

Websites

1. Legendary Coins & Currency
   http://americanhistory.si.edu/
   coins/printable/coin.cfm?coincode=1_02

2. The American Numismatics Society
   http://www.numismatics.org/

Websites continued

3. American Numismatics Association
   http://www.money.org/AM/Template.cfm?Section=Home

4. The History Place
   http://www.historyplace.com/
   unitedstates/revolution/index.html

5. British Battles.Com — The Battle of Trenton
   http://www.britishbattles.com/battle-trenton.htm

6. Family Tree Maker — Genealogy software
   http://www.familytreemaker.com/

7. Cyndi's List - Genealogy Sites on the Internet
   www.cyndislist.com/

Printed in the United States
75831LV00005B/97-120

9 781596 637825